I0735002

Red

HUNTED

SUBSCRIBE LIVE LOVE BOOK 1

ALLYSON LINDT

For my eternal dragon

Chapter One

If Fiona stood on the top-floor balcony of a New York skyscraper, would the city below look the same as it did from her Salt Lake City apartment—lights reaching out in neat rows for miles. Cars and people at quarter size?

Buildings would interrupt. The people would look like ants, and the cars like Hot Wheels.

Parker could tell her for certain. She glanced at the party behind her. With the patio door blocking her off, the only sound came from the couple of other people out here with her. It was an odd soundtrack, overlapping with the noiseless heads inside.

Parker stood more or less in the middle of it all, wearing a happy look that made Fiona grin even from out here. She wanted her best friend to herself for at least a few hours, but the two of them could catch up when his *welcome back* party was over. She didn't blame their friends for tying up his time. He'd been gone for months, seeing the world and sharing his video diary with the internet. Everyone wanted to say *hello* but also get the details Parker didn't share on YouTube.

Fiona turned her gaze back to the city below. The same one she'd seen every day, her entire life. The angle had changed as she moved from place to place, but the details were the same.

Behind her, the door slid open and shut with a soft *woosh*, but she didn't turn. A second later, someone rested a hand on the small of her back.

"Why are you hiding out here?" Parker asked.

She couldn't fight her smile. "It's not my party. I figured I'd let your adoring fans have you for a few hours, and I'd steal your time tomorrow, when you'd be too hungover to hold your tongue."

"It's an evil plan. I like it."

She spun to face him, and he wrapped her in a hug. More than six inches taller than her five-four, he lifted her feet off the ground when he gave her a tight squeeze. She couldn't help but notice the months on the road had been kind to him. His body was chiseled and hard beneath her, and if he weren't her best friend, she'd be tempted to drool. Would it be appropriate to trace her finger along those lines shadowed under his T-shirt, down his chest, to feel that yummy *V* he didn't have a problem showing off in his videos?

She shook the thoughts aside and stepped back so she could see his face without having to tilt her head too much.

He studied his shoes and the open air behind her but didn't meet her gaze.

"What's up?" she asked. They'd known each other since they were kids, and she was decent at reading him, but a nearsighted kitten with a fresh plate of food would see he had something to say and was hesitating.

"I have a question for you, but I already know you're going to say *no*. I'm trying to figure out how to build up the hype around it."

"The odds of me telling you *no* to anything are pretty slim." Which she didn't mind. He would do—and had done—the same for her.

He finally looked up, green eyes pale in the night. "This is different."

"Melodramatic much?" She tugged him toward a pair of lawn chairs in the corner and sat across from him. "Dragging it out like this isn't hype; it's false expectation."

He chuckled. "I don't want that. Here's the back story. I've been invited to participate in competition sponsored by Rinslet Multimedia. Think reality TV, but actually real. They've extended invitations to some of the top-watched streaming channels. Basically, we do what we've always done, but with some of their rules. Basic stuff. Livestream at least eight hours a week, in segments of an hour or more. Post a minimum of an additional eight hours of footage a week."

"So… what's the hook? What's the contest?" It didn't sound very unique to her.

"Every month, viewers vote one channel off, and Rinslet removes another that has the lowest views. In month twelve, there will be six remaining channels, and one of those gets a sponsorship contract. Salary plus expenses for another year, as an official Rinslet channel."

"That's fantastic. You're perfect for it."

He ducked his head, but it didn't hide his smugness. "Yeah. I am. There's only one thing I haven't figured out yet. I need a hook. Something more than what I'm already doing, to keep things interesting. Between you and me, we'll come up with something amazing."

"You want me to help you brainstorm?" That sounded like fun. "Why would I say *no* to that?"

He raised his brows. "I want you to go with me. You're not happy here. You're wasting your talent. I know you want to do more. Make it this."

"I'm fine here." The words slipped out without thought. She meant them too. Didn't she? She wasn't miserable with what she was doing. It was good work, decent money, and a place she knew. But the urge to take back her not-quite-*no* hovered at the tip of her tongue.

"Is that a *no*?" he asked.

Of course he'd call her on it. "Nick is working on a new project, and I'm helping. He needs me here."

"What's he doing?"

"Think GrubHub, but for home-baked goodies." Her brother's pitch flew to mind without effort. She'd heard it so many times, it repeated in her head whenever her thoughts were blank. "We have contracts with a series of couriers around the world, and, we match people who sell sweets with people who want to buy them, have them delivered as gifts, etcetera."

"That's brilliant."

"It's okay." It was brilliant. Nick had a solid

idea, and she loved it. But her part in things wasn't that challenging. Damn Parker for making her think about that. It didn't matter. Work was work, and it didn't have to be Disneyland fun as long as it was something that paid the bills and that she could get behind.

"Wow. Sell me some more." Teasing sarcasm lined Parker's words.

The patio door slid open. "You two going to come back inside? Join the fun?"

"On our way," Parker said. He stood and tugged Fiona to her feet. "Think about it. When I leave to do this, I want to take you with me."

"You were right the first time—the answer is *no*. I'm sorry."

He shook his head. "I'll give you a few days, but I won't mention it again. Probably."

"Thanks." She stuck her tongue out. They headed back inside.

As the party wore on, then wound down, Parker's offer never left the front of her thoughts. She wanted it to go away, but it clung to her. She had a life here. Bills to pay. A lease. Nick's business. It wasn't as though she could just pick up and go.

A pit inside grew larger each time she thought of another reason she had to be here. But of course she'd want to go with Parker. That was carefree and whimsical. Staying was the adult, responsible thing to do. That was life, plain and simple.

The pounding beat of *Something in Your Mouth* throbbed against Wyatt's eardrums. His issue with that, besides the fact that the song wore out its welcome in strip clubs years ago, was it wasn't the kind of music he thought should have teeth-rattling bass.

He shouldn't complain about the environment. He was surrounded by gorgeous women taking off their clothes, and the drinks went on his expense account.

And Chuck Edwards looked like a boy at Christmas, with his face all-but buried in Ginny's tits.

If the client was happy, Wyatt was happy. What would the clientele of Grammie's Pastries say if they saw how the company's Vice President of International Distribution defined *Goodie Basket*?

Wyatt slipped a twenty into Ginny's garter, for another table dance. She glanced at him, lips drawn in a thin line. She was less-than-impressed with Chuck and his tendency to *accidentally* grope her whenever he got the chance.

Wyatt mouthed *thank you*.

She turned back to Chuck, who was too focused on what was below her neck to notice the exchange of looks. Wyatt owed Ginny a bigger *thank you* later, though the tips would help make it better. The two became instant friends the first time he brought a perspective sale here, and she knew how to work the table.

Chuck reached for her, and she shimmied away with a giggle.

That was at least the fifth time tonight. Wyatt was losing count. He was trying to be patient, but they'd been here four hours. The blend of sweat, perfume, cologne, and alcohol that lingered in the air had become one with his suit jacket. There were blasts of cool, if someone was lucky to get a seat under a vent, but he hadn't been lucky.

"Did you have any other questions about the contract?" Wyatt asked. This signature meant great things for the courier service he worked for. Having the smiling Grammie next to their beige-colored logo, would do amazing things for marketing. It also meant a Senior Vice President of Sales position for Wyatt.

Chuck waved a hand, not sparing Wyatt a glance. "No, no. I've got the information I need."

Then why the fuck are we still here? Wyatt didn't have a problem with the dancers or anything about the club itself, but too many of the clientele reeked of desperation and shame. Chuck included. It was a pity. People should own their pleasures, not tuck them away in a room where they could barely see past their table.

Forty-five minutes later, they stumbled out to Wyatt's car, Chuck's arm slung around Wyatt's shoulder. Chuck more fell than sat in the passenger seat.

Wyatt breathed deep, searing the humid night air into his lungs, then exhaled and got in the BMW sedan. He pointed the car toward Chuck's hotel. "Can I tell my boss we've got a done deal?" he asked. He had to get at least a handshake and a *yes* before the client flew out tomorrow.

"I don't know." Chuck managed to slur the hard syllables.

Fuck-fuckity-fuck-fuck-fuck. "What can I do to

make that a *yes*?"

"Listen… We're looking for something with a more personal touch. You're an international conglomerate. We don't want guys in navy shirts and shorts manhandling our sweets on delivery. We're Grammie's Fucking Pastries."

Which was a bullshit answer, because the way the delivery drivers dressed wasn't new information. "We can do personal." As Wyatt spoke, he searched for how he'd spin a proposal like that to the people at the office. It didn't matter; this contract had to happen. "A change in appearance, specifically for you, if that's what's required. And no manhandling. We have years of experience and a solid insurance policy to back up our reputation."

"And you can do that all at a lower cost? Because we're considering a company that already offers the personalized touch and is more cost effective."

All of which Chuck knew five hours ago, before Wyatt spent hundreds of dollars on boobs and booze.

"Tell you what." Wyatt never let his friendly tone waver. "Now that I have a better idea of what you're looking for, give me time to come back to you with a customized proposal. I'll work the numbers, I'll speak with Global, and I'll come back to you with a new quote."

Chuck frowned.

"I'll get you new numbers within a week. You'll be back in town in a month, for the Grammie's Pastries Bake-Off. Fly in a few days early, and we'll do another night on the town. You can give me your final answer then."

Still no answer.

Wyatt swallowed a growl. "Ginny would love to see you again. I've never seen her warm to someone like she did with you." He was going to owe her *big time*.

"All right." Chuck sounded like the answer took all his effort. "One month. But I'm signing paperwork that weekend, whether it's with them or with you."

"I wouldn't expect any less." Wyatt felt as though his smile was plastered in place. There was no way he could pull this off for less than the existing quote, especially with the *personalization* requirement. It would cost the company a fortune.

But it would do amazing things for their marketing, and he was going to get that fucking Senior Vice President promotion. He didn't care who he had to go through.

Chapter Two

How long would it take for Parker to get used to being bound to a single location? He'd like to think he wouldn't have to find out any time soon, but the odds weren't leaning in his favor.

He always felt awkward being at Fiona's when she wasn't around. Something as simple as taking a shower made him feel out of place.

He stayed here whenever he was in town. She'd told him countless times to make himself at home and that she didn't have a problem with it.

That didn't rid him of the feeling of not belonging, but this did feel closer to *home* than any other place he visited. He didn't keep his own place. He was never in a single town long enough for it to matter.

He opened the shower door to grab a towel. The bright-red terrycloth made him smile. The vibrant color matched the rug, the accent wall, and even the loofah hanging on the wall behind him. It was one of the few places in the house that reflected the real

Fiona.

He stepped from the shower into a bathroom of steam, wrapped the towel around his waist, and stared into the mirror. A flesh-colored blur stared back. He shook his head and turned away, to make his way back to the guest room.

The faint scent of vanilla that always drifted through Fiona's place like the hint of fresh cookies, was marred this morning by a hint of beer. Between the two of them, they got most of the spills cleaned over the weekend. She even did something miraculous to remove a burgundy wine stain from the taupe carpet… that blended into the beige couch… that merged with eggshell walls. But the scent of the party lingered.

In his temporary quarters, he flipped his laptop open in its spot on the desk. He switched the webcam on, angled it to focus on him just above the waist, and hit *Record*. He wasn't livestreaming this morning, so the footage would be edited later, but he'd discovered even the trimmed clips worked better if he captured things as they happened, rather than scripting any of it.

"Hey, everyone. As promised, I'm back in Salt Lake City." When he started doing this, it felt strange, talking to an empty room as if it could respond. Now the conversation tone came naturally. "The valley isn't as big as some places, and it's much larger than others, but like with Goldilocks, it fits just right."

The worlds tasted sour, but he wasn't sure why. "It's always wonderful to be back home." He stumbled over the claim. "Edit that out later," he told the camera.

He grabbed some clothes from his luggage and stripped off the towel. "I'm going to visit my best friend, Fiona, today." He talked as he dressed. Another lesson learned—a lot of his viewers liked the hint of skin and the possibility he'd one day slip and show more than he was supposed to. "I'm taking her to lunch, and I'm going to beg her again to go with me for this competition."

He winked at the camera. "Don't worry. Things with her and me aren't *like that*. She's my oldest pal, as in we've known each other forever, but there's no threat of her taking me off the market." Another fumble as he spoke. "Edit that out."

What was up with his brain this morning? Whatever he'd hoped to have romantically with Fiona vanished years ago. He hadn't figured out how he felt about her until he was in another relationship, and she wasn't interested in being his fling or rebound girl.

He finished getting ready, switched to the mobile cam in his hat, and headed outside. The microphone rested near his ear. "There aren't a lot of cabs in this town. It's the kind of thing you have to call for here. But we have an awesome public transportation system, so I'm going to take the light rail and show you the view from there."

He'd mostly be filming on the ride, rather than talking. Any narration would be overlaid later. He might be okay holding half a conversation with no one else around, but it caused too many interruptions if he did it in public, unless he had a friend with him.

Fiona was at the edge of downtown, so it was a

short walk to a train station. At ten thirty in the morning, the car he stepped onto was only a quarter full. He scanned the faces of everyone there, and sat next to a man a few years older than him who traveled with a younger girl. Father and daughter, he assumed.

The girl was probably eight or nine. She looked up the moment Parker sat, blue eyes wide. "Is that a camera on your head?" she asked.

Her father clenched his jaw and pursed his lips.

"It is," Parker said. "I'm making a movie."

"Like on YouTube?"

The train lurched forward and continued on its route. "Exactly like that. I have my own travel channel."

"On the internet." Disdain hung heavy in Dad's voice. "It's not a real channel."

Parker wouldn't argue the semantics of what constituted *real*. He'd done that past the point of nausea enough times. Instead, he shrugged.

"Why?" Daughter asked.

"Why do I do this?"

She nodded.

Dad studied Parker, as if willing him to say something brilliant yet knowing he wouldn't.

"Have you ever wanted to go to Disneyland?" Parker kept his focus on the child.

"*Yes*. We went last year, and I met Snow White and the White Rabbit and Goofy."

"I went there when I was about your age, and I loved it." This wasn't the first time Parker'd had this conversation. There were variations of it smattered through his videos. He used it to fill in back story for new viewers, and he liked hearing people's responses. "When I got older, like now— Guess how old I am."

"Late twenties, maybe," Dad said.

Daughter's jaw dropped open. "You're so old."

Dad huffed, and Parker bit back a laugh. The man was probably in his early thirties. "*Old* is a relative term." Parker kept his voice kind. "Anyway, a little while back, I decided I wanted to see more places liked Disneyland, but bigger."

"Bigger that Disneyland?" God. The child could be reading from a script. She was perfect.

"Yup. But it's expensive to go a lot of places. Your dad works long hours to take you to on vacation, but if you went every weekend, he wouldn't have time to work. That's why I started making videos that are good enough people pay me so they can air their commercials while the vids run."

"Sell out." Dad spat out the words.

Jealous? Parker kept the retort to himself. "My stop is coming up." He flipped the remote in his pocket to shut off the camera, then looked at Dad. "Professional stuff time. I don't ever use a minor's images in my clips, but I would like your written permission to use the audio portion of that conversation."

"You're asking me to sign a release?"

"This is my livelihood. The form is digital. You can either sign on my tablet now, or give me your email address, and I'll email it to you for review." Parker's conversation tone was gone, replaced with the professionalism that helped keep him from getting sued.

"All right." Some of the disdain vanished from Dad's voice. "I'd like to review it first." He rattled off his email. "Do you really make money at this?" The professional aspect of things seemed to have shift his mood.

"Enough to pay the bills and buy souvenirs. Most of my sponsorships come in the form of pre-paid expenses. Tickets, hotel rooms, and food."

"Best of luck to you." Dad extended his hand, and Parker shook it.

He took the next stop and strolled about a block until he found the address Fiona gave him. He stepped inside the correct suite and paused in the doorway. The sheer contrast of the room was an exercise in manufactured dichotomy. The communal office space was filled with tables—like a cafeteria but steel, glass, and electronic. People occupied about three quarters of the spots.

Despite the room being mostly full, the loudest sound was the tapping of keys.

He spotted Fiona across the room, head down, earphones on, and gaze focused on her screen. Nick sat across from her, his back to Parker.

Fiona looked gorgeous. The tip of her tongue was caught between her teeth. Her dark auburn hair was pulled up top of her head and knotted in place around a pen, and the way she hunched over her laptop pushed her round, full breasts together and out, to strain against her shirt.

He dragged his gaze away. *Don't ogle her.*

She didn't look up as he approached. He crouched in front of her and rested a hand on her knee.

She squealed and jumped, before focusing on him.

Behind her, every head turned in their direction with a glare.

"Sorry about that." He couldn't keep the amusement from his voice.

"You're not, really." She pushed back and stood, and he joined her. When she hugged him, her body molded to his. He could get addicted to this kind of greeting. He didn't remember hugs being like this last time he was here, but he wasn't complaining.

She grasped his fingers, tugged him toward one of the rooms along the back wall, and closed the door behind them once they were inside. The space had windows that showed the rest of the office, a desk built into the wall, and a chair. There wasn't space for much else.

"People come in here to take calls. It's mostly soundproof, so it keeps more of those nasty glares off us," she said

"It's kind of creepy out there." He nodded toward the room. "It was like some Children of the Cube-Farm thing. I was going to film, but I'm afraid if I piss off the wrong person, their irritation will devour my soul."

She laughed, light and soft. He liked that sound. "That's probably wise. You can take a wide-angle shot when we leave, as long as you blur it to hide faces."

"I promise." He made a cross over his heart. "I know I'm a little early, but can you sneak away for lunch?"

She let out an exasperated huff, but it didn't mar

her smile. "I guess, just this once." She reached for the door handle.

"Wait." He grabbed her wrist.

"Hmm?"

"I'm going to warn you up front—I'll have the camera on during lunch. I'll keep it on me," he added the last bit when she opened her mouth. "I know how you feel about that. But I'm going to nag you again about joining me on this trip."

"Asking me in front of five hundred thousand of your most distant friends isn't the way to change my mind."

Chapter Three

Nick's friendship with Parker went back almost as far as Fiona's. That didn't stop her from feeling a twinge of something she couldn't identify, but that tasted bitter, when Nick invited himself to lunch.

Though Parker was staying at her place, their schedules were such that they hadn't had much time with just the two of them to catch up, and she'd hoped to get him alone today, before he left again.

The guys spent most of the meal talking about the video-editing software Parker used, and whether he could hook Nick up with an expert to help him build Facebook video ads. Food came and went, and they lingered at their table, sipping soda refills, while Parker and Nick talked.

Parker nudged Fiona's foot with his. "You've been quiet."

"Just soaking in the knowledge." She gave him a weak smile.

"I'm sorry. This must be draining as fuck for you," Parker said. "I was supposed to take you away for lunch, but I dragged your office with us."

Nick's phone jangled, as if chiming its agreement. He looked at the screen. "Speaking of… I have to take this." He swiped. "This is Nicholas Walters… Hey, Chuck. Great to hear from you."

Parker tugged Fiona's fingertips, and she gave him her attention. She much preferred that to hearing Nick's half of a conversation with their contact at Grammie's Pastries.

"I didn't get to implement my master plan." Parker's voice was quiet. "Can I convince you in the next thirty to sixty seconds, while he's on this call, to go with me when I leave?"

Her *no* lodged in her throat. It should be easy to turn him down. She'd been doing it since he brought up the subject.

"As we discussed before, I've signed agreements in every city where you do business." A thread of stress wove into Nick's words. The client probably wouldn't notice, but to Fiona, he might as well be shouting.

She tried to block out his words, to focus on Parker. Nick would give her the details when he was done. *Say no*, reason chanted in her head. "Why me?"

Parker gave her a lazy grin. "You'll have my back. We always have a blast together. And you want to. This is your chance to see the world on the sponsors' dime. Or dimes."

"Not on such a large scale, no… Of course we can put that in a guarantee."

Fiona swore Nick's tension was contagious. She rolled her neck, to chase away the growing tightness. "What about my apartment? My bills? My student loans?"

Parker twisted his mouth, then opened it.

"It's complicated." Nick's voice rose a notch. "I'm not implying that at all. I have no doubt you'd understand, but I don't want to misspeak. Legal ramifications and all that."

Fiona's lunch soured in her gut, as she pieced together the basics. If they lost this deal, they wouldn't have enough for salaries in about three months, which meant another job for her. A second, most likely, because she couldn't stand the idea of abandoning this company.

Parker studied her, brows pinched. "You all right?"

"Of course. Let me speak with my team, and I'll get you an updated proposal. We'll be in touch soon, Chuck." Nick disconnected. "Shit. Fuck. God damn it."

Fiona looked at him in surprise. Nick never lost his cool like that. This was bad.

"Problems?" Parker asked.

Nick scrubbed his face. "Did Red tell you what we're working on?"

Normally she hated the nickname, because as a kid it meant someone was teasing her about her hair color. From Nick and Parker, she was okay with it.

"Uber for cookies?" Parker said.

Nick's chuckle was strained. "More or less."

"We have a huge client lined up." Fiona's mind worked separate as she spoke. "As in... it's Grammie's Pastries."

Parker's eyes grew wide. "*Huge* is an understatement"

"Right?" Nick smoothed a crumpled straw wrapper, then folded it into tiny squares. "They were an easy sell. Said they liked our personal approach. Individuals delivering their goodies to homes had that *Grammie cares* feeling."

"It was supposed to be a done deal." Fiona struggled to find a solution, for what they'd do if they lost the contract. Get rid of the space in the communal office? That would buy them another month, maybe.

Nick sighed. "Chuck wants proof we can operate effectively on such a large scale."

Fiona swallowed the frustration that tasted like bile rising in her throat.

"So give him proof." Parker made it sound like the simplest solution in the world.

Fiona shook her head. "Right now we're doing a handful of deliveries a week. They want dozens a day in every one of their locations."

"Our proof is a theory on paper," Nick said. "He's seen that, and as of today it's not enough." He slid down in his seat. "Without them, there's no way to do it in practice. *They're* our proof, and they're not interested in being our beta group."

Parker, who had listened to the explanation with his brows bunched together, grinned. "Convince them it's in their best interests to become your pilot."

"I don't think you understand." Fiona tried to keep her words kind, but this was the wrong moment for one of Parker's flights of fancy.

"I get it. Catch 22, right? You can't prove you can handle their business without their business, which they won't give you without that proof."

"Yeah...?" Nick dragged the word out.

Parker's grin grew. "I need a hook for this contest. Fiona needs an excuse to go with me."

"So our company falls apart, and you kidnap my sister?" A growl cut through Nick's question. "Wait. What contest?"

Parker gave him a rundown of the year-long, streaming, reality competition he'd been invited to. "Here's what you pitch to Grammie's. Arrange a batch of deliveries in each city. It doesn't have to be a full-scale implementation. Do a day's worth of business in each town. I'll do a ride-along, stream it, and it becomes free advertising for them and proof of what you're capable of."

"That sounds..." Nick sat straighter. "It's brilliant. I'd have to sell them on it, but I love it. How does Red fit into all this?"

"If you do this, her going with me is for the business. Excuse managed."

Irritation tickled Fiona's nerves. "I already told you *no*."

"But you wanted to say *yes*." Parker sounded pleased with himself.

Nick looked back and forth, as if preparing for a tennis match.

"That's not for you decide. I'm not going." Fiona wasn't going to let this get to her.

"Because you're terrified of stepping outside your boundaries." Parker snapped his jaw shut with a scowl that probably mirrored hers. "I didn't mean that."

But it was out there, shaking the fence she sat on and taunting the insecurities she tried to keep locked behind a gate. "Sorry we can't all live our lives based on whimsy, and run from anything that looks like it might mean establishing roots."

"*Whoa.*" Nick unfurled a napkin and waved it between them. "Truce. What's wrong with the two of you?"

Fiona was done here. She shoved back from the table. "Nothing. You both like this idea, you figure out the details. I'm going back to my desk, to find out a real solution for when Chuck laughs at you." It was a bad way to finish things—Parker had a good idea—but her ego was limping, and the reasonable part of her said she was being anything but. She needed to put some space between herself and the situation before it slid from *bad* to *unrepairable.*

There was no protest as she walked away, reinforcing the fact that she was making the right decision. That didn't make it sting any less.

For the remainder of the afternoon, Fiona tried her damnedest to focus. When coding didn't keep her attention, she shifted to profit and loss projections, and how they'd change if Grammie's didn't work out. The numbers blurred and taunted her, screaming they weren't going to behave without something drastic. Like Parker's idea.

Which brought her frustration rushing back, both with him for refusing to hear her, and with herself for wanting to be convinced but at the same time being unable to make herself say *I'll go.*

He's not a mind reader, logic taunted her.

Chapter Four

The afternoon crept up and then past, and Nick didn't come back. Five rolled around, and still no sign of him. She packed up her laptop and his, sent him a message telling him she'd drop his computer off at his place, and headed out.

Parker was waiting for Fiona when she left the building. His lopsided smile made her stomach flip and flutter, and she mentally growled at her reaction. "Do you have a minute?" he asked.

He wasn't getting away with pushing his will on her by being sexy. It wasn't fair. She adjusted the two laptop bags on her shoulder and stepped around him. "I have a busy night of anything else waiting for me."

"Red, please."

The sincerity in his voice shattered her resistance.

"Let me." He took both bags from her, and fell into step beside her as they walked toward the parking garage. "I'm sorry about earlier."

That was generic. She didn't want to gloss over Parker's making decision on her behalf. "Did you and Nick get the details worked out?" She stepped up to her car, unlocked the truck, and gestured for him to set the computers inside.

"I'm serious." He offloaded his bundle and turned to face her. "I'm not just saying words, to get back into your good graces. I was being selfish about this whole thing. You made your stance clear, and I won't mention the contest again. Except for…" He winced.

She clenched her jaw. "Except for what? Does it have anything to do with the question you avoided?" At this point, she was taking her indecisiveness out on him. It wasn't fair, but it kept her from blaming herself.

"Nick wanted to be the one to give you the news, but I talked him into letting me do it. We worked up a preliminary proposal, and he sent it to Chuck. They signed off on a one-week trial run, with the option to extend to a month and then longer, if things work out. I have my hook, and the two of you have a path to proof. I'm hoping you'll come celebrate with me."

"And…?" She waited for him to sneak in a line like, *so I have one more chance to talk you into going with me.*

"No *and*. This is you and me, hanging out the way we used to. A few hours of *us* time before I go."

"Deal." She smiled. She still hated that she was torn about whether or not to go with him, but she'd take the rest without question.

♥♥♥

Wyatt took a seat at the bar, and he scanned the room. It was a Monday night, so there weren't a lot of people. That was fine. He needed to sit, unwind, and decide if coming to Salt Lake was as wise as it sounded twenty-four hours ago. The competition was in town, and he was going to pay them a visit tomorrow. See if he could side-step Chuck's manipulation and make a deal that guaranteed Wyatt the contract.

He glanced at the beer list for the micro-brewery, then waved the bartender over. "I'll take an oatmeal ale." Might as well enjoy the local culture while he was here.

Drink in hand, he cast a lazy gaze around. A redhead sat at the far end of the bar, her blank stare locked on a half-empty martini glass, while she poked a thin red straw at the cherry in the bottom of the drink.

Her lost, almost sad look called to him. He didn't come here for a hookup, but he wouldn't say *no* to a distraction.

He grabbed his glass and relocated to the seat next to her. "Have you found any answers in there?" he asked.

She looked up, and it took her a moment to smile. "I'm sorry—what?"

"I figured, for as intensely as you were watching that cherry, it must hold the secrets to the universe. I was wondering if you'd uncovered any." He kept his tone light and teasing.

"Not yet."

He liked the hint of defiance in her tone. "Maybe that's not the right cherry. Time to let that one serve its purpose and let me buy you another drink so you can try again."

She gave a tiny laugh. "I'm all right. Thanks."

"I never said you weren't."

A guy approached and draped his arm around the redhead's shoulder. He was as intriguing as she was, but on the other side of the coin—pale green eyes, light-brown hair, and a carefree smile. Wyatt wouldn't hesitate to hit on him under other circumstances. If the two were a couple, he was moving on.

"Who's your friend?" the guy asked.

"I didn't get his name," she said.

Wyatt extended his hand. "Wyatt. And I apologize. I should have realized you were taken."

"I'm Parker, and this is Fiona." He returned Wyatt's handshake. "And—I'm sorry—taken?" The two exchanged a look Wyatt couldn't interpret. "We're not a couple, just close friends."

Wyatt doubted it was that superficial. The spark flowing between the two was intense enough, he could almost taste the ozone. But if they were going to deny it, who was he to argue? He only wanted company for the night. The tough part would be picking which of them he was more interested in. Or convincing them to trap him between them and let him absorb some of that electricity. "In that case, let me buy you both a drink."

Parker's *I don't think so* overlapped Fiona's hesitant *Sure*.

Wyatt focused on her. "You don't sound sure."

"We're celebrating."

He didn't know what one had to do with the other. "Champagne it is, then." He grabbed the bartender's attention and placed the order. If the company could pick up the two-grand strip-club bill for Chuck, they could foot tonight's drinks, for sending Wyatt out here. "What's the occasion?"

"I'm getting my own TV show." Parker settled in the seat on the other side of Fiona, and scooted it a few inches closer to her. "Competing in a YouTube reality TV contest, to earn a sponsor. We're going to deliver sweets."

Wyatt would argue that wasn't real TV, but he didn't want to shatter his tentative link with these two. What were the odds they were in the same business as Grammie's? But Utah was famous for its bakeries. Sweets plus streaming videos wasn't the same as a multinational effort to deliver hand-baked goods. "Sounds like something worth celebrating."

"Do you do this a lot? Buy expensive champagne for strangers in bars?" Parker studied him with a guarded expression.

"Only the ones who catch my eye."

Wyatt's response drew a blush from Fiona. The pink dotting her pale cheeks was its own type of alluring.

"Besides, I should have been having a party of my own tonight, instead of traveling. This way, at least someone gets to enjoy it," he said.

"What was the occasion?" Fiona asked. Her tone was demure but she kept her gaze on him and her bottom lip snagged between her teeth.

Parker was harder to read, but he listened,

curiosity lingering behind his eyes.

"I've been negotiating a huge contract for months. The deal was as good as done, then *poof*, they walked away." Wyatt hated admitting he failed, under normal circumstances, but the Grammie's deal didn't technically fall through, and the story should be good for sympathy points. Once upon a time, he wouldn't have dreamed of going for the of emotional manipulation. Then he met, fell for, and lost Devin.

A lot of lessons learned there, that were helpful in both business and keeping Wyatt's personal life complication free.

Fiona sighed, but she gave him a half-smile. "Been there, done that."

"Are you in sales?" Wyatt wouldn't have pegged her as a salesperson, but he'd been wrong before.

"No. I'm a programmer. Salesmen make my skin crawl."

Parker chuckled, and Wyatt raised his brows.

"Oh, God. You're one of them, aren't you?" Fiona buried her face behind her palms and peeked at him through her fingers.

This was fun. "I fit the stereotype of *salesman* as well as you do that of *software developer*. As in, you don't."

"Got that bit. Thanks for the clarification." Parker's tone was flat.

Wyatt should walk away from this situation. Fiona was interested, but as much of her reactions were politeness. Parker radiated moderate levels of stand-offishness, though some of that was a mask. Wyatt was intrigued by the combination. His path to next steps with the not-couple was through Fiona, not Parker, so he spoke to her. "Besides, your friend here is probably an epic salesman."

"Take that back." Despite Parker's protest, a hint of pride at the compliment lay underneath.

Fiona laughed. "He really is. Except for—"

"What are you selling in Salt Lake?" Parker asked.

Curiouser and curiouser. "Me. I'm always selling me. The product doesn't matter if the person behind it can't back it up."

"What's your product?" Fiona leaned in, arm on the bar and hand near Wyatt's.

"Packages."

"Really?" Parker didn't sound impressed, but a smile peeked through. "Do you follow a line like that with, *mine is nine inches long, and you'll never regret the purchase*?"

Fiona's blush darkened.

Wyatt had to know if he was right to assume Parker was bisexual. "I don't know what kind of guys hit on you, but you deserve better, if anyone's ever said that to you."

"What do you consider better?" Parker shifted in his seat, moving closer to Fiona and Wyatt.

"I'm a fan of the direct approach. For instance…" Wyatt dipped his head toward Fiona's ear. She radiated the faint scent of lilacs and dryer sheets. "We'll have a lot more fun if we take this upstairs. Not *that* kind, though I'm not ruling it out; I figure it'll be easier for us to talk up there."

"I can't argue with that." Fiona's reply was breathy.

"Talk?" Parker studied him. "What happened to preferring the direct approach?"

Wyatt had definitely read him right. Desire raced across his skin. "That's as direct as it gets. We'd talk. If the clothes came off, that would be incidental fun."

Fiona downed the rest of her champagne with a single swallow and reached for the bottle. "I'd have to be a lot more drunk to agree to that."

Parker covered her hand to stop her from refilling her glass.

Wyatt was glad to see he wasn't the only one who disagreed with Fiona's logic.

"We either drink or fuck. Never both." Wyatt didn't have a lot of rules, but that was at the top of the list. "If you need the alcohol to convince you, I'm not interested."

"Another round of drinks on Mr. Suit." Parker filled everyone's glasses.

Wyatt liked this, which defied all logic. The conversation was fractured, bordered on antagonistic, and wasn't getting him laid, but it was fun. Might as well see where the rest of the night took him.

Three hours and two bottles of champagne later, the three had moved the conversation to Wyatt's hotel room, mostly to avoid the harsh glares of the other patrons in the bar.

He sat in one easy chair and Parker in another, with Fiona perched on the arm of Parker's seat. They were laughing, and try as he might, Wyatt couldn't remember what started this round.

He hadn't had this kind of a pleasant buzz with

his drunkenness in a long time. Fiona and Parker were probably only a few years younger than his thirty-two, but they had a carefree attitude he couldn't grasp. The professional, uptight portion of him thought it was childish. Relaxed, chilled-out-him thought it was charming. "You know what I'd like to see?"

"The biggest ball of twine in Minnesota?" Amusement danced in Parker's eyes. "'Cause I've seen it, and you're not missing anything."

The combination of absurdity and logic made Wyatt laugh. "No. But yes. But no. I want to see the two of you kiss."

Fiona blushed. She seemed to have a shade for every occasion.

"Not a good idea," Parker said.

A frown whispered over Fiona's face.

"Why not?" Wyatt wouldn't be half the salesman he was if he couldn't read people, and the energy racing between these two all but glowed. "You've done it before, right? Fooled around? Experimented? You've known each other for years."

"We haven't." Fiona's scowl deepened. That wasn't good. "That is, *yes* to the knowing each other for ages. But not the other stuff. Why would you want to see that?"

Wyatt could bring the fun back on track. "You're serious? Because the two of you look good together. The voyeur in me is imagining it and likes what he sees."

"I couldn't." Fiona shook her head, and this time it was Parker's expression that fell.

"Why not? It's easy." Wyatt closed the distance

between himself and Parker. "I'll show you." He cupped Parker's face and kissed him. It was supposed to be a quick brush. Enough of a moment to raise everyone's pulses a notch. But Wyatt didn't want to pull away. He slid a hand to the back of Parker's neck, holding him captive and deepening the kiss—dancing their tongues together.

When Parker grabbed Wyatt's shirt in his fists and gripped tight, flame raced across Wyatt's skin, snarling for more. Urging him to nudge Parker back. To press him to the wall and remove the clothes putting too much distance between them.

Fiona's whimper penetrated Wyatt's thoughts, both mingling with and disrupting the moment. He forced himself to let go and sit, but Parker's impish half-smile made him regret the decision.

"See? Easy as pie." Wyatt looked at Fiona. That didn't help calm him any.

"I can't top that. Wow," she said.

"Sounds like a challenge." Parker pulled her to him. He knotted his fingers in her hair and tugged hard enough Wyatt felt it in his scalp.

Parker claimed Fiona's mouth, swallowing her gasp. Wyatt's cock strained against his slacks, begging for attention. He didn't know if he wanted to be one of them or simply sit back and watch their unrealized energy explode into something nuclear.

This was supposed to be playful fun. At least one of them was too drunk for it to be more. The thought didn't calm the need spilling through him.

Parker broke the kiss and rested his forehead against Fiona's. "Holy fuck, Red." His voice was an octave lower and breathless.

Wyatt seized the nickname as a chance to shift the climate back toward neutral. "Red, as in Red Riding Hood?" The moment the joke slipped out, a new slew of fantasies teased him. The shy redhead in nothing but a cloak and garter belt. Parker would have to be the sexy woodsman. Shirtless. Too kind for his own good.

But that made Wyatt—

"Then are you the big bad wolf?" Fiona's question overlapped his thoughts. She turned to face him. Her lips were swollen and dark pink, and fuck if he didn't want a taste. "You're definitely up to something wicked."

He'd like to be. "In that case— My, what big eyes you have."

"That's my line." Fiona studied him with those stunning peepers.

"No, it's not." He should back away from this, but a little more teasing wouldn't hurt—a promise to make sure he haunted her fantasies the way she and Parker would linger in his for at least a few days. He stepped closer and dipped his head to hover near her ear, never making contact. "Because I'm not eating you tonight." He spoke softly, but Parker should hear. "When I do, you'll be begging me not to stop. Quivering maybe, but not in fear."

"That's a big promise." Her voice cracked.

"I'm a big guy."

Chapter Five

Two kisses—one rough, one sweet, both hungry—lingered on Parker's lips. Fiona stood between him and Wyatt, her fingers still tangled with Parker's.

He was tempted to pull her from the room. To take the Big Bad Wolf comment at face value and walk away far and fast. But Parker couldn't drag his gaze, or any of the rest of him, from Wyatt.

Wyatt dragged his mouth along Fiona's neck, eliciting the softest of gasps.

"One taste won't hurt, though." Wyatt's voice was a low growl that flowed over Parker's skin and left electricity in its wake.

Wyatt nipped her neck, then followed a line along her jaw and to her mouth. Claiming. Devouring. He trailed his fingers down her arm, to cover her hand where it was tangled with Parker's. He guided them both to cup Parker's erection through his jeans, stroking and teasing while he swallowed Fiona's groans in an eternal kiss.

Parker balanced on a knife's edge between pleasure and concern, but the touch, the sounds, and the fuzz of champagne tilted him toward the pleasure side. He'd embraced his bisexuality years ago, but a guy like Wyatt was different—the suit, the disdain for the world around him, the arrogance…

Wyatt was one hell of a kisser, and—fuck—the things he was doing with his fingers… Tracing the outline of Parker's shaft. Pressing down, then easing up.

Parker was tempted to fuck his hand.

Fiona, though… Parker couldn't get that kiss out of his head either. He shouldn't see her in that light. That kind of lust had the potential to destroy a friendship, especially since she was drunk too. Would regret this in the morning. Was leaning into Wyatt, who glided a hand up her chest to tease her breast.

Parker wanted to take a step back, free his erection from its prison, and watch while this scene unfolded. He wouldn't. He summoned the last of his willpower and broke the contact between everyone. "We should get going." He was surprised he kept his voice steady.

"Already?" Fiona jutted her lower lip.

Wyatt stepped back. "You're right. Yeah. Good call. It was a lot of fun. Good luck with your streaming… video thing."

"Thanks." Parker gave him a thin smile. What was an appropriate *goodbye* in a situation like this? He settled for wrapping his arm around Fiona's waist and saying, "See you around."

"Sure." Wyatt sounded as insincere as Parker

felt.

Parker and Fiona made their way to the elevator. She leaned into him on the ride downstairs. "I see why you like this."

"Like what?" Anonymous hook-ups with men whose individual suits were worth more than Parker's wardrobe?

"Going where the wind takes you. Following your impulses, instead of being bound by responsibility."

He wasn't sure he cared for the way she phrased it. It echoed their earlier argument too closely. He led her to the curb and called for a Lyft. The busses in this town might be efficient as hell, but they also didn't run after midnight. Fuck. It was after midnight. Fiona was going to be pissed in the morning, waking up hung over and running on little sleep on a work day.

"It's got its ups and downs," he said.

"Still. The meeting strangers. The letting go. Experiencing… things." She slurred the last word.

"You're drunk."

She moved to stand in front of him, her back to his chest, and pulled his arms around her waist. "That doesn't mean I'm stupid. Just a little less with the inhibitions. I liked Wyatt."

"I'm pretty sure he was actually bad a guy as he claimed."

"I don't think so, but if he is, you can rescue me. In fact, you can rescue me in general."

Parker pulled her closer, enjoying her weight against him. "Did you have something in mind?"

"I want to go with you."

Of course she'd pick *now* to say *yes*. He wanted to jump on her answer.

"Still believe I'm too drunk to think?" She glanced over her shoulder at him.

Shit. "If you want to go in the morning, I'll make arrangements."

He was grateful when their car arrived and the conversation faded. Not because he didn't want to talk to Fiona, but her proximity and her faint scent and the cool night air were wreaking havoc on his control.

A little sleep, and they'd both be fine. And as long as she didn't take back her answer, he'd be better.

♥♥♥

Wyatt tugged the hotel-room curtains tighter together, blocking out that last sliver of morning sun. He massaged his temples and sank onto the edge of the bed. He didn't remember the last time he drank that much the night before when he had to work the next day. College, probably.

Then again, the entire evening with Fiona and Parker reminded him a lot of those days. Silly, reckless, and too horny for his own good.

The thought brought another—a reminder of some of the horrible lines he used. The ache in his skull grew. Christ. He couldn't believe he'd compared himself to the Big Bad Wolf. And that bit about eating her…

Aspirin. He needed it. And coffee. It was a good thing his schedule was open ended today. He could let the hangover fade, gather his wits, and in a few hours, track down this Nicholas Walters guy.

He skipped the room-service menu and turned on the coffee maker. Did he really charge those drinks to his corporate account?

At least, unlike Chuck, Fiona and Parker were good company.

Images of the round of kisses they shared flooded back, searing his skin and blanketing his nagging headache. He smiled. Definitely worth it. He wouldn't mind seeing them again. Parker said something about videos. What were the odds Wyatt could find him on YouTube?

Probably about one in a billion. It would be more entertaining that local news and early-morning television, though. He opened his laptop and pulled up the site in question. He typed *Parker,* then paused. This was ridiculous. He hit *Enter*. Only four million results. Was that all?

He leaned back and scrubbed his face. Yup. Absolutely ridiculous.

He straightened up again, to close the browser, and his gaze landed on a familiar face, three videos down. *Parker Travels* was the name of the channel. Not the most original title, but the guy had over two million subscribers. Whatever the hell he was doing, it was working. And the most recent upload was from early this morning.

The scent of brewing coffee filled the room, and the drip sputtered into the pot. Wyatt clicked *Play*. An ad for the latest mobile phone ran, and he let it finish. Might as well let this guy get his monetization. He grabbed a paper cup from the short stack, filled it with coffee, and added a generous amount of sugar.

"All right guys—I think I screwed up, but maybe not." A tinny version of Parker's voice filtered through Wyatt's speakers.

Wyatt settled back into his chair to watch, drink in hand. Parker's face was illuminated by the screen he sat in front of, that cast the room behind him in shadows that reflected those under his eyes. Lines creased his forehead, and a day's worth of scruff darkened his chin. Wyatt lingered on the memory of the rough burn that five-o-clock shadow left behind.

"Fiona said she's going with me, but she was drunk. But she was lucid. But" — Parker raked his fingers through his hair—"I should back up."

Wyatt didn't usually care for this kind of thing. He didn't understand the appeal of an under-produced piece of footage, especially someone narrating to the camera with nothing else going on. Parker had a captivating kind of honest charisma, though. Wyatt would wonder if it was clever editing, but the guy had the same thing in real life.

"So here's the deal," Parker said. "I'm doing the contest, and I'm going big. I have a sponsor, signed, sealed, delivered. Never expected to snag one out of the gates, but we drew up the paperwork yesterday, and you guys are going to love it. Grammie's Pastries are letting me be their face for at least the next month. Longer, if y'all keep voting me from round to round. We just have to use this app Fiona and her brother wrote to schedule some deliveries."

Wyatt didn't hear the rest. The words *sponsor* and *Grammie's Pastries* were stuck on a loop in his head. He opened a new tab, and searched for

Nicholas Walters. The first result was the same app developer he discovered the other day. The one Grammie's said was his competition.

This time, Wyatt clicked over to their website. It was clean, attractive, and tiny. He navigated to the *About Us* page.

Nick and Fiona are a dynamic sibling team who want to share their enjoyment of—

Wyatt closed all the tabs in his browser and shut his laptop. A stunt like this, some charming-as-fuck YouTuber delivering cookies in person and telling the world about it for the cost of room and board? That was the kind of gimmick Grammie's would get behind, and if it went well, it would destroy Wyatt's chance at the contract.

He could fix things. Make this work in his favor.

He'd wanted to see Parker and Fiona again, and if they were hitting up cities Grammie's was in, he had a built-in excuse to travel to wherever they were.

Every company wanted to jump on board with the latest social media gimmick, but very few wanted to be associated with anything less than *family friendly*. All it would take to send this potential deal into a tail spin was footage of something like what the three of them got up to last night, making it into Parker's feed.

It was time for Wyatt to ensure he landed this contract.

Chapter Six

Fiona glanced at the guest bedroom door on her way to take a shower. *Closed.* An odd concoction of relief and disappointment mingled inside. Traces of last night lingered in her head, both the memories and the nagging ache of having drunk too much.

She had fun, and looking back, there were no regrets. She drew a finger over her lips, sinking into the memory of Parker's kiss. It wasn't the first time they'd done that, but she'd forgotten how intense it was. The rush that flowed between them… The way he made her feel like the only person in the universe with such a simple gesture…

Fiona shook the thought aside and let Wyatt glide in to take its place. He was dark to Parker's bright. Consuming, engulfing, and drawing her into a pocket of intensity she never wanted to emerge from.

The overlapping images danced along her skin, tightening in her nipples and making her grateful her vibrator had fresh batteries.

She forced the loose thought away and pushed herself through the motions of getting ready for another day in the office. An hour later, she gave Parker's closed door one more look before heading to work.

As she walked into the hallway, she heard a latch and Parker's, "Fiona, wait."

She locked the front door behind her. She hated to pretend she hadn't heard him, but if she stayed, he'd want to know if she felt the same as last night. She wasn't sure if she could walk into this Grammie's-live-streaming thing with him, but if she'd stayed around and talked to him, she'd say *yes* before she figured it out.

One thing was for certain—she wasn't ready to dive into that kind of life the way Parker had, even if she went with him. He'd been running since Gretchen passed away. Always looking for the next way to escape. To hide. To pretend that part of their past didn't exist.

At least Fiona had dealt with it.

She walked into the parking garage under the building and paused in front of her empty spot. *Crap.* She'd forgotten she left her car behind last night.

At least the busses were running now, and thanks to Parker, she knew which one would get her to the office fastest. She'd have Nick take her to pick up her car at lunch or something.

When she strolled into the office a short while later, the room was immersed in an eerie symphony of different keyboards being used by people who typed at different speeds.

Nick glanced up when she took her seat, a tiny

smile playing on his face.

What was that about? She tried to ignore it, and set up her workstation for the day. The moment she was online, her messenger pinged.

How was the celebration? Nick asked.

Amazing. Terrifying. Hotter than she thought was possible, between that stranger and Parker. She shoved the last thought aside, to revisit it later when she was alone. *It was fun.*

I didn't think you wanted to go with Parker.

She stared at the words, trying to make sense of them. *Who else would I celebrate with? It's his news.*

I meant on his trip.

Fuck. Even after promising he'd wait for a real answer until she was sober, Parker had run his mouth to Nick. She stood with a huff. "Did he call you before I got here? Because—"

Every head in the room turned a glare on her, and heat flooded her face. She sank back into her seat and ducked her head, wishing she could disappear behind her monitor.

He didn't call me. Nick's reply was followed by a YouTube link.

Fiona made sure her earbuds were plugged in and clicked *Play.*

She watched as Parker told the camera—and five hundred thousand of his closest friends, according to the page views—that she'd said *Yes* to going with him.

It's not set in stone. She resisted the urge to send the message in all caps. No reason to yell at Nick over this.

It is now. Grammie's has seen it, and they love

it. You're part of the contract, or they're pulling it.

Jaw clenched, she stomped to her feet again and met Nick's gaze. He shrugged. She nodded toward one of the sound proof offices at the edge of the room.

"Before you say anything," Nick said the moment the door was closed, "it's just for a month initially. You'll still be on salary. You auto-pay everything, so your bills and your rent will be covered, and I'll watch your apartment."

She stalled on a retort. That was what she wanted, right? She was free to go. So why was she hesitating?

"I know, you think staying is the responsible thing to do, but I've got you covered. If this goes well, it'll be huge for us. And I know you want to do it. Go, Red. Take off, keep Parker company for the next four weeks, and enjoy the fuck out of seeing the world on someone else's dime."

With her excuses gone, and his support and permission taking their place, her earlier fear came back. What if this was a bad idea? It was safe here. Familiar. Comfortable.

"Take the day off," Nick said. "Go tell Parker you're going. Figure out what you need to do on that front. For the rest of the week, we'll make sure everything is under control in the office."

"You make it sound so easy." She found her voice.

"It is."

"I'm going to need a ride to my car."

Nick opened the door. "Sure."

As they headed toward the parking lot,

excitement bubbled inside, dancing with her doubts. This was going to be an incredible ride. With a little luck, that would be a good thing. She prayed to God things went that way.

Parker stood in the parking lot of the local Grammie's offices and led his camera up the three stories of glass and steel. "Used to be their corporate offices," he said to the camera. "They moved to Colorado a few years ago but left a lot of their setup here. We're about to step inside. I have Fiona with me, but I've promised I won't make her go on camera unless she wants to."

"Hello." Fiona wiggled her fingers in front of the lens, her tone light and playful.

For the first day or so, she'd grumbled about being corralled into this, but as the week went on, her scowls vanished, replaced with smiles and excitement as they planned each leg of their trip.

Parker wasn't complaining. He loved having her here with him—Fiona the Voice—keeping him company while they showed the world how cookie delivery was awesome. "We promised Grammie's we would only film in designated areas, so you're about to see a whole lot of lobby, until we meet our first delivery driver," he said to the camera. "But stick with me. I promise the fun is just getting started. You trust me to show you the ins and outs of wherever I go, and that's what we're up to."

He and Fiona walked into the reception area of Grammie's. In contrast to the modern exterior, wood paneling, area rugs, and plush furniture greeted them.

A man a few years younger than them smiled and approached the moment they walked through the doors. "Are you Parker? I'm Will." He extended his hand. "It's great to meet you. I'm super excited to be your driver for the day. Is the camera on? I can't believe they're letting me do this. I'm so excited."

"Will. Hi." Parker shook his hand and talked over him before the poor guy could ramble them through another week. "This is Fiona. We're thrilled to have you showing us around, and yes, I am streaming this live."

"Oh." Will's smile froze in place.

Parker draped an arm over his shoulders and pulled him in, as if they were the only two people about to hear this. "There's a secret to doing this right. Forget the camera is there. Or if you have to, pretend it's another person you're talking to. One who doesn't talk back." He stepped away again.

"Isn't that frustrating? Not getting real-time feedback from whoever you're talking to?" Will asked.

"Are you kidding? I love it."

Fiona and Will gave him matching confused looks.

"You ever think of the perfect comeback a couple hours after the fact?" Parker said.

Will nodded.

"Me too." Parker winked at him. "But I get to add it in post."

Will and Fiona laughed. Perfect. Everyone was at ease. They could get something done. Parker and Fiona sat in the back of Will's car, and the delivery boxes were nestled in coolers in the trunk, protected from being jostled and melted.

Part of Parker's contract with Grammie's kept him from saying certain things on camera. Streaming was more difficult—no swearing, no lewd comments, no blatant innuendo—but for the most part, he avoided those anyway, to keep access to all the good sponsors. Part of the prep for this venture was that Nick's app ran a promo—anyone placing an order with Grammie's today got delivery for free and agreed to be filmed.

Up-front releases signed, this was about to be the perfect start to the perfect hook, so he could win the perfect prize.

Three hours later, as the three of them stopped for lunch, Parker wasn't so confident anymore. Every single delivery went smoothly. Which wasn't a big deal, but it made for shitty views. The most exciting event they had was the young boy who wanted to wave to the camera while his sister watched it inside, on the computer.

Their grins made it worth it, but Parker could almost hear his ratings dropping off with each stop.

Apparently, he'd agreed to a month-long Grammie's commercial, complete with milk and cookies, and living, breathing Normal Rockwell paintings.

If he didn't figure out a way to inject some flavor into this, he wouldn't even get the month. His time would be up at the end of the week.

He glanced at Fiona, who was chatting with Will and doing her best to stay behind the camera. Would she go home early if that happened? And which was more important to him? Winning this competition and securing the sponsorship, or keeping her by his side?

He didn't know why it was even a question. He'd pick Fiona in a heartbeat if it came down to it, but that was one of the amazing things about their friendship—she wouldn't make him choose.

Chapter Seven

Fiona's sneakers echoed off the tile of the airport floor. With no chatter around them, to drown out the noise, her and Parker's footsteps sounded unnaturally loud. Apparently, not even the most dedicated traveler wanted to catch a flight at five thirty in the morning.

She bit back her five-billionth yawn, as she and Parker made their way to their departure gate.

"This is Salt Lake airport, at un-Godly a.m.," Parker said.

Fiona wasn't expected to answer; he was talking to the camera. She was adjusting to the fact that he did that out of the blue, as well as getting used to the idea they were really doing this. Preparing to leave work behind for a month, making travel plans, and figuring out schedules with Parker and Grammie's—seemed to take an eternity and at the same time didn't give her enough of a chance to prepare mentally.

"Do they let you leave that on during the

flight?" She walked a few steps back from Parker, rather than next to him. It was the easiest way for her to keep out of the filming line of sight.

Parker shook his head. "Nope. I'll turn it off before we board."

"But you're subjecting your viewers to an empty airport terminal in the meantime?" she teased.

"Don't know. We'll find out." He turned the lens toward him, and she stepped to the side. "She's got a good point, friends. We haven't had a chance to drink our coffee, and it's too freaking early to be witty. I'm signing off for now. When we land in Denver—which will seem like two seconds to you, thanks to the magic of editing, I'll be fun again, and Fiona will be her sweeter-than-cookies normal self."

She nudged him with her shoulder. "Shameless flatterer." This was the one thing she slid into without hesitation—spending more time with Parker. It was as fun and natural as she remembered.

Parker yanked the camera up again, to talk into it. "One more thing. Tell Fiona in the comments how much you want to see her on camera."

"Not likely." She laughed, but as they reached their gate and she saw a familiar face, she faded off.

Wyatt sat a row back from the gate, several seats between him and the sparse smattering of other flyers. Mr. Big Bad Wolf had teased her dreams a couple of times since their encounter. Sometimes he stripped her down, and others she watched him with Parker.

She wasn't sure which dream was her favorite, but as the memories of both raced over her, they drew her senses to life, dancing over her skin.

Wyatt looked up from his phone and treated her to a delicious smile that made her feel like she was the main course.

"Not signing off quite yet," Parker said to his audience as they drew closer to Wyatt. "Want to meet one hell of a smooth-as-fuck bastard?"

Wyatt covered his face. "Not on camera. I want whatever immunity Red has from being filmed."

The nickname carried a new meaning, rolling off his tongue. More unpredictable, but also tantalizing. Fiona wasn't sure how she felt about it, but it sent a new wave of fantasies spilling through her. Wyatt pressing her to the wall. Tangling his fingers in her hair. The deep, throaty growl of the way he said *Red*. Or maybe her imagination would have filled in those blanks regardless of what he called her.

And she should be talking to the people outside her head, rather than letting imaginary versions of them undress her. "I never would have pegged you as camera shy."

"Professional expectations and all that." Wyatt smiled.

"Fine." Parker's sigh was exaggerated. "I won't subject my audience to two disembodied voices, but I will share highlights with them later, including any new lines from Fiona's favorite *Big Bad Wolf*."

Wyatt winced. The hint of discomfort made him more approachable, but not any less delicious.

Fiona shoved the thoughts aside. She needed some coffee, stat, to get rid of her wandering lust. And Parker had a point—the *Big Bad Wolf* line didn't sound as seductive when it didn't come through a champagne filter.

"You give the camera a much cooler *goodbye* than you do a stranger in a hotel room," Wyatt said, as Parker stashed his baby in its padded carrying case.

Parker clenched his jaw.

At least the tension was still present without the booze. Fiona resisted the urge to roll her eyes, and turned to Wyatt. "Are you stopping in Colorado, or flying through?" It seemed a little convenient he'd be on the same flight as them, but if he had to head east, it made sense he'd want to leave early.

Besides, she and Parker were the only people here not wearing business suits, so they were the ones who would seem more out of place on the painfully early commuter flight.

"Flying through." Wyatt patted the seat next to him. "Heading to Indianapolis."

Too bad he'd probably be gone by the time she and Parker got there. "That's wh—"

"One hell of a city." Parker talked over her.

She stared at him. What was his problem?

Wyatt knew Fiona was going to say *That's where we'll be in a few days*. He might not be Chuck's favorite guy right now, due to Grammie's contract's being up in the air, but it only took a five-minute call to Tony, who worked reception for Grammie's, to get a copy of Parker and Fiona's schedule for the next month. A little flirting on Wyatt's part, accompanied by the assurance they were telling the internet anyway, and he had what he needed.

He handed Fiona a card with his name and number scribbled on it. Not an official business card. The last thing he needed was them figuring out he worked for the competition. "If you're in Indianapolis in the next couple of weeks or Atlanta after that, look me up," he told her. "I promise no more Big Bad Wolf lines."

"Don't extend the offer to be polite." Parker's retort had a bite to it.

Wyatt apparently had rubbed Parker the wrong way in more ways than one.

Fiona took the card and gave Wyatt a warm smile. "Ignore him. He's not a morning person. Maybe we'll run into each other again." She was almost like a different person this morning. Still reserved, but not as shy. He liked that.

"I hope so," Wyatt said. He figured things would go one of two ways—either Parker and Fiona wouldn't make it past Week One, which meant Wyatt didn't have to worry about them, or he'd find a way to become a part of their adventure by the time they left Indianapolis. He was hoping for the second. There was a lot of potential with these two, and he wanted to have some fun before it all came crashing down.

"Good morning, ladies and gentlemen." The airline employee's greeting over the loudspeaker cut into the conversation. "We have a short flight to Colorado this morning, with continuing service to Indianapolis. At this time, we'd like to invite all platinum members to board."

Wyatt gave Fiona and Parker one final smile,

stood, and slung the strap of his laptop bag over his shoulder. "Enjoy your flight, and good luck with the competition."

"Thanks." Parker's reply was flat. He and Fiona fell into step behind Wyatt, to join the platinum members' line.

Wyatt glanced at Parker's camera bag. He should have noticed the conspicuous silver tag earlier. The guy traveled a lot, based on his videos. Of course he'd have things like frequent-flier miles racked up.

Wyatt kept half an ear on their conversation as they drifted from one topic to the next.

"*...looking forward to Tampa...*" That was Fiona, excitement lining her words.

"*...roller coaster you'll love...*" Parker's voice held as much enthusiasm, but with a hint of adoration. "*...the gulf, but from the Texas side...*"

Wyatt tuned them out. He already had their schedule, and the ease and affection of their conversation gnawed at a part of him he needed to keep dead—the pit inside that tried to remind him not everyone was out to screw someone over. That pit lied and got him in trouble every time he listened to it.

A few minutes later he boarded, stashed his laptop in the overhead bin, and settled in his seat. One of the best things about flying this early was the lack of other passengers. A plane this small didn't have a true business class section, but at six in the morning, there weren't so many people squeezed in here that it was difficult to move.

When Parker and Fiona took the seats across the

aisle, Wyatt hid his smirk. This should give him the chance to get better acquainted with one of them during the flight. He'd put money on Fiona sitting by the window, after the awe in her voice at the idea of seeing Tampa Bay and Disney World for the first time. She'd probably read when she wasn't watching the scenery below. Parker struck him as being the chatty guy who would want company, which gave Wyatt a chance to break past that defensive barrier.

His theories crumbled when Fiona nudged Parker into the row first. "I'll take the window next time," she said. "You know you want to sleep a little longer, and you'll be more comfortable there."

Parker grinned and dropped into his spot. "You're too good to me. When we get to Denver, we're going to brunch. Best place this side of the country."

"You don't have to bribe me." Fiona sat and pulled out her phone. "But I'm not going to turn you down, either. Brunch. Dinner. Mountain hikes. I want to do it all."

Wyatt would rather spend the flight working than listen to the two of them in their too-good-to-be-real bubble of glee. He scanned his email while the flight attendants went through their standard demonstration, and then he grabbed the magazine from the seatback in front of him, to flip through while the plane taxied.

Ads. Articles posing as ads. Hype. Several of them for his employer. They spent millions a year on these stupid promo pieces, but his boss had grumbled at the expense request Wyatt made for this trip.

But the Grammie's contract was too important

for them to let slip away, so Wyatt talked his way into approval without too much drama.

He turned at the sound of a frustrated huff. Parker was already asleep, and Fiona stared at her phone with a scowl.

"Problems?" Wyatt asked.

She looked up. "Nothing big. I thought I synced my books onto the device, but the one I wanted isn't here."

"What are you reading? Or hoping to read?" Maybe he'd found his conversation after all.

Pink tinged her cheeks. "Nothing you've heard of."

He wasn't sure if that was disdain or discomfort. "Don't judge." He winked. "Despite the good looks, I'm also well-read and intelligent."

Her raised brows said more about what she thought of that than her lack of response.

"It's true." He chuckled. "I've even read the classics, though I was never a fan of Dickens."

"Me neither. He's wordy, pedantic, and dry."

Wyatt nodded at the empty window seat next to him. "Join me? And tell me what you're reading. You'd be surprised what I've heard of. Or if you prefer to watch the landscape below…"

"I can't impose."

"You'd rather stare at the seat in front of you for the next hour, while your buddy sleeps?" Wyatt asked. "Keep me company."

She chewed on her bottom lip. He'd seen that a lot in his life—usually a conscious effort at flirting or seduction. Fiona doing it looked unintentional, and that was far more attractive. "All right." She unsnapped her seatbelt and moved across the aisle.

He half-rose to let her slip past, and her intoxicating scent—jasmine and soap—drilled into his thoughts.

They both sat again, and she turned her attention to the window. "The ground always looks fake from this high up."

"A bit like a children's playset." That was a more appropriate response than *a lot of things do if you examine them from the right angle.*

"Exactly." She continued to stare through the Plexiglas. Seconds ticked away.

"It was *The Siren*," she said. "Told you you'd never heard of it."

She meant the book missing from her phone. Sexy, aggressive-but-lost heroine. A not-hero. And the ending… He understood why she'd blushed; the book had its share of hot, explicit sex. It seemed Red had a wicked streak hiding underneath. Electricity rolled over him. He wouldn't mind uncovering and feeding that streak. "I've not only heard of it, it's one of my favorite books."

"You don't have to say that to make conversation." She looked at him.

No, he didn't. But he did feel obligated to prove he wasn't an illiterate chest thumper. "Is this your first time through the book, or are you re-reading it?"

"I've been through it a few times." The corners of her mouth twitched in an unformed smile.

Given the book's in-depth exploration of BDSM lifestyles, his dick jumped to about fifty conclusions in half a second, all of them involving ropes or spanking, and none of them making it easy for his big brain to carry on the intelligent side of this conversation. *Ask her if she wants to join the mile-high club.* No. He needed this relationship to last beyond sex in an airplane bathroom. And he, not his penis, needed to talk to her. "Then the ending, with the gift..."

"And the leaving and the getting back together." She grinned. "Such a good story." Reservation faded from her voice, leaving excitement and joy in its place.

"I completely agree."

She twisted her mouth.

He didn't know what to make of it. "What?" Now that he had her talking, he wasn't ready to let the conversation lapse.

"I wouldn't have pegged you as a romance guy."

He couldn't hide his disgust. Romance—the concept in general—was for suckers and idiots. No reason to say that out loud. "Romance is for suckers and idiots." *Oops.* "I used to like the illusion of happily-ever after, but it's one of those things that reads as so fake to me now, I can't do it. The Siren is literary. It's erotic. It's not romance."

"Does it hurt to be so jaded?" A current of seriousness marred her teasing question.

"Hurts a lot less than the alternative." He clenched his jaw. He shouldn't be skimming the surface of this part of himself with a stranger. Then again, she was smart. She'd see through his bullshit if there wasn't at least a hint of truth to it. The best lies were based on reality.

She studied him, green eyes seeming to reach

past his surface, for secrets he didn't even show himself. "Almost all stories have romance in them. What are you reading instead?" she asked.

"You tell me." He wanted to steer this back to superficial. Twice now they'd talked, and twice now she'd nudged him toward an intensity he didn't like. He needed to watch himself with her, going forward. "Are you thinking I'm more of a Stephen King kind of guy? Or John Grisham?"

"Honestly? I'm having a hard time thinking past the image of you, reading a Harlequin paperback with some shirtless cowboy in the front, and not caring who saw you in some random airport terminal."

"Never cowboys." His disgust was more playful this time. "Grew up around the not-quite-real thing. They're not for me."

She wrinkled her nose and searched his face. It was a cute look on her. "Hmm... Not CEOs or Sheiks. That would be too close to your reality. Firefighters, maybe."

He wanted to ask what *too close to your reality* meant but was concerned it might take them down that serious path again. "The books have heroines too. Maybe I don't care what he's like, as long as she's the perfect combination of intelligent, reserved, and loyal." Not that anyone was actually loyal.

"Sounds very specific." Amusement danced in her eyes. "Policemen, then?"

He chuckled. "I'm a sucker for uniforms of any kind. Or I was. These days, I prefer high fantasy."

"Because romance is too unrealistic." She rolled her eyes, but her smile never faded.

"Yup. Give me dragons over love any day."

"In that case, back to your question. I would have pegged you as a suspense guy," Fiona said.

Stalkers and psychopaths? No, thank you. He didn't know if it was worse when the authors got it right or when they got it wrong. "Too much like reality for my taste."

A whisper of a frown crossed her face, and he was grateful when she didn't push for details. The conversation drifted from books to how different the mountains looked from twenty-five thousand feet, to her work.

He was looking for an excuse to not give her more details about his job, when the attendant announced they were beginning their final approach.

"I should get back to my seat before we land." Fiona stood as much as was possible under the overhead bin.

Wyatt shifted to let her pass, but grabbed her wrist when she stepped into the aisle. "Wait."

She watched him with expectation. He rested a hand at the base of her neck and brushed his lips over hers. The light contact sparked over his nerves and stole his breath. A silly kiss shouldn't do that to him.

She blushed. "What was that?"

"I had to know what it was like when I had my wits about me," he said smoothly.

"And?"

"Worth it." He dipped his head to her ear. "Look me up when you get to Indiana."

She looked surprised when he pulled back. "How did you…?"

"Anyone could have guessed that was what you

were going to say in the airport. I'll be there for a week. Bring your friend, or not. It's up to you."

"All right." She gave him a shy smile and returned to her spot next to Parker.

That went well. Possibly too well. If this was a movie, he'd be half a scene from getting fucked in a very bad way.

Fortunately, real life wasn't a movie.

Chapter Eight

Fiona shifted against the upholstery of the Ford Fiesta—who drove these anymore?—and tried to find a place to put her knees that didn't leave them pressed to her chest. She settled on a position with her legs tucked to the side.

When she got back home in a month, she was adding a feature to the delivery app that required drivers to specify how big the back seat of their car was. She wasn't sure how she'd justify it, once the Grammie's marketing push was over and the drivers didn't need room for three people in order to do their jobs, but she was making the change regardless. Out of some sort of after-the-fact spite or something.

Parker sat next to the driver, chatting about random topics, camera rolling. He'd offered to let her take shotgun, but he needed to film, and it made more sense for him to do that from the front seat.

"Why delivery driving?" Parker asked their guest star for the day. "Choice? Convenience? Nothing better to do?"

The woman—Sally? Sharon? Fiona felt horrible she'd forgotten the name already—wore a pasted-on smile that showed off all her teeth. "I like not being in an office. The tips are nice. I get to meet new people."

The next day, their driver said something almost identical. The two might as well have been reading from a script. Driver number two looked more comfortable being filmed. He glanced at Parker. "You know what I mean. About the freedom, that is. You get to see the world."

"Are you a fan of my show?" Excitement nipped the edges of Parker's voice.

The driver's smile wilted. "I watched an episode when they told me I had this chance. It's a cute gig."

Fiona winced, grateful no one was looking at her, and Parker sank a few inches in his seat.

The three days of deliveries in Denver blurred together as much as the conversations with the drivers.

I can't believe I'm on TV.

Parker smiled widely and said "It's YouTube. Which is the same, but better."

Of course. I knew that.

Or, *Sure, those videos for kids. Can I say* hi *to my mom?*

And, *Can I wave to my dad?*

Even, *I want to wish my kids a Happy Monday.*

Parker's smile grew each time, until it looked stretched, but Fiona was certain only she saw that. "Of course," he said. "Are they fans of my channel?"

Your what? Oh. No, they're not.

Fiona knew Parker didn't expect everyone to

watch the show, but when they checked into their hotel in Omaha, the morning of Day Four, he didn't stand as straight, and his words were strained during his morning *conversation* with his viewers.

Fiona hated seeing him like this. There were days when she'd watch his videos at home and see the circles under his eyes or hear the exhaustion in his voice. She'd always drop him a text or an email when she saw that, to make sure he was all right.

He'd already assured her several times that he was fine.

They had today off. With luck, that would help him recharge. They'd agreed they could share a room, since they were taking this trip together and it didn't make sense to ignore each other at the end of every day. Maybe she could convince him to not film for a few hours, and they could stay in and unwind. Or go see the city through their own eyes.

Because tomorrow was the last day of their week-long trial run for Grammie's, and she didn't want to see it flop.

She tossed her bag onto her mattress and sat next to it. "What should we do first?"

"Um… Hang on." He pulled his laptop from its bag and set it on the desk. "Is there a Wi-Fi password in the hotel directory?"

She opened her mouth to answer, and he said, "Never mind. Room numbers. I forgot." His fingers flew across the keyboard, then tapped on the desk's wood surface while he waited for pages to load. "*Come on,*" he muttered.

She flopped onto her back to stare at the ceiling. Of course he had to check his insights first. The plummeting stats made the frown lines on his face deeper every evening.

"I know your views aren't as high as normal, but at least we're doing this together. And having fun. That's something," she said.

He made a sound that was half-growl, half-sigh. "Are you, really? Jammed into the backs of too-small cars, listening to people babble about how amazing cookies are and get offended they won't see themselves on network TV? Are you really having fun?"

"I'm enjoying your company." Rather, she would be, if he'd spend less time pouting. She sat again and fixed a glare at his back.

"Me too. But that's not getting my stats up, and it doesn't pay the bills." He dropped his face into his hands. "That came out wrong. I'm sorry."

"I get it." She struggled to keep the irritation from leaking into her voice. "You're trying hard to balance the Grammie's contract with the status-quo, and it's not as carefree as you're used to."

He scrubbed his face. "You *don't* get it. Every time you say shit like that, I can tell you don't even come close to getting it."

The venom in his voice caught her off-guard. "I'm trying."

"That's part of the problem." He looked at her, gaze boring into her. "What you're *trying* to do is make this lifestyle fit in with the one you've built up as the *Parker doesn't care about anything* world in your head. I know you don't have a lot of respect for what I do, and for some reason, even though you know me, you think the person on camera is the same as the person in real life. And none of that is helping right now."

She bit the inside of her cheek, anger and hurt warring inside. She wasn't interested in a repeat of the argument they had before she agreed to this, and snapping at him when he was in this mood wouldn't solve anything. "What can I do?" That should be a safe question.

He worked his jaw up and down, his frown deepening. "I don't know. We're locked into this contract. If it all crashes and burns, we can keep going within the rules of the competition, without having to do this dull-as-fuck Grammie's bullshit. Unless my ratings kill my chances before then."

"This was your idea." She struggled to keep a grasp on sympathy.

"I *know*. God damn it, I know that."

She wouldn't shout back. She wouldn't let this escalate. "Maybe do some brainstorming before tomorrow's deliveries? Ask your viewers what they want to see. You've done that before."

"I've given them multiple-choice options, like *sushi or barbecue for dinner*. I'm not stupid enough to open up the forum and let them just toss ideas out. What good is that going to do me?"

She let out a long, slow breath between clenched teeth, and glared at him. "I'll call Nick now and tell him to cancel the contract with Grammie's. This isn't supposed to make you miserable." That meant she and Nick would lose the contract as well, and it gnawed at her that Parker might be selfish enough about his drive to escape the world that he'd do that to them.

She reached for her phone.

Parker groaned, pushed to his feet, and came to sit next to her. When he covered her hand and took her phone away, a shock of heat seared from his palm and up her arm. "Don't." The frustration had bled from his voice, leaving tiredness in its place. "We'll figure something out. You and me. Please?"

"All right." The agreement didn't take the sharp edges off her mood, but she wasn't ready to give up and go home, and she hated fighting with Parker.

He wrapped his arm around her shoulder and pulled her into him. "There's an art museum in town. I'll leave the camera at home, and we'll go see Omaha."

"Sounds fun." She forced happiness she didn't feel into her response.

♥♥♥

Parker had a lot of practice wearing a mask for his channel. He rarely missed a day of posting, regardless of how he felt. Today, as he knocked on the door for their final delivery, he hated that mask. Wanted to rip it off and never pick it up again.

Fiona was trying to be nice. Which made things worse. If she'd listen to him, rather than shut him out for the sake of getting along, he might be able to make her see.

Scratch that. She might never understand. Sure, this was a lot of fun, and he was one of those lucky few people who got to do what they loved for a living, but it was still his fucking job.

When the door opened and he found himself face-to-face with Cora Welton, his simmering anger seared through his gut and landed in his shoes.

"Oh." Fiona's voice was soft behind him.

Parker was grateful for the mask again. "Hey. It's been a long time." What else was he supposed to say to the sister of the girlfriend he lost to a car accident nearly a decade ago?

"Delivery from Grammie's." Their driver-de-jour stepped forward and handed Cora the box.

"Thanks." She never took her attention off Parker, as she set the cookies out of sight. "Wow. It's really you. I had to see it for myself to believe it. I just… I can't." She looked past him, at Fiona, and he followed her gaze, jerking his head back at the last second, so he wouldn't catch her in the shot. "I always knew he was an asshole, but not only is he still running, you're with him," Cora said to Fiona.

Bile burned up Parker's throat at the accusation that he was running, and he fumbled for a retort. An apology. Something.

"We all miss Gretchen." Fiona stepped up next to him. Her voice was kind but didn't leave any room for argument. "But it's been ten years. Moving on doesn't mean he didn't—*doesn't*—care."

Cora sneered. "Which might sound more sincere if the two of you hadn't moved on while she was still here."

An invisible fist clenched around Parker's heart. No one knew he and Fiona were almost a couple back then.

"I'm gonna wait in the car," the delivery driver said.

"That was the only reason she was out that night," Cora said. "Drunk. Leaving me tear-filled voicemails. Not paying attention. She found out about the two of you."

"I'm sorry. If I could take it back, I would." Fiona's voice cracked.

No. Bullshit. Parker didn't like the way that part of his past had unfolded, but he didn't regret anything that happened with Fiona. "We didn't do anything." That was true. He and Fiona agreed he'd break things off with Gretchen first, and then they'd figure out where they stood. "I hate how things turned out. Every day I wonder how it would be if it went differently, and I beat myself up over her death, but we have to go on living."

"Why? Gretchen didn't get to. You lied to her. You broke her heart. And in return, her name was smeared across local papers for being an irresponsible killer, while you're seeing the world, pretending the past doesn't exist." Hate spilled from Cora.

Parker forced ice through his veins. It was the only way to keep himself from saying something he'd regret. He shut off the camera. "I'm sorry. I can't say that enough, but it won't change things." It took more strength than he thought he had to get the words out without choking on the past.

"Fuck you." Cora slammed the door.

"We're done." He couldn't look at Fiona. Didn't dare see the pity or fury or grief in her eyes. He turned and stared at the delivery driver instead, surprised the guy was still here. "You'll have to finish the rest of the route alone."

"Yeah, no. It's cool. I mean, obviously the whole thing isn't, but... Do you need a lift somewhere?"

"No, thanks. Our hotel is only a few blocks away." It was actually a mile or two, but he needed to collect his thoughts.

Neither he nor Fiona spoke on the walk back.

His guilt and anger hadn't faded, when they reached their room. He flung the door open, and cringed at the *bang* when it bounced off the wall.

"I didn't realize." Fiona's voice was soft behind him.

"What?" He forced himself to look at her. "That Gretchen knew you and I lov—cared about each other? She wasn't blind. Or that I still feel guilty about how she reacted?" If they kept talking, he'd push Fiona's buttons, and he didn't know if he had the power to care. The hurt in Fiona's gaze—the way it reflected his own—was worse than anything else she could have thrown at him.

"I figured you still cared. Still felt bad about it. Or you wouldn't be running."

He was so fucking sick of people accusing him of hiding from this. "For the last God damned time, I'm not fucking running from anything, except—" He snapped his jaw shut before he could say what he was thinking. There was no way this was the right time for admitting he still harbored a ten-year-old crush to go with that ten-year-old guilt.

"Except what?" Fiona asked.

"Forget it. I'm sorry. About what happened back there, about… Forget it."

"No." She squared her shoulders. "We've got at least three more weeks together—longer if this goes well—but you've been hiding something from me since you asked me to come with you on this trip. What do you want from me, Parker? Why am I here? Why are you making yourself miserable, to do this? What's the point?"

"We're not having this conversation. Not now." Not while emotions raged and wounds were fresh and he wasn't thinking straight.

"And if I push the issue, then what? You'll send me home? Because you twisted and manipulated things to get me here, and I want to enjoy it. It's taking some adjusting, but I'm willing to admit this might be good for me. And what happened back there with Cora? That hurts. Believe me, it's gnawing me from the inside out. But it's an old scar, and I cried myself out ten years ago. And nine. And eight. And now I want to know why you're shutting me out. Is it about what Cora said? Because I have a feeling there's more."

"Fine." If things were going to hurt, might as well reopen every wound associated with the past. "I didn't leave because of Gretchen. I'm sorry, and I hate that it happened, and everything I've already said, but I left because of you."

"I... What?" Fiona frowned.

And Parker's resolve faltered. He steeled himself. "I can't stand the way you push me to arm's length. All. The. Fucking. Time. You go out of your way to convince *everyone* we're just friends. Each time you say that, you might as well knife me in the heart." He stepped closer, gaze locked on hers, as he searched for any reaction to his words. He didn't know how to interpret the flicker he saw.

She moved back as he advanced, watching him,

her brow furrowed and her bottom lip caught between her teeth. Fuck, why did she have to do that? She stopped when she collided with the counter in the kitchenette. "What am I supposed to say instead?"

"I don't want you to say anything you don't mean. If that's what we are, it's fine. But I want to know what happened to the almost-more we had back then. I wanted you here because I want to see if that still exists. This trip, this invitation—all of it is about you. How much I want you and how much I need you to start seeing me. Not the guy in front of the camera, but *me*." He didn't mean to let that much slip out. Hell, he'd never put it all into words in his own head before. It left him raw and exposed.

"Okay."

He didn't know what she meant by that, and he didn't have the brainpower left to interpret it, so he let instinct drive his actions. He tangled his fingers in her hair and crushed his lips to hers, needing to feel something besides pain.

For a blink, when she froze at his touch, he swore his heart stopped. When she kissed him back, molding her body to his and digging her fingers into his chest, a wave crashed over him, muffling everything bad.

He gripped Fiona's hips, lifted her to sit on the counter, and slid between her legs. He needed to be closer. To lose himself in the moment. A tiny voice in the back of his head whispered this was the wrong way to do things, and he silenced it. Fuck propriety and consequences and tomorrow morning. He needed this *now*, and the way she clung to him said she did too.

Chapter Nine

Fiona groaned against Parker's mouth and dove into need—his, hers, all of it. Logic tried to point out she wasn't doing this for the right reasons. It was the same logic that almost talked her into passing up this trip and that picked fights with Parker, and she was sick of listening to it.

She could vanish in this—his grip in her hair and the way it tugged at her scalp, his legs against the inside of her thighs, and the soft fabric of his T-shirt against her fingertips.

He yanked her head back, to suck along her neck, and she gasped at the sharp sting. Her head was a mess, her heart wasn't doing any better, and he felt so good. She'd wondered for ages what it would be like to have more with Parker, and damn it, she was going to find out. This was better than thinking.

She wanted to experience more. She pulled he bottom of his shirt, and he took the hint and broke away long to yank it over his head and toss it aside. Parker's scent, musk and deodorant, drilled into her senses and helped shove all thought further to the back of her mind.

She raked her nails up his back, drawing him closer, and he hissed against her neck.

"I don't have any condoms." His lips vibrated on her skin.

One more thing she didn't want to think about it. "I'm on birth control. Anything I should be worried about?"

"No." He unhooked her bra, and stripped that and her top off. When he lowered his head to one nipple and trailed his tongue along the swollen skin, any response she had evaporated.

He alternated between sucking and nibbling, sending a rhythm of pleasure and desire dancing through her. The sensations focused in her belly, as if yanking a cord, and then traveled lower. Every time he ground against her, his erection digging into her mound, she felt the dampness between her legs.

Every touch from Parker, no matter where, was a new spark of need. It was as if her entire body was an erogenous zone. She dropped one hand, to cup his shaft through his jeans. He pressed into her palm with a moan, pumping his hips in response to her stroking.

"God. I need you, Red." His voice was gravelly.

"Me too." She undid his pants and worked him free. His dick was hot against her skin. Hard and eager. When she dragged her thumb over the head, she smeared a drop of precum.

"Fuck this. I've been dreaming about you too long to be patient."

His words flared white hot inside her, burning away the last of her reserve. He dreamed about her? In a fumble of hands and shifted weight, she helped him tear off her jeans. His hung off his hips, and she wrapped her legs around his waist, to pull him back to her.

When he thrust inside her, fast and slick and without hesitation, it stretched her out. It was an exquisite ache, and she arched her back.

She tried to set the pace, wanting to feel him pound against her, but he gripped her hips tight. "I'm already going to have a hard time lasting," he said. "You feel incredible. Don't rush it."

She pouted, and he nipped at her bottom lip before kissing her hard again. Despite his words, he built to a fast pace, slamming deep. She'd never had sex like this. Not this intense or desperate.

With each thrust of his hips, he hit something inside her that made her clench around him, needing more. She was pushed near climax, but she didn't think she could come from penetration alone. She'd never even done that with toys.

He lowered his head to her breast again and drew a nipple into his mouth. The hard sucking mingled with the well already brimming in her, and orgasm washed over her. She gripped him tighter with her legs, not wanting him to stop—needing to ride this wave.

"Jesus." He moved his mouth back to her shoulder, bit hard, and fucked her harder. His groans became short grunts, and he spilled inside her. She didn't want to let him go. They should be able to stay wrapped in this moment forever.

As the heightened pleasure faded, he slowed, then stopped.

She rested her forehead on his chest, not daring to speak. Not wanting to ruin the invisible shell encasing them. He leaned more of his weight against her and the counter.

If she spoke, she'd have to reach into the part of her brain that could think. The bit that would assault her with logic. She wasn't ready to deal with that.

Watching Parker's channel had become part of Wyatt's morning routine more quickly than he wanted to admit. The first few days, he told himself it was research for work. He needed to know if Parker and Fiona would make it past Week One.

Wyatt settled into the easy chair in the corner of his hotel room, coffee in hand and laptop perched on the edge of the bed, and clicked *Play* on yesterday's delivery video. He was at the point where he had to admit he enjoyed Parker's work, though it took him sifting through a few months of archives to reach that conclusion.

Parker had earned his subscriber count and page views; the guy oozed charm in front of the camera. He was the perfect balance of relatable and confident.

This week, with the Grammie's shots, something was off. Parker still shone, smile in place and easy-going attitude at the forefront, but it wasn't genuine anymore. The guy was hiding fifty shades of misery.

Wyatt had a feeling the Grammie's contract was one yawn away from crashing and burning for the competition. By the time his meeting with Chuck rolled around, he'd have a proposal in hand and no little startup delivery app to contend with.

A shout from his speakers drew his attention, and he watched an argument unfold between Fiona, Parker, and someone who had a lot to say about an ex-girlfriend. Correction—*deceased* girlfriend. It was beyond awkward to watch, but Wyatt couldn't tear his gaze away.

Parker was quick to defend the past and just as diligent in keeping Fiona off-camera. As he cut the recording, he faltered on both parts before the screen went blank.

He stared at the black rectangle on his laptop, processing what he'd witnessed. Parker and Fiona were almost more once. That explained the spark between them and why they fought against it so hard.

He almost felt guilty, watching that intimate moment unfold. It was worse realizing that a few hundred thousand other people had done the same. He looked at the views. Correction—more than a million. The clip was climbing toward being the top viewed ever on Parker's channel.

As Wyatt studied the pained look on Fiona's face at the end, the anguish in Parker's voice... There was definitely a bit of feeling bad for them going on.

A look at the comments told him the audience wasn't as sympathetic.

It's about time this show got good.
Fcking selout got what he desrved

Dude, ditch the corporate chains and go back to making kick ass clips

Some of it was variations on what Wyatt had read over the past week, and coincided with the dropping views each day. But some of the remarks were in a brand new vein.

That's fiona? You're fucking her right?

I can't believe you gived up truer love for someone like that. Pig.

Maybe you're show wudn't suck so much if it was just the redhead. Takin off her clothes.

As Wyatt read more comments about Fiona, he frowned. For almost every one, someone named lumb3rjck76 jumped to her defense. It looked chivalrous at first.

Watch your mouth. She's a person.

Hey, asshole, apologize.

Then he reached the comment that said, *fucking beotch needs to smile. I'd rhape her ass until she was happy.*

Lumb3rjck76 replied with, *When I find out where you live, I'll personally ensure you know how unpleasant a threat that is.*

With the chivalry, it could be Parker using an alias, but the tone wasn't his. Not from what Wyatt had seen. Then again, the guy was part chameleon, so perhaps—

Don't listen to these assholes, gorgeous. I'll meet you at your next stop and make sure nothing happens to you. Lumb3rjck76 had repeated the same comment every fifty or so, meaning it always appeared on-screen.

Ice ran through Wyatt's veins. It was too

familiar. Or he was overreacting. He prayed for Fiona's sake it was the latter.

His cellphone rang, jarring him from the trip down memory lane. He glanced at the screen, snarling when he saw his boss's name.

Wyatt swiped *Answer*. "Morning." He kept his tone cool.

"How's the contract chasing going?" Brett's voice was snide.

"Fantastic." Wyatt wouldn't rise to the challenge of a pissing match. "Grammie's is still my priority, and as of now, it looks like we'll be able to make onsite adjustments to this office, to meet their requirements. Once I'm done here, on to the next one."

Brett knew this—he'd signed off on Wyatt's trip—but he also knew that a deal like this meant Wyatt would climb over him on the promotion ladder.

"Keep on top of it." Brett sounded anything but sincere.

"Sure. Anything else?"

"Now that you mention it… Some guy called the main offices looking for you. Devin, maybe?"

The name yanked back Wyatt's uneasiness about the comments on yesterday's video. He might be hoping for Fiona and Parker to fail, but he didn't wish a stalker on her. Or anyone. "Thanks for the heads-up. I have to be at the local offices soon. I'll keep you updated." He disconnected before Brett could reply.

As Wyatt finished getting ready for work, a sick ache gnawed at his ribs. He was never a direct victim of Devin's obsessions, but he'd been an ignorant accomplice on more than one occasion. He'd never forgiven himself for unwittingly helping Devin stalk and assault a series of women.

And he didn't want to see Fiona end up in a similar situation to Devin's victims.

Chapter Ten

A haze lingered in Fiona's mind, keeping her on the edge of sleep and treating her to snippets of the night before, with Parker. She didn't know what was most appropriate—*wow* or *finally* or *what have we done.* Scratch that. She wasn't thinking that last one.

She rolled over in bed, and when she felt the cool sheets next to her, consciousness tore in. She opened her eyes to see Parker's side of the bed empty and a soft glow filling the room. Kind of like what a laptop would cast.

Most of the feathers tore away. She sat up and turned toward the source of the light. Parker sat at the desk, computer open, headphones on, and video editing software up.

Irritation snaked through her, followed by a memory of his irritated accusation that she didn't understand what he was doing. Why it was so important to him. She tempered the hurt of him abandoning the warm bed in favor of his channel.

The clock said it was almost six, and she rarely saw him up before nine, so this must be important.

She wrapped the comforter around her like a cape and climbed from the bed. When she touched his shoulder, Parker jumped.

He had his earphones off in a heartbeat and whirled to face her. "Fuck. You scared me."

"Sorry. Are you getting a lot of work done?"

"I am." He cast his gaze away from her. "But I'm glad you're up."

Her gut did a flip that ended in a nosedive. "Why's that?"

"I'm sorry about earlier."

"You mean the fighting? The scene with Cora? It needed to happen, even if the situation wasn't ideal." The gnawing on the lining of her stomach insisted that wasn't what he was talking about.

He shook his head, gaze turned to his feet. "That. What came after. All of it. I shouldn't have— We don't— I'm sorry."

He meant the sex. Anger and hurt surged forward, making her want to gag. "Of course you are. In that case, me too. It was an outlet, right? It didn't mean anything? We were both hurt. You've been under a lot of stress. Nearest port in a storm." As she spoke, she yanked on her clothes. She shoved everything of hers into her duffel bag, not caring what order it landed in as long as the zipper still worked after.

"Red." He grabbed her wrist.

She jerked from his grip. "*Don't.*"

"Where are you going?" He was finally looking at her.

Away from the guy who was supposed to be her best friend but used her for sex. Really good sex. Who she would have been happy to talk with about what happened, agree they were better off as friends than as lovers—anything other than *I'm sorry I fucked you.* "Anywhere that isn't here."

"Fiona, please. It came out wrong. Stop and we'll work through this?"

"I'm taking the shuttle to the airport." She didn't know why she was sharing her plans with him. "If you find me at our gate before your flight, I didn't decide to take a different plan home." She slung the strap of her bag over her shoulder and placed her hand on the doorknob. "But don't hold your breath."

She stalked toward the entrance, unable to keep a few simple words from repeating in her head. *I'm sorry. I shouldn't have.* Like it was all his decision? And it was a bad one, at that?

Then there was the fact that he refused to look her in the eye.

Tears welled up, and she wiped them away until her cheeks stung. She didn't dare look at anyone, let alone talk to them. She kept her gaze on the ground—like Parker had—and made her way out to the shuttle.

Fortunately, it was empty. She sat near the back, not sure if she wanted Parker to chase her down now or let her walk away with any dignity she might have left.

The driver climbed aboard and glanced at her. "Waiting on anyone?" he asked.

Apparently not. Fiona couldn't make her voice work. She settled for shaking her head.

The vehicle rumbled to life, and a moment later,

they were navigating city streets. They stopped at three other hotels. Fiona was grateful only a few other people boarded and they all sat in their own corners.

As the road rumbled through the floor and the tires thwapped on pavement, she was lulled back toward her center. Last night she knew there was something off about the interaction. She wanted it. She couldn't count the number of times she'd lain in bed fantasizing about being with Parker, especially a few years back. And the sex was good. Better than, even.

But it was for the wrong reasons. She knew it while they did it, though it was easier to admit now, with the sun cresting the mountains and glinting through tinted glass.

That didn't mean Parker's approach to breaking the news hurt any less. His apology looped in her head, crawling under her skin with each repeat, until she wanted to scream for it to stop.

She pressed her palms to her eyelids until stars danced in her vision, and gritted her teeth, willing the ache out of the memory.

The bus slid to a stop, and she opened her eyes. They were at the airport. Did she buy a ticket home, or wait six hours for her scheduled flight and for Parker?

She didn't know, but at least she had a little while to figure it out. She grabbed her bag, gave the driver a brief smile, and made her way inside. Fiona headed toward security. She could check in online, or purchase a new ticket the same way once she figured out what she was doing.

There were only a few people queued up for the metal detectors, and Parker stood near the rear of the line, scanning the airport.

She wanted to hide her smile, but it slipped out, complete with the conflict that raged inside. "How did you get here before me?" If she said anything else, it would either be an accusation or a plea to forget about what an asshole he'd been. Neither felt like the right answer.

♥♥♥

"I hitched a ride with someone else checking out. I wanted to stop you before you got on the shuttle, but I didn't know if you would listen." Parker enjoyed the fuck out of last night, then falling asleep with Fiona in his arms, and waking up next to her.

But guilt gnawed at him. That same lingering feeling that never left, and surged back so strong after Cora's accusations, it threatened to devour him. He *did* hate what he did to Gretchen and the way he left things with Fiona after.

He'd needed to catch up on work this morning, so he tried to use that to clear his head. Instead, he stumbled on a series of comments on yesterday's video. Drooling over Fiona. Offering to take her away from him.

That led him to pull up old clips he had of her. Movies he'd promised would never see the light of day, because she was embarrassed to be on camera, with her laughing. Smiling. Being carefree.

And when she woke up, he was in that half-gone place, mentally, that made his words come tumbling out all wrong.

"Let me try again, please? To explain what I mean, that is," he said now.

She clenched her jaw and folded her arms, but she stepped away from the security line. "Knock yourself out."

"I…" He had to get this right. "It wasn't a mistake. The sex, that is. I don't regret it. Fuck—it was incredible. But I don't want to relegate our relationship to the strictly physical. You're my best friend, and I'd never forgive myself if I lost that in favor of getting laid."

She gave him a half-smile. "That's only marginally better, but I understand where you're coming from."

"Yeah?"

"Yeah. Friends first. Last night was a remnant of the past. One of those things we didn't get to explore back then, that's loomed over us forever, and now we've gotten it out of our system."

That wasn't what he'd been going for, but if she was forgiving him, they could work out the rest later. "Come to Indiana with me?"

"I'd like that."

He rested a hand at the small of her back and nudged her into the security line again. The brief contact seared through him with longing, and he suppressed the desire. They'd figure this out, but letting lust take the lead wasn't the way.

They shuffled through the line, silence hanging between them. This wasn't right.

On the other side of the metal detector, they put their shoes back on, stuffed phones and wallets away, and grabbed their carry-ons.

He didn't know if he was relieved or not when Fiona's phone range. She glanced at the screen. "It's Nick." She swiped. "Hey… Right next to me… We're in the airport. Hang on. Let me find someplace quieter."

Parker took the cue and guided her toward an empty departure gate.

"Just a sec," Fiona said into the device. "Okay. You're on speaker."

"Hey." Nick's greeting sounded filtered.

Parker wasn't in the mood for chit chat, but this was most likely business. That, he could do. "Morning."

"I caught the feed yesterday." Sympathy filled Nick's voice.

"You and about a million other people." Parker should be grateful for the high views. The video was going viral. He couldn't plan for this kind of publicity. That didn't mean he liked what caused it.

Nick gave a nervous chuckle. "Including Grammie's. But first, are you two holding up okay?"

"We're fine. Great, even." Fiona answered before Parker could. "Tell him what you told me."

"Right," Nick said. "So, like I said, I talked to Grammie's. They love your numbers from yesterday's feed, and since the footage didn't paint them in a bad light, they're okay with that, too. They want to extend the contract with Parker to be a month to month, starting with two months up front. They'll give you more freedom to film what you want, as long as you don't mar their name."

"That's awesome." Parker clung to the excitement. It was nice to have a little good news this morning.

"But…" Nick trailed off.

Fiona frowned. "I don't like the sound of that."

"You'll like it even less when I tell you what it is. They want more of you on camera, Fiona."

Parker clenched his jaw. "She's not part of the contract."

"And he doesn't speak for me." An edge lined Fiona's voice. "That's fine. I'll do it."

What? Parker stared at her, looking for some hint of what she was thinking. She looked back, expression blank.

"It's not going in the contract," Nick said. "It's just a request. Think about it before you decide. Are you two certain you're okay?"

"We're fine." Fiona's answer came too quickly and was too sharp. "Look, we're starting to draw stares. You know—speakerphone plus airport equals rude. Can we call you back when we get to Indiana?"

"Sounds fair. Talk to you soon," Nick said.

Fiona disconnected and dropped her phone back in her purse.

"Are we really fine?" Parker asked. He knew the answer was *no*, but wanted to give her a chance to speak her mind if she had more to say.

She scrubbed her face, a sigh escaping through her fingertips. "It hurts. I'm still processing, but we'll get there. We've had cracks for a while now. This way we give them attention, right?"

He returned her smile, wondering if his looked as strained. "Exactly. We'll find that middle ground we should have worked through years ago." Or they'd lose a wonderful thing. He wouldn't let that happen, though. He refused to.

Chapter Eleven

Parker insisted Fiona take the window seat. He was going to be *working* most of the flight, anyway. "I've put too much off, the past couple of days. I need to catch up on edits," he said.

She gave him a bright smile. At least she remembered to sync the books on her phone this time, so she'd have something to read. She settled into The Siren, as the plan climbed toward cruising altitude. The book reminded her of the last flight she took and that Wyatt's business card was tucked in the pocket of her purse.

She had a feeling he wasn't the kind of guy who apologized after sex as though he was the sole reason it happened.

The thought left a bitter taste in the back of her throat, and she hated herself for having it. And what was she doing, making out with one guy, fucking another, then letting her mind drift back to the first?

She was unattached. She forced the words to stick in her head. She didn't have any sort of exclusive arrangement with either of them—she glanced at Parker, who had his head down as he worked—and no one seemed to be interested in redefining things.

Her mind drifted into the vividly erotic world on the page.

An hour or so into the flight, Parker nudged her. "Do you have a minute?"

"Sure."

He slipped his headphones over her ears. The gesture pinged inside with familiarity, longing, and a resentment she didn't like. He turned his laptop toward her and said, "I want your thoughts."

It was a video on the Rinslet Media's channel. A petite brunette with blonde roots stood in front of a green screen that shifted scenery when she spoke. "Hey, world. Chloe Nielson here. For those of you who don't know, I'm the corporate representative for this year-long affair. I know—sounds kind of dull, right? But I swear to you we want this competition to be anything but.

"This message is for our contestants. It's been a great week one, and all of you are doing great. We hope your subscribers love what they're seeing as much as we do, but we've got a little issue with your streaming. Each and every one of you."

Fiona frowned. That didn't sound good, so why was the woman grinning?

"You guys are doing a great job of keeping it clean and running smoothly. Even your live feeds are going off without a hitch. But let's be honest. Part of the reason millions are tuning in is for the unscripted content. It's time for your first challenge. In the next week, every single one of you will be given a time and a place and twelve hours' notice. Nothing else, though we promise to keep it legal. This is corporate-sponsored content, after all."

Fiona's thoughts drifted over the impact of something like this. It meant Parker had to step into the unknown and keep the cameras rolling in order to stay in the competition. Her instinct was to recoil, but the longer the idea rolled in her head, the more she liked it.

She handed Parker back his headphones.

"What do you think?" he asked.

"It sounds"—*terrifying*—"like a lot of fun." The randomness had an odd kind of appeal. "I'm in."

Parker looked surprised. "As in *in*, in? Are you going live with me?"

Was she? "Yes." Agreeing made her gut churn, but it also made her pulse race with excitement. "Absolutely."

Besides, it would be a good chance to show Parker how emphatically she agreed with the idea they were friends and nothing more. Hell, she'd play wingman if he wanted.

The conversation drifted off again, and a comfortable silence fit between them as they disembarked and caught a shuttle to the hotel.

Within a few minutes of checking in, Parker had his laptop out again. "I'm not caught up yet. I'm sorry. Give me a few hours—I'll hurry—then we'll go get dinner. See the city."

"Don't worry about it," she heard herself say with more nonchalance than she felt. "You need to focus." Was she being spiteful? No. This was support. He wanted her to understand this was his job, and she was trying. And this way, he had the room to do what he needed. It wasn't up to him to entertain her twenty-four-seven.

"Are you sure? What are you going to do?" he asked.

She pulled Wyatt's card from her purse. "See if I can find some company for the evening, and give you time to think."

He scowled and worked his jaw up and down. "Cool." His casual tone didn't match his expression. "Text me your details when you get there, and I'll catch up when I'm done."

"Good idea." She grinned. Was he making the offer because he was jealous? No. He'd made his stance clear. He only suggested it because part of the point of this trip was to spend time together. And even if he was being possessive or envious, it wasn't up to him. When it came to their relationship, he'd made his stance clear.

♥♥♥

Wyatt was surprised but pleased when Fiona called. He'd been figuring out how to put himself in their path again.

"I've got a free night, and you've been in a town a few days. If you're available, maybe you could show me the highlights of the city?" The blend of hesitation and boldness in her request was tantalizing.

He also didn't miss the singular pronouns. "I haven't done a lot of the tourist stops, but I can show you a few places the locals love," he said.

"You sound like P…" Her chuckle and words trailed off. "Never mind. Yes. Okay. I'm in."

She was going to say he sounded like Parker. The guy was drawn to dives and locals-only spots. It was one of the things Wyatt enjoyed about his clips. How much nudging would it take, to get her to talk about what happened after the camera stopped rolling the other day? Did it have anything to do with her solo request tonight, or was this coincidence?

"I know the perfect place to start," he said. "It looks like an armpit from outside, but it's the best Korean barbecue in the Ohio River Valley."

"That's oddly specific." This time her laugh didn't fade.

"It's not fine dining, but it's worth a visit. How's that?"

"Sounds perfect. I'll be there."

He gave her the address and said he'd be out front at eight, and he swore he heard breathy giddiness when she said, "See you then."

Fiona was waiting on the sidewalk when he arrived, five minutes early. She faced away from him, fidgeting with a strand of hair. Her jeans hugged her hips and ass, and accentuated her long legs. Her top was wispy and black, and he swore he saw a hint of red bra beneath. If the sun weren't fading behind the skyline, it might be easier to tell.

"I hope I didn't keep you waiting." He rested a hand on her shoulder.

She jumped and whirled, a shy smile and a blush spreading across her face when she met his gaze. "I just got here."

"Perfect." He dropped his hand to her hip, to

nudge her toward the door. "Shall we?"

A mouthwatering combination of scents greeted them when they stepped inside. Spices and meat. Bright fluorescents bounced off wooden seats and tables with grills in the center.

Wyatt's decision to meet here had more to do with how the meal was eaten than the food itself.

A woman showed them to a table in the back. "Careful of the middle—it's hot," she warned as she handed them menus.

Fiona hovered her hand a few inches over the metal surface, and Wyatt laughed.

"What?" she asked as she sat.

He shook his head. "That's what I did, too. The woman says *it's hot*, and the first thing most people do is check for themselves."

"I wonder why that is."

"People inherently distrust other people?"

"That's cynical."

"I'm a cynical kind of guy. What would you guess, if not that?"

Fiona trailed her thumb along the crease of the paper wrapper holding her chopsticks. "People are naturally curious. We want to learn. Experience. Grow."

"Is that why you're here?" That wasn't what he meant to ask, but it would let him drive the conversation anyway.

"Do you mean tonight, or this trip in general?"

"Yes."

She twisted her mouth into a crooked smile that pushed her lips into a plump, kissable heart shape. "Then, yes," she said.

Fuck—he liked sparring with this woman. "In that case, I hope your curiosity isn't sated after tonight."

She ducked her head, tucking a strand of hair behind her ear.

The waitress interrupted, to take their orders.

"May I?" Wyatt asked Fiona.

"Considering I have no idea where to start? Please."

He ordered a little bit of everything.

"Why the hot table?" Fiona asked when the waitress left.

He held up a finger, indicating she should wait. "It's more of a *show* thing than a *tell* thing. Until then, are you doing all right? I saw the clip from the other day." He let sympathy bleed into his tone.

Her skin paled several shades. "I'm good. Fine. An old wound, is all." Her voice was tight.

He hit a more sensitive nerve than he expected. "Does that *fine* have anything to do with why Parker isn't here?"

"He's got work to do. I left him to do it."

"Lucky for me, then." Wyatt wasn't going to call *bullshit*. He wasn't dragging this up to spoil the mood. Or maybe he was, in a way. He'd rather see the boundaries now, or at least get a loose idea of where they were, before he pushed her too far in the wrong direction. Wyatt would either be the supportive shoulder to cry on or the rebound guy. Perhaps both, if he played his cards right.

Their food arrived—two bowls of frozen raw meat, one of lettuce leaves, and a variety of dipping sauces.

Fiona raised her eyebrows. "Well?"

"Steak." He plucked from the first bowl and dropped a bite-sized piece on the grill. He repeated the movement. "And pork." Grease sizzled and popped between them. He unwrapped his chopsticks and tugged to break them apart. "Spicy or sweet?"

"Sweet." The way she licked her lips drove straight to his cock, but her ghost of a frown said he needed to shift her mood back to playful.

He selected a piece of lettuce, wrapped it around some freshly grilled steak, and dipped it in the plum sauce. Roll pinched between chopsticks, he held it across the table for her.

She leaned in and let him feed her. Her movements were an alluring combination of grace and hesitation. Lust danced across his skin.

"That's how it works." He kept his voice smooth and steady.

She pulled her chopsticks from their wrapper and snapped them apart. She tried to balance them between her fingers and thumb, but fumbled.

"Like this." He demonstrated how to hold them and pinch the ends together.

"You say it like it's an easy thing." She fiddled with the chopsticks for several seconds, the tip of her tongue caught between her teeth. One of the sticks clattered to the table, and she huffed.

He picked up the fallen utensil and covered her hand with his, helping her hold her fingers correctly. "Better?"

"No." She dropped them again the moment he pulled away. A short laugh slipped out. "Maybe I'll just go with a fork."

From there, conversation slid toward the mundane. Each time he asked her a question meant to draw her out, she deflected back to him, with something tame. Was he enjoying his trip? How was the weather here?

A soft chime echoed from Fiona's purse, and she grabbed her phone. She scowled as she stared at the screen.

"Everything all right?" Wyatt asked.

She showed him the text message with Parker's name at the top. *You be back soon? I'm still working, but we can watch movies while I half-ass edits.*

She pulled the device away, typed something, and then dropped it in her purse.

"What did you tell him?"

She met Wyatt's gaze, green eyes shadowed with something he couldn't identify. "That his videos were more important, and I'd leave him in peace. Or, if you prefer, *I'm good. Catch up with you later.*"

"Ouch. You not a fan of movies?"

"It's not that." She poked at a drop of mustard on her plate. "But if I'm watching movies with someone, I'd rather they were watching too, and not using me as a warm body."

Wyatt kept his shock from his face at the casual way she tossed out *using me*. "I have movies in my room."

"Last time I went back to your room, things got weird."

But in a spectacular way, as far as he was concerned. "And they might again, but we're not drunk, you're capable of thinking for yourself without the chaperone, and this isn't some poorly wrapped euphemism. What kind of movies do you like?"

"Action-horror sci-fi."

The oddly specific genre almost made him smile, but he forced himself to frown instead.

"What?"

He shrugged. "Fifty Shades of Grey is on Cinemax."

Pink dotted her cheeks.

That was worth it. "I'm teasing. This time." He winked. "You pick, and I'm serious about that. Vampires. Black ops. Marvel. There's probably something on with Jason Statham or Sylvester Stallone… What do you say?"

The way she chewed her bottom lip as seconds ticked away sank into his veins and heightened his anticipation. He didn't know how she had this effect on him, but he was looking forward to the long game of finding out.

Chapter Twelve

When Fiona said, "All right, I'm in," Wyatt's anticipation scaled from hopeful to rock hard.

He paid for dinner, stood, and offered his hand. "Hotel's across the street."

"That's convenient." Her tone was dry, but amusement glinted in her eyes. Her fingers were smooth and soft against his palm, tempting him with notions of where else he'd like to feel her touch. She pulled away sooner than he would have liked.

"Intentionally so. It's within walking distance of a lot of good restaurants."

The warm night air didn't cool the need scorching across Wyatt's skin. After a week of wheeling and dealing and negotiating with the local outlet, he needed a night for him. He rested a hand at the small of Fiona's back, to point her in the right direction, and let his touch linger when she leaned into it.

They stepped into an empty elevator. An impulse snaked through him to press her against the wall and explore what lay beneath that gauzy black top. *Long game.* He had to remember the point was to set their Grammie's contract on a path toward crashing and burning. Getting laid was a bonus, not the goal.

The car stopped on his floor, and she fell into step beside him on the short walk to his room, arm brushing his. He unlocked the door and held it open for her. "My temporary and humble abode."

"I know the feeling." She stepped inside, hovering in the entryway. "Does it get old?"

"What's that?" He brushed past her, stripping off his tie and undoing the top button on his shirt. He slipped off his shoes. "Make yourself comfortable, by the way."

She stepped out of her flats and lined them next to each other near the closet. "Spending so much time living in hotel rooms."

"It's not bad. I see a new city every week, and I meet fascinating new people I wouldn't get to know at home." He met and held her gaze, until she blushed and ducked her head.

The way she wore her emotions on her face was as enticing as the rest of her. "That does sound nice."

"Parker does the same, doesn't he? What does he think of it?"

A scowl ghosted across her brow and lips, before a flat mask slid in. "He thinks a lot of things. I wanted a different perspective, though."

Each time Parker came up, Wyatt's curiosity grew another notch. What transpired between the two? How to get it out of her without cutting the evening—the overall goal—short? He'd work on that. "Can I get you anything?"

"I'm good."

He settled at the head of the bed, back against the wall and legs stretched out. He patted the mattress next to him. "You'll be more comfortable over here." *I promise—no biting unless you beg.* No reason to scare her off.

She hesitated, then moved into the room and sat next to him, leaving several inches between them. It was a start. He grabbed the remote and pulled up the list of pay-per-view movies. "Pick your poison."

"You can't rent something. Not for that cost."

"Why not? The perks of an expense account."

"It's so expensive, though." She took the remote and flipped through the channels until she landed on an explosion. "See? Now we don't have to decide, and we still get eye candy."

"I like the way you think."

Someone raced through the halls of what looked like a spaceship. Wyatt was curious about what they'd landed on, but it might be more fun to figure it out as the movie played.

The character on screen helped two people through the rear door on the ship and ushered them toward the med-bay. The music and frantic action set a tense pace. The man was pale and unsteady on his feet, on the verge of collapse when they helped him onto an examining table. One woman helped strip off his gear, and was examining his back when spikes perforated his skin and sprayed her with blood.

She panicked and backed from the room, locking her shipmates inside.

Fucking stupid.

Fiona made a *pft* sound.

Wyatt raised a brow, and glanced at her. "Something on your mind?"

"Nah. I don't want to ruin the movie."

"You can't say something like that and expect me not to push for answers." Did she have the same issues with it that he did?

She rolled her eyes. "Fine. She locked them in quarantine. She's got bodily fluid on her face and is running around the ship screaming, but she locked *them* in quarantine."

"Right?" He glanced back at the same woman stumbling then collapsing from whatever the contagion was, and grabbing a gun from the weapon's cache. "And they're encouraging the rest of their crew to return to the ship? Burn the thing to the ground."

"Exactly." The movie continued to play. "And the mothership, with more than two-thousand people on board, is going to breach atmosphere, to save one person who's probably lethally infected and risk the lives of the entire population in the process?"

"No discipline." Wyatt agreed. This was more fun than watching the movie. As it continued, he and Fiona picked apart every detail.

"Oh, come on," she said with mock exasperation. "That's David. How do you not know that's David?"

He laughed at her frustration, and moved on the mattress to face her. She was much better scenery than the movie. "Give the woman a break. She's been traumatized."

"Because she's an undisciplined officer." The

fight bled from Fiona's voice when she looked up at him. Her mouth was twisted with amusement that reflected in her eyes.

Definitely better than the movie. "Bad movie. Horrible movie. Now I feel like a poor host."

"You didn't force me to watch it. But I do kind of wish I could forget it."

He rested his hand on the back of her neck. "I know how to do that. At least temporarily."

"How?" She licked her lips, leaving a shine.

He could have this and still play the long game. It was easy to convince himself of that, with his cock digging into his zipper and her breath falling against the inside of his arm. "Like this." He kissed her.

She hesitated, and his brain stalled, but then she leaned into him, hand on his chest, pressing her mouth to his. Desire sang through his veins. This was better than he remembered. She parted her lips, and he slid his tongue in, to dance with hers.

Each gasp she let out was another shard, feeding his growing need. He knotted his fingers in her hair, holding her prisoner and diving into her.

She gripped his shirt in her fist and moaned against his mouth. If he broke contact, it would leave room to think, but he only wanted to feel. Everything. As if reading his mind, she straddled his legs.

If she lowered herself, she'd feel the length of his erection dig into her. He dragged his tongue down her neck, and she tilted her head to allow a better angle.

She settled into his lap and gave a half-chuckle when she pressed against his cock. Her gentle rocking sent pleasure spilling through him, until it tightened in his gut and traveled to his balls.

He slid his free hand under her shirt and up her bare stomach, cupped her breast, and dragged his thumb over the fabric of her bra and the hard nub underneath. When she moaned and arched her back to get closer to his touch, her heat engulfed his shaft.

Fuck—he wanted to bury himself inside her.

He slid his hand to her back, to unsnap her bra.

"Stop." Her voice was breathless. She rested a hand on his wrist and pushed him back. Lust shadowed the green of her eyes as she looked at him. "I'm sorry."

Sorry was a pale descriptor for what he felt. Apparently she wasn't as enthralled as he'd hoped. He struggled to find his voice. "Is something wrong?" It took the last of his willpower to keep the words even.

"I can't use you like this."

If the blood hadn't rushed from his head, he'd laugh at the notion and the way she applied it. "It's okay." He needed her off his lap, though. Hands on her hips, he prompted her to move.

"I'm sorry," she said again, as she knelt next to him. With her fingers intertwined, hands tucked into her lap, and gaze cast down, she was still sexy as hell, but now in a submissive way.

"You don't have to apologize. You don't owe me anything because you came up here. Or because I bought you dinner."

She managed half a smile but wouldn't meet his gaze. "I'm lucky you're a gentleman."

She had no idea.

His cock was raw with need, and his balls

ached, but he shoved the gnawing desire aside. "I promise to keep my hands to myself if you want to stay." Why did he say that? He needed to see her on her way, jerk off, and pass out.

"I do, but I shouldn't."

"You don't want to go back yet, so don't." He extracted himself from the bed with great reluctance, and moved to the chair next to it. "I'm enjoying your company."

She glanced between him and her shoes, then nodded at the bed. "You don't have to sit all the way over there. I'll behave if you will."

Fuck. This woman was going to short circuit every connector in his brain before he was finished, and he'd enjoy every minute of it.

♥♥♥

Parker pulled himself from the meditative work state that had consumed his thoughts for hours, and glanced at the clock on his computer. It was almost one in the morning, and Fiona was still gone.

Jealousy spiked inside. He didn't have the right to feel that way, but he couldn't help it. He checked his phone. No text since the reply she sent several hours ago, shrugging off his movie offer.

Was she still with Wyatt?

Of course she was. And it was her right to be there.

Envy gnawed at Parker's senses.

He sent her a quick text. *Making sure you're all right.* Though she probably wouldn't reply one way or the other.

That didn't stop him from sending her another

note every half hour or so, until he drifted off around three.

The buzz of his phone jarred him awake, and he grabbed for the device before he finished prying open his eyes. He focused on the screen and the lack of response from Fiona.

It was a text from Rinslet. *You're up, traveler. Outside the Old Town Tavern. 6 pm.*

Fuck. He wasn't in the right frame of mind for this. He forwarded the message to Fiona, along with a note of his own. *I understand if you're not there, but I'd like you by my side. Please? At least tell me you're all right, so I don't call the police.*

He didn't mean it to be a threat, but she'd gone out with someone she barely knew, and vanished. Parker might be jealous, but that didn't mean his paranoia was irrational.

♥ ♥ ♥

Something chimed in Fiona's dreams. A chirp. A digital bird? She frowned. No. That sounded like her cellphone. She opened her eyes.

"It's an insistent thing, isn't it?" Wyatt's voice, deep and heavy with sleep, sank into her core. He lay behind her, arm draped over her waist and erection digging into her ass.

Last night drifted back—watching another bad movie, poking more holes in the plot, falling asleep talking about the most random things.

Her cellphone chimed again, and she untangled herself from Wyatt. "I'll shut it off."

"See what they want." His voice mingled with the sound of rustling bedding. "Don't ignore them on my account." There was no animosity in the words.

She scrolled through the string of texts from Parker, asking if she was all right. Guilt filled her at his concern. The spite that drove her last night was gone, lost in hotel pillows and a no-pressure evening.

"What's Parker have to say?" Wyatt asked.

She was surprised he knew who the messages were from.

He unbuttoned a wrinkled shirt and shrugged out of it. The thin fabric of his undershirt hugged every line of muscle along his chest and upper arms. "The two of you are attached at the hip. I'm surprised he didn't call the cops." He was casual, despite everything that happened.

"He's threatening to," she said as she read Parker's last message. His challenge was today. If she were still riding last night's spite, she'd tell him to do it alone. She fired back a quick, *I'll be there.*

She looked at Wyatt. Her spite wasn't completely gone. She was being a child. What good would it do to invite Wyatt along? Then again, maybe it was what she needed. What happened with Parker wasn't going to happen again—he'd gone out of his way to make that point. So there was nothing wrong with her focusing her attention on another guy. Especially one she'd never see again. "What are you doing tonight?"

"Same thing I do every night." A smile danced on Wyatt's lips.

"Try to take over the world?" she said at the same time he did. She laughed. "Jinx."

Wyatt sat next to her. "I'll put world domination on hold for the night, if you have a better suggestion."

She gave him a brief rundown of the challenge, including time and place.

He shook his head. "I really don't do on-camera."

It was an odd hang-up for someone with Wyatt's confidence, but Fiona wasn't judging. "Come watch from the crowd. It's sure to be amusing."

"I'll see what I can do."

That was as non-committal as it got. "What would you have done if Parker called you yesterday instead of me?" She wasn't sure where the question came from.

"I'd have enjoyed his company and wondered why he left you behind."

Was Wyatt wondering the same about her? Why she didn't bring Parker? Did she read last night wrong? The questions left an odd bittersweet tang in the back of her throat. "Would the night have ended the same?"

"Probably not."

She would have been comforted by the answer, but his cool tone didn't reassure her. "Why not?" she asked.

"He doesn't kiss the way you do. And probably wouldn't have stopped me. Not that I'm saying you were wrong to," Wyatt added the last bit quickly. "But... Parker seems like the kind of guy who would have kept going."

Yeah, he was. The reality of Wyatt's observation sank deep into Fiona, unsettling her more than the rest of the conversation. She couldn't keep spinning this thing with Parker around in her head, getting dizzy, guessing and second-guessing his motivations. Or hers. And Wyatt…

She looked up to find him watching her. She didn't even know where to start there.

Life was so much simpler two weeks ago. And the idea of going back to that terrified her on a level she didn't expect.

Chapter Thirteen

Parker jolted from his half-snooze when the hotel door clicked open. He blinked the dryness from his eyes and focused on Fiona.

"Hey." His greeting came out a croak, and he cleared his throat. "Are you all right?"

Her hair was mussed and her top wrinkled. It drooped off one shoulder, and she shrugged it back into place. "I'm fine. We fell asleep talking."

"He was that boring, huh?" Parker tried to keep the teasing in his voice. Jagged jealousy shredded him. Would it be worse if she'd fucked Wyatt, or if she was comfortable enough with him already that falling asleep made sense?

She glared, then her expression softened and she sighed. "I'm sorry if I worried you. You look tired."

I was up all night, worrying about you. That was passive-aggressive. *I was working all night.* And that was callous. "I didn't get a lot of sleep, but I was working until after one, so I would have been shitty company."

"How long do we have before we need to leave for filming?"

He hated the tight rope stretched between them, threatening to knock someone off if he stepped wrong. "We don't have to go until tonight. I called our scheduled driver for the day, and Grammie's is fine with us taking a break, as long as I mention them in the live stream." He raked his fingers through his hair, to keep himself from reaching for her. "I meant what I said yesterday. I don't want this to destroy us."

"I don't either." Fiona sighed. She pulled a chair out from the desk and sat. "We'll get back to all right. I promise."

"Don't shut me out in the meantime."

Her lips twitched, threatening a smile. "I could ask the same."

"It's a deal." It wasn't a conclusion, but it felt like a good next step.

A week ago, Parker in nothing but his boxers was a nice sight but nothing to lose her mind over. Now Fiona had to force herself not to stare. To pretend she could ignore the way his back flexed when he stripped off his shirt. To look away from his elongated form when he stretched, and push aside the rush of memories of him lifting her onto the counter… Sliding inside her…

"You okay?" he asked.

She nodded. "Planning my day. Get some sleep."

"All right." He gave her one more look, brow

furrowed, then climbed into bed.

She sank low enough in the chair to rest her head on the back and stare at the ceiling. Trying to bury images of sex with Parker left room for Wyatt to slide in. Need tingled between her legs with the reminder of how he felt, hard and thick, pressing against her through their clothes, his rough hands sliding under her shirt.

She shook her head and sat up again. Distraction—that was what she needed. She'd read.

Fiona grabbed her phone and pulled up her book. In the background, Parker's breathing evened out. He must have fallen asleep.

She forced her gaze to the screen, and… landed right at the beginning of Nora handcuffing Zach to the desk. Which Fiona had been saving for when she was alone.

What was she thinking last night, going up to Wyatt's room? He was a gentleman about it, though she suspected he didn't appreciate having to be. And there were more of those images again, complete with whispers of sensation—his hungry kisses, his low growls…

Parker turned over in bed, drawing her gaze, and his blankets slipped off, leaving his back exposed.

What the hell was wrong with her? She'd seen him shirtless more times than she could count. Logic didn't erase the desire throbbing in her thighs, begging for attention. Her nipples ached, and she twitched her fingers, wanting to slide a hand under her bra, for a pinch.

She'd watch TV. On her laptop so she could

stream movies, and to keep the noise from waking up Parker.

She grabbed her computer, plugged in her headphones, and drummed her fingers on the keys, not pressing any. What should she watch?

Porn.

No. She wasn't doing that. Especially on hotel wireless.

She needed an outlet. To grab her vibrator from where it was tucked under her clothes in the bottom of one bag, head into the bathroom, and take care of business. A quick self-polish, and then she could focus again.

But the toy was loud, and she didn't want to wake Parker. Did she? She glanced at his sleeping form again and shifted in her seat. Each time she adjusted her weight, the seam of her jeans pressed against her.

Stay out here. The idea jolted through her, making her pulse scream and her heart hammer against her ribs. With Parker sleeping a few feet away?

She undid her jeans and slipped her hand inside, over her panties. Damp warmth teased her fingertips.

What if Parker woke up?

The question tugged an invisible string that ran from her nipples to her core, making her sex beg for attention. If he did, would he watch? She liked that idea.

A new boldness filled her, and she pushed her jeans to the floor. Fiona shoved the crotch of her underwear aside and dipped between her folds. She was soaked.

Maybe he wouldn't say anything. Or maybe he'd stroke his cock while he watched her.

The idea amplified her desire, and she moved her free hand under her bra, to pinch and twist her nipple. She sought out her clit and traced circles around the swollen button.

Would he be bothered if she told him she was fantasizing about both him and Wyatt?

Would he want to make things more hands on? No. She wouldn't allow that. Not this time.

She stroked herself faster, lust coursing through her veins, and her head swimming.

She'd let him give her directions, though. Tell her where to touch. And she'd listen to his grunts as he got close to climax. Watch him come as he watched her.

The images danced in a collage in her head, until stars sparkled behind her eyelids. Orgasm built inside with the image of Parker jerking off while he watched her.

She bit the inside of her cheek to keep from crying out, and the bitter taste of copper hit her tongue. *So close.*

She came hard, grinding against her hand and tugging her breast until she was too tender to keep going. Her body shuddered away from her touch.

She sank back in the chair, letting euphoria wash over her. It took her a moment to catch her breath, and then the cool air of the room rushed in, pushing away her haze and letting reality back in. A glance at Parker told her he'd slept through her masturbation session.

It was probably for the best, but that didn't quiet

the voice of disappointment.

At least her head was clearer now. She'd take a shower, give her hair plenty of time to dry before tonight, so she could tame it for the camera, and then *actually* watch a movie.

♥♥♥

Fiona expected to be awkward around Parker after he woke up. Would he know what she did? Instead, the thrill and risk of it all kept wickedness dancing inside.

The address he had for his Rinslet-appointed event was on the edge of downtown. A cluster of buildings formed an alley that passed through from one block to the other, and had a couple of cafe's dotting the sidewalk.

There was still plenty of light for filming, though long shadows ran along the concrete.

"You sure you're okay with this?" Parker asked.

A hostess seated them at a wrought-iron table with matching chairs and brought them each an ice water.

Fiona was terrified of being on camera. "No. But yes."

"You've seen me walk people through this before?"

She nodded.

"It'll be the same thing with you. I'll keep the conversation going, and you'll to talk to me like you normally do. Not that you need to worry. You'll shine."

"Thanks." She gave him a shy smile. His

confidence would have to bolster her until she got more comfortable with the idea. Despite the flutters in her gut, she was excited. Would Wyatt show up? No. Any promise he made was to be polite, especially with the way she left things last night. She mentally slapped herself for letting her mind wander.

Parker studied her while he fidgeted with his camera equipment. The handheld was tethered to his phone, to ensure he could stream, and he could clip the device to his head if he needed that perspective on things. "Is there anything you want to know before I start filming?"

"I'm good." God knew she'd watched enough of his clips in the past to have an idea of how things would go. "I'm going to duck into the restroom one more time and make sure I look okay."

"You look stunning." Parker squeezed her fingers.

"Thanks, but you have to say that. I'll be right back." As she pushed away from the table, she swore he heard him mutter, *No, I don't.*

In the bathroom, she let the icy water run on the inside of her wrists, and took several deep breaths to calm her nerves. She needed to not make such a big deal out of this. So what, if she'd agreed to let her best friend film her during an event they knew nothing about, for hundreds of thousands of people to see?

She shouldn't have thought down those lines.

She stared at her sandaled feet and forced her surging panic down. One foot in front of the other, back to the table. This would be fine. The mantra repeated in her head.

Parker's sneakers appeared in her line of sight, and she looked up. "I'm ready…" Her thoughts trailed off when she saw Parker was talking to Wyatt. "Oh." The word came out breathy. "I didn't think you'd show."

Wyatt gave her one of those dangerous smiles that made her feel like the only thing on the menu. "And miss my favorite up-and-coming celebrities, performing live? Not for the world."

"You're welcome to join us, if you'd like." A thread of contempt undercut the sugar in Parker's voice.

"Nah." Wyatt never flinched. "My table's a few over. I'm happy watching from there." He extended his hand. "Good luck."

Parker eyed it warily, then shook it. "Thanks."

"And you too." Wyatt grasped Fiona's fingers and kissed the back of her knuckles.

She swore she heard Parker growl.

Rather than watch Wyatt walk away, she took her seat as Parker took his. "All right, Mr. Carney. I'm ready for my close-up," she said in her most sultry voice.

That brought Parker's grin back, and he grabbed his camera. "It's two minutes to six, so we're going live. You know how it works. Little red light goes on—we're on the air."

She took one more deep breath, then nodded. The light on his camera flicked on, and he pointed the device at himself. "Evening, all. Before the big event starts—and before you ask, no I don't know any more than you do—I've got a special treat. A lot of you requested we bring Fiona onscreen, and after a lot of begging, and possibly a little soul selling, as far as you know, she's agreed." He twirled the lens in her direction. "Say hi, Fiona."

She wiggled her fingers in a wave at the camera and smirked. "Hi, Fiona."

Parker's laugh was drowned out by the blare of music. "What the fu—" He self-censored and pointed his camera away from her.

She twisted in her seat, in time to see one person push back from a table a few feet away, singing at the top of their lungs. Another joined them, and then someone walking by added their voice to the mix. In about thirty seconds, there were a couple dozen people gathered in the middle of the walkway, evenly spaced and harmonizing.

"Are you freaking kidding me, Rinslet?" Parker asked, and Fiona looked back to see him talking to the lens. "A flash mob is so two-thousand ten."

"I think it's neat. And they're really good." Fiona alternated her attention between him and the singing, dancing crowd. "Besides, I've never seen something like this in person before."

"In that case, and because you're right—they are decent—we'll watch. This probably took a bit of effort, so you'll have to share your debut with about twenty-five other people."

"I'm fine with at." Fiona was fascinated with the choreography. The tune was a sort of medley of Broadway songs, complete with the corresponding dance steps.

Parker kept up a light monologue for his viewers until the performance was over. As the singing faded, applause broke out around the plaza.

"Looks like everyone is a fan," Parker said. "Including Mister Big Bad Wolf, who I won't show you, because he insisted."

Fiona glanced toward Wyatt, who was clapping along with everyone else. He met her gaze and winked, and she turned away with a shy smile. Seriously, what was her deal?

"Excuse me." An unfamiliar voice broke into her thoughts. A man from the flash mob stood in front of her, a rose in hand. "A lovely flower for the lovely hostess."

"Thanks." She took the gift with a tentative smile.

"That's a bit off-theme, don't you think?" Parker asked.

Fiona thought about snapping at him for ruining the moment, but she agreed. On top of the odd gesture, everyone else had dispersed, while the stranger was watching her, unblinking.

"You're amazing. I'm so glad you decided to go live." He grabbed Fiona's free hand.

She tried to be polite about pulling away. "Thanks."

"I mean it. You're so gorgeous, and really, you put this guy to shame. Am I right?" He chuckled and nodded at Parker.

"Yeah. I'm a real putz." Irritation crept into Parker's voice. "We're going to get back to our coffee now."

"Sure. Of course. I mean, I didn't want to interrupt. I can't believe I got to meet you." The stranger grabbed Fiona's hand again, his grip tight and his skin clammy.

She wasn't as kind about wrenching from his grasp this time, and she wiped her palm on her jeans.

Wyatt seemed to materialize from nowhere as he stepped up next to the stranger and clapped him on the shoulder. "My friends are too polite to say it, but they want you to leave."

"Fuck off, assh…" The stranger's retort died when he turned to face Wyatt.

"Don't make this more cliché than it already is." Wyatt's voice was firm.

The stranger gave Fiona one last look. "We'll talk again soon. I promise." He turned and left.

Fiona's heart was in her stomach as she tried to wrap her brain around what just happened.

"And that, dear viewers, is the Big Bad Wolf," Parker said.

Chapter Fourteen

Wyatt clenched his teeth when Parker introduced him to YouTube-land. That nickname was going to haunt Wyatt for a while, apparently. And he'd been hoping to avoid getting caught on camera so early on. Now the clock was ticking down toward someone recognizing him. How long until that information got back to Fiona? Her brother knew who he was. Was he watching every second of video?

Wyatt hadn't been able to help himself, though. The stranger with the rose set off all his warning bells. While he understood Parker and Fiona's desire to be polite, especially during a live display, some people shouldn't be encouraged with things like kindness.

At least Parker had the good grace to turn away the camera within moments of Wyatt stepping into the shot.

Wyatt grabbed an empty seat, spun it, and straddled it so he could rest his arms on the back and face the pair. He nodded at Parker's camera and the flashing red *Record* light. "Is that thing still on?"

Parker looked at the lens. "We've gotta cut and run, folks. Hope you enjoyed the show. I'll be back later. Eat Grammie's cookies."

A quiet snicker slipped from Fiona, and Wyatt couldn't hide his smirk.

He waited a heartbeat after the recording light turned off. "That sounds so dirty if you take it out of context."

Parker rolled his eyes.

"Thank you for stepping in," Fiona said.

"I'd say, *Anyone would have done the same*, but…" Wyatt let the thought hang there. "Anyway. I'm not going to imitate your creepy admirer. I'll leave you two be."

"We're fine. Go ahead and stay." There was a sarcastic sneer to Parker's words.

Wyatt didn't know if the attitude was related to that first night of drinking, or if Parker's irritation had been renewed after Fiona's night out. He also wasn't sure it mattered.

Fiona's, "Please. We'd enjoy the company," was too sweet to ignore.

It sent a surge of need through Wyatt, growling to hear her beg for more. All in good time. The desire was compounded by the fact that every time Parker unleashed the attitude, Wyatt wanted to break him. In the most tantalizing way possible.

For now, he settled for waving down his waitress. "I'm moving tables. Will you bring my drink here when it's ready?"

"Sure." The woman gave him a warm smile and

walked away.

He turned to Fiona. *Path of least resistance.* "Are you enjoying the city and all its hidden wonders?"

"We haven't had much of a chance to go sightseeing yet."

"We were planning on getting some of that in later tonight," Parker said.

"I can give you a tour if you're interested." Wyatt was pretty certain of what Parker's answer would be, but he'd be remiss if he didn't offer.

Fiona leaned in, chin resting on her palm. "Last night *was* a lot of fun. I wouldn't mind seeing more like that."

"I'd be happy to show you a few spots," Wyatt offered.

"Sure. Sounds great. Maybe another time." Parker clipped off the words.

They weren't making eye contact with each other. Interesting.

The waitress brought them all their coffees at the same time, and set a muffin in front of Fiona, who picked a few crumbs and nibbled at them.

Parker slide the sleeve around his cup up and down.

"Correct me if I'm wrong, but the dynamic has shifted between the two of you," Wyatt said. It might be due to their interaction with the ex's sister, but that seemed like the kind of thing they could talk through. It could be a result of Fiona's staying out all night with Wyatt, but that shouldn't matter unless she'd lied to Parker about what happened between her and Wyatt. And the biggest reason for her to do that would be to make Parker jealous…

Then again, Fiona called Wyatt in the first place. Pieces clicked in his head, and he understood her comment from last night. *I can't use you.*

"Same dynamic as always." The end of Parker's statement was muffled when he took a long sip of coffee.

Fiona glared at Parker.

"You fucked, didn't you?" Wyatt assembled the rest of the puzzle. "As in, each other."

"I'm not sure how that's any of your business," Parker said.

Fiona's flush darkened.

That answered that. "What's the big deal?" Wyatt asked.

Parker looked at Fiona. "Do you want to get out of here?"

She turned to Wyatt. "We're taking off, if you still want to keep us company."

"I was thinking we'd head back to the hotel." Parker spoke between clenched teeth.

Wyatt sipped his drink, watching the tennis match.

"Perfect." The sweetness was back in Fiona's voice. "Our hotel, right? Because things always get weird when we go back to his room." She nodded at Wyatt.

While he was entertained by the exchange, the tension was getting heavy. Leave these two be, or watch the drama unfold?

Parker's expression went blank, and then a casual smile slid in that didn't quite reach his eyes. "Come with us. We're going to hang out. Be boring.

If that's your thing."

"I'd love to." Wyatt wasn't passing up an offer like that, as disingenuous as it might be. He left enough cash on the table for all three of their orders, plus a tip.

Parker said, "You don't have to—"

"I don't. But it's no problem." Wyatt stood when they did, and fell into step beside them as they strolled down the street.

"It makes things awkward. That's what the big deal is," Fiona said. She was talking about Wyatt's earlier question.

"It's really not a deal." Parker's tone had evened out. The way he'd flipped the switch was fascinating and eerie. "We don't have that kind of relationship."

"The kind with sex?" Wyatt was going to prod this for all he was worth. He walked next to Fiona, his arm occasionally brushing hers, Parker on her other side.

"The romantic kind." Parker sounded like he was trying to shrug off the topic.

Wyatt side-stepped for someone walking in the other direction. The evening sun warmed his face, and a cool breeze slid over his skin. "You fucked, right? It wasn't a confession of love."

"Sounds right." Fiona's response was flat.

"Did it suck?" Wyatt knew the question would cause some bristling.

"No." Parker's response came quickly.

Fiona shook her head. "Definitely not."

This was a simple conversation. Wyatt didn't understand what their hang-up was. "So... let yourself admit you enjoyed it, and move on."

"That would suit your purposes, wouldn't it?" Parker maintained his even tone, despite the accusation.

"How so?" Wyatt asked.

"You've been eying Fiona since that first night in the bar. I'd bet my subscriber list you'll say whatever it takes to fuck her."

Fiona ducked her head and fell back a few steps. Wyatt slowed his pace to match hers, and Parker followed suit. No reason to hide *that* intention. "You're not wrong. I'd do the same for you."

Parker faltered, but he recovered quickly. They reached the hotel, and he held the front door for them, following when Wyatt was through. They headed toward the elevators. "Telling the truth doesn't make it any less manipulative," Parker said. "Sometimes truth is the biggest deception."

Wyatt wasn't surprised Parker's facade slip, and he wanted to back Parker into a corner on this. They stepped into the elevator, and Wyatt was impressed Parker was keeping up the charade of being okay with all three of them heading up.

"You'd know, wouldn't you?" Wyatt said.

Parker's back stiffened. "What the fuck is that supposed to mean?"

"*I care about you Red. You're my best friend. I'd do anything for you.*" Wyatt deepened his voice, mimicking Parker.

Fiona crossed her arms over her chest. That wouldn't do.

"That's not a deception." A growl ran through Parker's voice.

The elevator slid to a stop, and they stepped off. "No?" Wyatt was about to take a stab in the dark, but he knew people and these two were transparent. "You ever follow that up with, *And I know what's best for you?*"

Fiona let out a tiny cough and paused in front of a room to unlock it and push inside.

"You don't know what you're talking about." Parker's aggravation was growing.

Wyatt held his hands up in surrender. "All right. I don't know what I'm talking about. It was just sex. It wasn't a big deal. I'm running my mouth."

"Exactly." Fiona rolled her eyes and moved further into the room.

The tension was back, but it held a different current this time. It was lined with lust and repressed desire and self-deception. And God, Wyatt wanted a taste. "Good." He turned to Parker. "Because I don't want the obstacle of a relationship."

He was stunned when Parker grabbed his tie and met his gaze, eyes hard and angry. Parker crushed his mouth to Wyatt's, and lust raked through Wyatt's nerves, lighting his senses up with need. Fury and desire and irritation spilled through the connection.

Parker let go and stepped back, never dropping his gaze. "Is that what you're after?"

It was a fascinating contrast. Where Fiona was innocence and temptation, Parker was barely contained chaos, sprinkled with fire.

Wyatt shook the thought away, to focus on keeping control of the discussion. His approach was working. "Let's call it a favorable step in the right direction." He pressed closer to Parker, feeling the other man's frame hard and unyielding against his own, until Parker was backed against the wall.

Parker raised his brows but didn't pull away.

"I want to taste you." Wyatt let a rumble slide through his words. He was intensely aware of Fiona's attention, and that amplified his desire to play the game this way. He shifted his weight, pressing his erection against Parker and noting the flicker of satisfaction he received in return. "To take you in my mouth and suck your dick until your balls are blue, while Red watches, enjoying every agonizing minute," Wyatt said.

The room was so still, it was as if the walls held their breath.

Parker didn't flinch.

"And you're not going to come." Wyatt let the captive audience fuel him. "Not while I'm licking your cock. Because I want you both, and I think you'd like to watch and stroke yourself raw, while Fiona and I fuck. Because—God—I want to feel what it's like to be buried inside her."

Parker stared him down, jaw clenched. Wyatt was two seconds from either getting decked or laid.

"Is that an empty promise, or are you two going to get to it?" Fiona's voice, sweet but with an edge, added to the heavy air, rather than slicing it.

"Do you live on that pedestal you've placed yourself on?" Parker asked. "Because that's got to be a mighty fall, when you misstep."

Wyatt smirked. "I take my bruises and learn from my mistakes. And I don't make promises I'm not prepared to back up." He kissed Parker again, and

Parker kissed back, his tongue dancing with Wyatt's and groans filling the air.

Wyatt dropped his hand to stroke Parker's cock through denim, enjoying the jolt every time Parker bucked against his hand. He thought he heard Fiona whimper, but his pulse pounding in his ears made it difficult to be certain.

Without breaking contact, he nudged Parker toward a chair. One of them stumbled, or maybe it was both, but they caught themselves. Parker dropped into the seat, and Wyatt unzipped his jeans, still enmeshed in the kiss. He was used to being yielded to. With Parker it was push and pull, and that was a new flavor of delicious.

Parker tilted his head back with a groan when Wyatt worked his shaft free.

Wyatt knelt at his feet and trailed his thumb over the head of Parker's cock, smearing away a drop of precum. He watched Parker, enjoying the visual as much as the sounds, as he licked along Parker's shaft before taking him in his mouth.

"Oh fuck." That was Fiona, barely audible, and it was kindling on the need raging inside Wyatt.

He stroked while he licked. Parker knotted his fingers in Wyatt's hair, setting the pace and pushing him down until Wyatt almost gagged.

Wyatt listened to the cues, paid attention to the thrusting against his face, and caressed Parker's sac until it tightened. Then he pulled away and stood.

Parker let out a strained chuckle. "I didn't think you were serious."

"Always, when it comes to getting laid." Wyatt turned to Fiona, who stood near the bed, her lips flushed and swollen. He grinned, trying to decide where to start. "Why are you still dressed, Red?"

She worked her jaw up and down, but no sound came out.

"Shirt off, or tell me no," Wyatt said.

She hesitated, and he raised an eyebrow. She pulled her T-shirt off, then grabbed one arm with the other hand, as she shifted her weight from one foot to the other. Her bra was light blue, and perfect on her pale skin. The submissive posture drove straight to his erection, threatening to pop his zipper.

He wanted to glance at Parker, see if he was enjoying this as much as Wyatt was, but he didn't want to miss the display.

"Jeans next," he ordered.

She kicked off her sneakers, toed off her socks, and moved to her jeans, shoving them down her legs, and then bending at the waist to pick them up and set them aside. Yellow cotton panties. *Jesus*, she was fun.

He dragged his gaze over her body, enjoying the way a flush of pink spread over her skin everywhere he looked.

"Promises were made." Her teasing tone drew his attention back to her face and the smirk playing on her lips.

His dick roared with the need to drive inside her. "Slide your fingers between your legs. Tell me if you're wet."

Parker let out a slow hiss when she complied.

Fiona nodded.

"I didn't hear that." Wyatt couldn't keep up the teasing much longer.

"I'm soaked," Fiona said.

He stalked closer, and she gasped but stood her ground. He drew her hand up, so he could suck her fingers clean, taking his time with each one. Her taste almost broke his rein on control. He gripped her hair, eliciting a moan, and tugged her head back.

Another kiss—this one sunshine and flowers and dandelion dreams, compared to Parker's chaos. Wyatt didn't press into her. He forced his tongue into her mouth, massaging and owning and claiming. She reached for him, and he grabbed her wrist, holding her hand captive. He swallowed her groans like they were candy.

She pushed her body to his, until she was grinding against his leg.

Wyatt broke away, and she watched him with her bottom lip caught between her teeth.

There was no way she didn't know what she was doing to him. "You get to pick," he said. "I'm going to fuck you until you scream, unless you want Parker."

"Do I have to choose?"

Fuck. That single question, deviance wrapped in innocence, almost made him come. Someone needed to let her off her leash a long time ago. Or put one on her. Wyatt wasn't sure which she'd enjoy more.

Chapter Fifteen

"Do I have to choose?"

This wasn't what Fiona expected when she invited Wyatt up to their room. That little spiteful bit of her wanted to see how Parker would react, but it also felt safer, having both of them around. The encounter with the rose-guy shook her.

The way Wyatt and Parker watched her now chased that away and left a far more primal feeling singing through her.

"You want to ease into something like anal. Your guy isn't a starter toy." Wyatt wasn't one to mince words. She liked that. It helped wipe away her inhibitions.

Parker twisted his mouth. "I think I should be offended."

"You shouldn't be." Wyatt kept his attention on Fiona.

Wyatt and Parker together were oxygen and gasoline. And so help her, she craved being consumed by the flames. "I'll take care of myself if you two are still going at it," she said.

"As much as I'd like to see that… Maybe next time." Every time Wyatt summoned that wolfish grin of his, want pulsed between her thighs. He bumped her shoulder, coaxing her to sit on the bed and pulled a condom from the trifold wallet in his back pocket. Then he unbuckled his belt and undid his slacks. The line of his erection was distinct through his boxer briefs.

She pouted—that seemed to get her a good reaction. Then again, a lot of what she was doing was based on how he responded. Her first playful jab had been tentative, but the way Wyatt dove into this, with zero hesitation, made her bolder.

"What?" he asked.

She would be disappointed that misbehaving didn't get her spanked, but this was fun as well. She looked at Parker. "You're too far away. I want a taste."

Parker shed his jeans, knelt next to her, settled a hand on her cheek, and brushed his lips over hers. This was different than the other day. The desperation was sweeter. More sincere.

Wyatt nudged her shoulder again, and she took the hint, and lay on the mattress. Parker kissed a trail along her jaw, down her neck, over her collarbone, and to her breast. He worked her free from her bra and flicked his tongue over a nipple. She gasped and arched her back, pressing into his mouth.

Fiona didn't know if she wanted to watch him suck and nibble on the swollen pink nub, or pay attention to Wyatt, who rolled the condom on and fisted his cock.

Wyatt wedged her legs apart with his knee and dragged her to the edge of the bed. The friction of the comforter against her skin made her gasp.

He positioned himself at her entrance and thrust in without further warning. The way his cock stretched her out tingled over every inch of her, and she clenched her toes to keep the feeling from escaping.

Wyatt built to a steady pace, pulling most of the way out before plunging inside her again. Parker alternated between licking and nibbling, while he massaged her other breast.

She reached between Parker's legs, to grab his shaft, and pumped. He groaned against her skin and sucked harder. She lost track of the sensations as they blurred into each other, making her head float and filling her with fissures of pleasure. She didn't realize how hard and fast she was stroking Parker, until he pulled from her grip.

"Jesus, Red. I can't..." His voice was a breathy groan. He replaced her grip with his own, rubbing his shaft and grunting until he spilled on her stomach in thick, white spurts.

Her arousal surged, and she hovered on the edge of release. When Wyatt sought out her clit, teasing with his thumb while he pounded inside her, it was like he pressed a button. She came hard, clenching around him and grinding into him, wanting to ride the wave for as long as possible.

The way he gripped her thigh made her think he was close too. He dug his fingers in, tight enough she hoped he'd leave marks. His groans kept time with his thrusts, until he let out a long cry and shuddered against her.

For a moment the only sound in the room was the three of them catching their breath. Nothing else reached Fiona's ears. Then she heard a rustling noise. She watched, half-lost in bliss, as Parker grabbed a handful of tissues from the box by the bed and wiped her stomach clean. Wyatt stripped off the condom, wrapped it up, and tossed it in the trash.

He collapsed beside her and pulled her into him. It felt natural to curl up against him, with him mostly clothed. Parker lay behind her and draped an arm over her waist, his breath hot on the back of her neck.

The antipathy was gone, leaving a fuzzy glow in its place. Fiona wanted to climb into this feeling and live in it. Too bad her brain wouldn't let her. What was the appropriate protocol now? Did they tell Wyatt, *thanks, see you around*, and leave it at that? Did she and Parker backpedal to the stilted interactions they hadn't finished muddling through?

She didn't want that. If this was just sex, that was fine. The twinge in her chest disagreed, but that was post-coital denial. She was good doing *with benefits* when it came to Parker.

Her phone chimed with the opening notes of "We Are Family." Talk about awkward timing.

"Leave it." Parker held her more tightly.

She pushed past reluctance and sat up. "I can't. It's Nick."

"Nick?" Wyatt asked.

"Her brother." Parker sat as well. He stripped off his shirt and handed it to Fiona. It was a silly gesture, since her top was only a few feet away, but that didn't stop her from pulling it on. The cotton smelled like him and wrapped her in warmth. She tried to be subtle about inhaling as she grabbed her phone.

911. Call me now.

Her gut sank when she read Nick's message. "Shit."

"Everything all right?" Wyatt propped himself up on his elbows.

She shook her head and called Nick. She had to turn away from the pair on the bed, or she wouldn't be able to focus on the conversation.

"You got my message," Nick answered.

"Yeah. What's up?"

Wyatt wandered into the bathroom, and she heard water running.

"The app is crashing hard. It's not system-wide, but I can't keep it stable."

Shit-fuck-God-damn-it. "Give me ten minutes to get set up and remote in, and I'll call you back."

"Awesome. Thank you, Red."

Her brother's use of the nickname sent discomfort crawling over her.

Wyatt stepped back into the room, zipping up his slacks, as she was hanging up. She looked between Parker and him. "I have to take care of this." And finish getting dressed. And shower. She'd prefer it happen in a different order, but the last one had to wait.

"Don't let things get awkward between us." Wyatt's voice was firm. "We had fun. Fuck—we had a lot of fun." Everything had changed, but he made it sound so simple.

"So… um…" She wasn't sure what to say next.

"Parker and I are going to head out—"

"We are?" Parker looked at him, surprised.

"—so you can fix whatever this is," Wyatt continued as if he hadn't been interrupted.

The two of them alone together sounded like a bad idea, given how irritated Parker was with Wyatt before the sex, but she didn't have time to argue. She yanked on her jeans, reluctant to surrender Parker's shirt. He grabbed a fresh one from his luggage.

She hid a smile. "Play nice?"

"I'm not great at *nice.*" Wyatt said.

Parker rolled his eyes. "We'll behave. Call me if you need help or when you're finished."

"Thanks." She dug out her laptop as the men left. It didn't take her long to tether to her phone and log in remotely to the network. She dialed Nick up again and put him on speaker. "Bring me up to speed."

"The plugin you wrote for location tracking is glitching, and I can't figure it out." Nick's tone radiated stress.

She'd tested the hell out of that component. It was their most stable piece. "Glitching, how? Why? What did you do?"

"I… uh… tweaked something, and it freaked out."

She scrubbed her face, a sigh escaping through her fingers. Despite the critical nature of the situation, snippets of her fling—tryst? Experimentation?—with Parker and Wyatt teased her thoughts. She squeezed her legs together and forced herself to focus on the crisis. "I'm syncing with source control now. What did you change?"

"It's a feature Grammie's asked us to implement. It centers around the contract language for being filmed with Parker and getting a customer's approval. I can't pull it, but I also can't figure out how to make it work with what you had in place."

A string of foul words lingered on the tip of her tongue, but she swallowed them. "Let's patch it."

♥♥♥

Parker fluctuated between trying to wrap his head around what just happened, and wanting to enjoy the moment without needing to rationalize it.

"How long have you been doing the videos?" Wyatt asked.

And this guy—what the actual, ever-living fuck? He was arrogant. Irritating. Sexy as hell. And now he and Parker were buddies? "The filming itself? I've had a camera attached to my hand since I was in my teens. The travel blogging—earning a living at it, etcetera—five or so years."

"You're good. And lucky. You seem to have found your calling in life."

They were walking side by side toward a restaurant a few blocks away, that Wyatt insisted was worth the visit.

Parker was tired of letting his thoughts ramble with no answers. "I need to know, what are we doing?"

"Going for a beer. Giving Fiona a chance to work in peace. I'm not sure what kind of answer you're looking for."

"You've been pushy and aggravating since we met," Parker said. "And now we fuck, sort of? And we're best pals?"

Wyatt glanced at him. "You've been aggravated with me since we met; that's different. I think *best pals* is a bit of a stretch." They reached a building with a brick face, a glass door painted black, and the words *Brew Pub* etched on a tiny plaque. It was the only indicator there was an establishment here.

Wyatt held the door, and Parker shoved down the surge of masculinity and brushed past him. The inside of the place was as nondescript as the outside. Wooden tables and chairs. Dark booths with high-backed leather benches. Brick walls. No art or kitschy decorations.

"You were listening, weren't you? To that conversation we had on the way to the hotel? Not only thinking about your dick?" Wyatt said the last bit as they reached the host podium. The host looked surprised at the language, but Wyatt didn't flinch. "Booth. Two."

Parker held his reply until they were seated and didn't have an audience. While he didn't have a problem going off in public about most topics, there were some things people shouldn't be subjected to unless they volunteered. "You mean the bullshit about it just being sex? The laundry list of things you said to piss me off? Which part was I supposed to hear?"

Wyatt gave a short laugh. "You *were* paying attention. It wasn't bullshit. And you're cute when you're annoyed."

Parker swallowed an irritated retort. "What was

it, then?"

"It was genuine. I don't understand why the two of you would let something like sex, especially with each other, drive a wedge between you."

Their waitress interrupted, and Parker ordered a Coke. He needed mental clarity to have this conversation, and alcohol wouldn't help.

Wyatt ordered an oatmeal ale. "And bring us some of that queso you guys make. Extra chips." He looked at Parker. "No reason to hit up the local places if you don't try the specialties."

"Great. Thanks for the tip." Parker couldn't keep the sarcasm from his voice. That was one of his *things* when it came to his channel.

Wyatt leaned in when the waitress was gone, resting his forearms on the table. "As I was saying— what's the big deal?"

Parker didn't think he could put it into works if this guy didn't already get it. "It changed things."

"So? She's still Fiona, right?"

"Yes…"

"You're either okay with the casual sex, or you're not. But if you're not, don't lie to yourself and say you are just because you want help getting off." Wyatt sighed. "Fine. I'll stop talking the standard lines for a minute. The two of you have a connection. I saw it the first night we met. It's… I can't describe it, but I'm not trying to step on your toes or break up your friendship."

"Then what are you doing?"

"Helping you drop a few inhibitions, to keep them from getting in your way."

Parker snorted. "So this is an altruistic act on

your part."

"Fuck that. Everything I do is selfish. I got laid. If I'm lucky, I get to be part of that self-discovery process again."

Parker rolled his eyes. "Noble of you."

"Anything but. We covered that." Wyatt smiled at the waitress when she returned with their drinks and chips, and took a slow sip of his beer before setting it aside. "Whatever the two of you have going on, you've ignored it for so long, anything you do is going to feel out of place. You radiate sexual tension, and you have to ease into exploring it."

Parker couldn't believe he was getting relationship advice about his best friend from a guy they met in a hotel bar, whom Parker just watched…

He shook the thought aside, because it brought images with it images guaranteed to distract him. "And you're part of that *easing*."

"I was today. I wouldn't complain about another round."

Of course he wouldn't. No wonder this guy was in sales—he talked a fantastic pitch. The problem—or maybe it wasn't a problem at all—was Parker liked what Wyatt was selling. A Round Two or Three? And a chance to find out what Parker and Fiona might be? That was a hard thing to say *no* to.

Chapter Sixteen

"What happens if one of us falls for you?"

Wyatt was surprised Parker phrased the question that way. This entire conversation was odd, though. He still wasn't sure why he'd coaxed Parker into heading out with him. Logic said it was the Grammie's contract. Part of the game. Getting to know the other half of his prey.

There were easier, less draining ways to do that. He might enjoy Parker's company, but trying to drill this concept of *no-strings is okay with your best friend* was getting repetitive.

"It won't happen," Wyatt said.

"Why not?"

He had to explain this? It was all but painted on the walls. "Fiona is keeping me around because it makes you jealous." And because she had an inner sex-kitten, mewling for attention. "I'm not your type, and I'm not looking to get attached."

"You really will say anything to get laid."

"Only if it's true." Lying didn't serve any

purpose in the long run, when it came to sex. Covering the deception was more effort than the getting off was worth. "This afternoon was more fun than I've had in a long time."

"It was good." Parker grabbed a chip and dipped it in queso, then nibbled on it. "So's this. Wow. Not the same kind of *wow*, but this is good."

That was the point. "Are we on the same page now, or do you want to continue the third degree?" Wyatt asked.

"I still think you're hiding something. And I don't suspect no-strings with Fiona is going to be as easy as you make it sound. But I see where you're coming from. Though, that might be the afterglow speaking for me."

"How magnanimous of you." Wyatt drained his beer and waved down the waitress for another.

"It's too bad finding a way to kick up my rankings for the competition doesn't come with this kind of detailed instruction." Parker seemed to be speaking as much to himself as anyone.

The rapid shift in topic knocked Wyatt's brain off balance. "Why can't it?" That was the wrong question. What did he mean to say? He tossed Parker's musing with his own.

Parker twisted his mouth in amusement. "It's a family rated channel and competition. I don't think diagrams and charts about no-commitment sex will fly with the censors."

"You're losing me. Or I'm losing you." Gears turned. "Your contract with Grammie's—what kind of exclusivity does it have? As in, can you only film their food?"

Parker studied him. "I'm not allowed to show their competition, but they don't care if I'm eating somewhere else. I had to put that in the contract, or I wouldn't be able to do anything else."

"Does your footage of their deliveries have to be live?" What the fuck was he doing? Helping the competition do a better job at sealing the deal? No. This was about keeping himself in their lives.

Parker shook his head. "It just has to appear in at least one of my clips every week day. And I haven't taken advantage of the rest of the contract because we've been in these tiny little cities that don't have a lot of local color."

"You're serious." Wyatt stared at him in disbelief. "You've devoured half a bowl of *local color* while we've been talking." He nodded at the queso. "So limit your delivery footage to big events—weddings, parties, catered things. Then do what you'd normally do, but in these smaller cities."

"There's a problem with that." Despite the words, there was no argument in Parker's voice. "When I do those clips of the local dives and amazing hotspots in other places, I have time to scout out the locations. I'm not in this to wreck anyone, so I'd rather go someplace good. I don't have that kind of freedom with my schedule right now."

"The places I could show you in these small little towns no one thinks are worth visiting..." Wyatt would make Parker a list, but he wanted to be an in-person tour guide.

"Yeah. That'd be convenient."

He couldn't tell where Parker's sarcasm was directed. "Don't suppose you'll be in Philadelphia anytime soon." He knew the answer as well as he'd known exactly who *Nick* was. No reason to tip his hand.

"No." Parker shook his head. "We're going to Maryland next." He frowned. "Wait. There's a Grammie's hub in Chadds Ford, outside Philadelphia, isn't there?"

There was. It was the only reason for Wyatt to go there. "You tell me. You're their cameraman."

"There is. It's one of our later stops. I bet we could rearrange our schedule. Fiona's looking forward to seeing the place, so she won't complain about getting there sooner. If you were willing to show us the town and whatever else you thought we'd enjoy…"

This was easier than Wyatt expected. "I could do that. You'd have to promise to keep me off camera."

"I gotta know—why the camera phobia?"

"I don't care if you film me. Hell, if that's your kink…" Wyatt shook the thought aside. "It's a job thing. There are rules around sponsorship. As in, we can't do anything that carries the tiniest whiff of endorsement. Since all your videos are sponsored, I'm not willing to risk being disciplined over that." It was a half-truth, and a good reminder that the clock was ticking until someone saw Wyatt in the footage from earlier. He was grateful the information wasn't part of the call from Nick.

♥♥♥

Fiona tapped her fingers soundlessly on the desk while she waited for her latest changes to publish to the test server. A new text message chimed on her phone, and she pulled it up without thought.

When she saw a picture of herself, at the cafe with Parker, her gut flipped. The note with it said, *Loved meeting you today. I meant it. We'll talk soon.* It had to be from rose-guy.

"Freaking creepy," she muttered.

"What's that?" Nick asked.

She deleted the text and blocked the sender. "Nothing. There are a lot of people out there who are kind of skin-crawly, is all."

"I get that. We're up."

She logged into the sandbox interface and pulled up the appropriate emulator. It worked for the first several searches, but failed when she typed in a Grammie's location they hadn't tested yet. "Damn it."

"Short of pulling my code apart and writing it from scratch, I don't know what else to try." Nick's frustration matched her own.

"So get started." She couldn't keep the playful tone in her voice.

"I will. But in the meantime…"

"I know." She sighed. It was irritating, but not as big a deal as when she first got on the phone. As long as she and Parker stuck to their schedule for the next few weeks, she and Nick would have enough time to fix the app for other locations. "Keep me updated, and I'll check in as often as I can."

"Got it. And, Red? You're having fun, aren't you?"

The question drew a soft smile. "So much fun." Not that he would ever know the details or even the basics, but it was sweet that he cared.

They wrapped up the conversation, and she disconnected.

She stared at her screen a few minutes longer, feeling odd just closing up shop, but she'd done all she could, and Nick assured her he had the rest under control. She shut her laptop and set it aside. Silence descended over the room.

Now would be the perfect time to get that shower. The thought was followed closely by the reminder of the eerie text message. Maybe she'd wait until Parker got back.

Would things be stilted between them still? Wyatt didn't seem to have an issue with casual sex, but that didn't have anything to do with Parker

Second-guessing wouldn't help anyone. She turned on the TV and flipped through channels, but every time she heard a noise, she had to mute the sound and strain her ears.

This was stupid. She was getting worked up over nothing.

That didn't stop her heart from jamming in her throat when she heard the door handle wiggle. Relief flooded her when Parker walked in the room.

"You okay?" he asked.

"Better now. Did you have fun on your date?" The teasing slipped out before she could question the wisdom of it.

He gave her a familiar lazy smile that meant he was relaxed. "Oddly enough. It wasn't as horrible as I expected. And we have to talk. But first, how did things go with the app?"

She didn't like the sound of *we have to talk*, but

his delivery was casual. "It was good. Not great, but we got it patched. I'll dial in and work with Nick on a real fix whenever you're doing editing."

"You're supposed to be on vacation." A warning tone leaked into his voice.

She pushed aside her aggravation. "I'd like to be, but that's not an option. You want me to take your work seriously? I need you to return the favor."

She expected a protest. Instead he settled on the edge of the bed. His knees brushed hers. "That's fair. But don't work too hard. I want you to enjoy yourself."

That wasn't an issue earlier. The thought rushed into her head from nowhere, gliding hot along her skin.

"Speaking of—okay, we weren't, but I need a segue to what I wanted to talk to you about," Parker said.

"Right. That. What's up?"

"How do you feel about going to Chadds Ford a week early?"

"Why?" She eyed him suspiciously. It would be tricky with the patch she and Nick put in place, but it was a city already on the list, so it shouldn't be too bad.

"Wyatt offered to show us around, if we meet up with him while he's there."

Her pulse hammered in her ears. There was no way Parker said that so casually. "Are you and I all right?" she asked.

"I think so? We are. Aren't we?"

"Yes. Definitely." Did the raunchy threesome adjust his attitude that much? If so, she was great with tit. "And you're okay with him showing us around?"

Parker frowned and searched her face. "Promise me you're not falling for him?"

She let out a short laugh. "Definitely not." A guy like Wyatt wasn't falling-for material.

"Then you're blushing because…?" Parker let the question hang in the air.

Was she? Stupid pale, easy-to-read complexion. She searched for the right way to phrase her response.

"Well?" Parker asked.

She met his gaze. Looking away would be worse, but this wasn't easy either. "If I tell you this, it's because we're friends, and I trust you. I'm not saying it to make you jealous or incite an overprotective response." Jeez, she was getting wordy. "I need— Don't judge me?" Making the request was easier than she thought. Despite the bump in their relationship, she trusted Parker, and she prayed that wasn't about to disintegrate.

"I can't make promises about my initial reaction, but I'll listen, and I swear it's between us and it won't make me think any less of you."

"It sure as hell better not, since you were there, too." And here it was—the reason this was different than the other day. Besides the stress being gone, there was no guilt associated with what they did. It was fun. It was playful. No one was making a big deal out of it.

"Now I'm really curious."

"The blush is because… Wyatt's a really dirty lay. Like filthy-I'm-pretty-sure-he-was-holding-back-God-that-was-so-wrong-but-not."

Parker coughed and stared at her in surprise. "I don't have an argument for that."

"Good." She was more relieved to hear it than she expected. "This trip is about exploring, right? Stepping outside of boundaries? There's a lot of potential there with all three of us"

Parker grabbed her hand and pulled her to sit next to him. The contact sparked, but it didn't set her on edge. It felt natural. Friendly. No expectations. The way he and she were supposed to be. "Then it's settled. I'll change our travel plans, and tomorrow, after we're done with our Grammie's deliveries, we'll head for Pittsburgh."

Nervous flutters churned inside. This was a good idea, wasn't it? Rearranging their trip, to meet up with a guy, pretty much exclusively for hot sex with a little tourism thrown in? Sure. Sounded brilliant.

Chapter Seventeen

Parker expected tension the next morning, but aside from a few shy glances and a couple of fumbles, when they ran into each other, things with Fiona were pretty good. And definitely nothing like they were twenty-four hours earlier.

He filled her in more on the details of Wyatt's suggestion of to visit those spots typically only locals knew about, and his offer of expertise in that area, in lieu of Parker's limited schedule to explore.

When he emerged from the shower, ready to dive into one more round of filming before they flew out, he saw Fiona staring at a screen of comments.

"You shouldn't read those," he said.

"I know." Her voice held a tremor he didn't expect. "But I figured I'm a big girl; I can take a few cruel comments." She turned to face him, a frown etched on her face. "I didn't expect creepy."

"You're attractive and intelligent. Some guys are intimidated by that."

She shook her head. "That's not what I mean—though, yeah, some of this stuff is gross, now that you mention it. But there's this guy, lumb3rjck76…"

"Okay?" Parker had seen a few of his comments. Quick to defend Fiona and threaten anyone who said anything rude about her. He didn't blame the guy.

"I got a text last night, signed with that name."

His blood turned to ice in his veins. "What text?"

"It was a picture of you and me, and said he was happy to meet me. It came in while you were out with Wyatt."

"Why didn't you mention it sooner?"

Her frown deepened. "I deleted it because it squicked me out, and then forgot about it with everything else going on."

Parker didn't know that a text meant any more than a comment, except that someone had Fiona's number. And knew where she'd been. And even if it was the creepy flash-mob guy, it didn't make the situation any less nauseating. "You have to promise to be more careful."

"How am I supposed to be more careful?" Irritation snaked into her question. "We broadcast our travel schedule."

"Well, how did he get your number?"

"I don't know. I didn't give it to him, and I think that's a key point to keep in mind." Her voice grew in volume.

He didn't want to worry her more. "We're leaving this afternoon. Whoever this guy from yesterday is, he'll be here, and we'll be two states away. And if someone else took that picture, the same applies to them. Just be careful."

"Sure. I'll try." She spoke through gritted teeth.

During their deliveries, Fiona stayed off camera and said few words. Parker didn't like seeing her this way. The sooner they put some distance between them and the guy freaking her out, the better.

After they boarded the plane and the doors were closed, she wasn't sitting as rigidly, and the hint of stress that lined her forehead most of the day, faded away.

She settled in her seat as they taxied down the runway.

Parker wanted to draw Fiona out and help erase any lingering tension. "Are you still looking forward to Philly?" he asked. When they set up their schedule, she'd made him promise they'd spend time there.

"Are you kidding? So much history—the Liberty Bell, Independence Hall, Franklin Institute… We're still planning to do the sightseeing, aren't we?"

The question and the downturn in her tone caught him off-guard. "Why wouldn't we be?"

She shrugged and tucked a loose strand of hair behind her ear. "You said the point of meeting up with Wyatt was to film the local places. Go off the beaten path, where tourists don't tread. It occurred to me I shouldn't assume we'd have time for more. I did, though. Assume, that is."

"I know you've been looking forward to this." Parker nudged her arm. "I told him he had a maximum of two afternoons to show us the best he could find. Day Three is for you, and we'll stay for four if you want. It's your pick, including whether he comes with us or not, after he's done playing tour guide."

"I guess whether or not he's invited along after depends on what he's got to show us."

"Ouch," Parker said playfully.

"I didn't mean it like that." She laughed. "Well, I did, but what I was thinking was there's no reason to draw it out longer if things don't go well."

He swore her smile made the green in her eyes brighter. He was willing to agree to a lot, to keep her doing that. He was lucky she wasn't demanding, but she deserved so much more.

The string of realizations hit him hard, clenching around his chest and sinking into his thoughts. He'd do anything to keep her happy, and he'd been an idiot to do otherwise before now.

♥♥♥

Most of the concern Fiona'd had about if her relationship with Parker would stay strained, evaporated on the flight to Philadelphia. They spent the time talking about everything.

Well, almost everything. This arrangement with Wyatt, casual sex—was it only there for all three of them, or was there a chance she and Parker…?

Every time she traveled down that thought path, she had to stop herself. It brought too many uncertainties. Asking him might destroy this tentative peace. It reminded her of how not-smoothly their first time together was. There were still parts of their relationship that were undefined, that she didn't have an answer for what that definition should be.

"You coming with, or do you want to see if you can live on the plane?" Parker nudged her, teasing in his voice.

The rest of the passengers had finished disembarking while she was lost in her thoughts.

She smiled and stood. Parker grabbed both of their carry-ons from the overhead bin, and she hauled her laptop bag onto her shoulder.

It was almost eleven at night when they stepped outside.

Parker steered them toward a waiting cab. "I was thinking—we get the driver to stop on the way to the hotel, wherever he recommends, and we grab some dinner."

"Cheesesteaks and soft pretzels?" It was probably what everyone wanted when they got into town, but she wasn't going to skip it because of that.

He tossed their luggage in the trunk, held open the back door for her, and slid in next to her. Parker leaned forward, to give the cabbie their hotel address. "But we need to make a stop first. Greasiest, most Philly food we can get."

"You got it." The guy pulled into traffic and navigated them to the main roads.

As they drove, jet lag and a long day sank into Fiona's bones, and a yawn slipped out before she could stop it.

"Not fair. Those are contagious," Parker said.

"Too bad." She leaned her head on his shoulder. "I'm sleepy, and you're comfy."

He rested his head against hers. "Just don't pass out before we get dinner." The gesture was comfortable, with no expectation. It was *right*.

She replied with a loud, exaggerated snore, followed by a drowsy-sounding, "What? Huh?"

He chuckled and relaxed, supporting her weight. Heat spilled through her at the contact and threatened to *actually* lull her to sleep.

"You're that couple from the internet, aren't you?" The driver's question drew Fiona back to the conversation.

"That's us." The pride in Parker's voice was distinct.

The driver glanced at them in the rear view mirror. "My kid is watching that competition. That *twelve months, twelve contestants, a million dollars* thing? He's bouncing between the channels, but the little bastard got me hooked on you." His tone was affectionate. "Best third-person view I've ever seen of places I've never been."

"Thanks." Parker's smile was contagious.

Fiona swore she could feel the glee radiating from him.

"You filming here next?" The driver wove easily through traffic.

"As a matter of fact..." Parker furrowed his brow. "Hey, you wanna be on camera? Say *hi* to your kid, get some exposure in for your ride—that kind of thing?"

"Are you serious?" The cabbie asked.

"Dead serious. Give me your card. I'll call you tomorrow for a pick-up, and email release forms to you and your boss. We'll need a yellow chariot in the afternoon."

"I'm in." The driver parked next to the curb, in

front of a spot that was barely more than a shack with a window and a few benches out front. He twisted in his seat and handed Parker a business card. "And this is the place you want to get your food. Best cheesesteaks in the city, and they'd probably let you film too."

"Thanks. Give us five." Parker climbed from the car and offered Fiona a hand. She liked seeing him this way—confident, having fun meeting new people, doing what he loved.

She thought she understood before, but now it was clear. She'd blamed him for running away for so long, but he'd been building a career for himself. This was who he was.

They picked up dinner, and Parker chatted with the driver on the ride to the hotel.

When they got inside, half the lights were out in the lobby. Fiona wasn't surprised, since it was after midnight. The scents of grease and meat drifted from the paper bag she held, and her stomach growled. Exhaustion crawled through every inch of her, but the pleasant hum of she'd be up long enough to enjoy dinner and more of Parker's company.

As he checked them in, she let her gaze wander around the lobby. A movement near the dark gift shop caught her attention, and she squinted at the shadows to make out the shape.

It was the guy from the flash mob. Rose-guy. Her gut twisted in on itself, and the scent of the food turned nauseating.

It couldn't be, though. She stepped toward the man. Needed a better look.

"Hang on. Where are you going?" Parker

wrapped an arm around her waist, startling her.

She looked back at the gift shop. There was nothing there. "I thought I saw… Never mind."

"Saw what?"

"The guy with the rose." But she hadn't. Sleep deprivation and a lingering sense of *today is going too well* were playing tricks on her mind.

"You're tired and not seeing straight." That Parker's words echoed her thoughts wasn't reassuring. "He's two states away, and no one but the three of us knew we were headed here."

Doubt and confusion churned inside. "I guess."

"Even if he did want to follow, he wouldn't have known where to go."

"I guess." She'd seen *something*, but Parker made too much sense.

"Come on." He guided her toward the elevator and a waiting car. "Room. Food. Sleep."

"All right." She turned to face the door, and let him push the right button for their floor. As the elevator slid shut, someone stepped into view in the lobby. *Him.* Creepy rose-guy met her gaze and smiled.

A chill raced over her, as the lift rose.

Chapter Eighteen

Wyatt leaned against the wrought-iron fence outside the church, enjoying the warmth of the afternoon sun on his face. A taxi pulled up to the curb, and he smiled when Fiona stepped out. He shouldn't be happy to see the pair—this was a work venture, a means to an end—but he couldn't help himself.

Parker stayed in the back seat, talking.

"He's thanking the driver and signing off," Fiona said when she reached Wyatt. Faint circles were under her eyes, not quite hidden by concealer.

"Long night?"

A shadow of a frown crossed her face. "Jet lag."

"Sorry to keep you waiting." Parker joined them. His camera hung on a strap around his neck, no telltale red light flashing on it. He dug through a backpack slung over one shoulder, extracted a tablet, and handed the device to Wyatt. "Release form. I should have sent it to you before—I'm sorry—but we can't roll until you sign it."

Wyatt took the tablet but didn't look at the screen. "Why do I need a release form if I'm not going to be on camera?"

"Read it. You're not granting permission for me to use pre-recorded footage, but it indemnifies me if you appear on live clips, as long as I do everything within reasonable expectation to avoid that happening."

Wyatt was impressed with the professionalism and attention to detail, especially after he scanned the short but precise contract. He shouldn't be surprised, though. Even if Parker had fun doing this, it was his livelihood. "I want the option to look this over more in depth later, and modify it if I need to." As he spoke, he signed.

"That's fine, as long as you understand a signature now applies to the live shooting I do today."

"Got it." Wyatt handed him back the tablet. "Are we ready to go inside, or do you need to warmup first? Or whatever you do?" He knew what Parker did. Every sign-on was a variation on a standard.

"Give me a second. And if I'm trying not to film you, you have to make an effort to stay out of the shots."

That seemed fair.

Parker introduced the area to his viewers, then panned across the front of the building and to Fiona, before turning the camera back on himself.

Wyatt could see how avoiding being on screen could get old fast. He'd need to figure an alternative.

The building was under restoration, but parts of it remained open to the public. Because of the gorgeous stained glass, it was as much a tourist attraction as it was a church.

They strolled up the front walk.

"Whoa." Parker's exclamation made Wyatt pause.

"What's up?" Wyatt asked.

"Don't you catch fire if you step foot inside a church?"

Fiona laughed, but clamped her lips together when Wyatt raised his eyebrow. "It was funny." She shrugged.

"All right. It was." Wyatt opened the door. "But is it considered a sin if I don't feel guilt about it?"

Fiona brushed past him. "I don't think it's up for personal interpretation. The seven deadly sins are fairly well defined."

"In that case, I'm taking you both with me." He followed her into the building.

"I wish you could have seen that, folks," Parker said from behind. "Our faceless tour guide vanished in a plume of ash and smoke. I'd show you the remains, but I think that qualifies as putting him on screen."

"No comeback." Wyatt chuckled. This was so much better than the aggravation Parker projected toward him in the past.

Fiona skipped back out to grab Parker's arm. "Come on. I want to see this before the sun is gone. Or at least this decade."

Wyatt moved aside as they both joined him. He'd seen the sunlight streaming through the glass before. It was stunning and the reason he'd picked this time of day to visit.

He was more interested in watching Fiona's and Parker's reactions.

She made the softest *oh* sound.

"This is amazing." Awe filled Parker's voice, and he panned the camera around the building. "I'm not even going to try to describe it. You can see it for yourselves."

"It's beautiful." Fiona looked at Wyatt. She spun away and wandered through the chapel, brushing her fingers over hand-carved designs in the pews, meandering toward the windows, and pausing.

Parker followed. The few words he spoke were reverent and hushed.

Wyatt had been here more times than he could count. Philly was a regular stop for work, and this place was one of the few that filled him with a sense of peace. Though not as much now, with the renovations happening.

However, it had been a while since he saw the structure through fresh eyes. Watching Parker and Fiona explore breathed new life into the historic beauty.

Fiona approached the confessional booths, while Parker filmed something else. Wyatt wrapped an arm around her waist and pulled her to him. He waited until Parker was paying attention, then hovered his mouth near her ear. Her soft scent filled his head and teased him.

"He can't hear me," Wyatt whispered. "So I can say anything I want, and he'll fill in the blanks." He kept the teasing in his voice and was rewarded with an impish smile. "For instance, I can nod at the confessional, and he'll assume the worst."

Fiona blushed. "No, he won't." Her response was as soft as Wyatt's.

Parker turned the camera on himself. "Our faceless guide knows this is a PG show, and is pushing his luck. In a church, no less. How unfair is that?"

"See?" Wyatt said in a normal tone and winked at Fiona.

Fiona laughed and pulled away. "Don't go getting any ideas. I'm sweet and innocent and not breaking any ratings rules."

Wyatt couldn't suppress his snort of disbelief.

"Nick, if you're watching, she totally is. Sweet and innocent, that is. I promise no one is corrupting your sister." Parker kept the shot trained on himself.

"Because she doesn't need any help," Wyatt teased.

"Hush." There was no force behind Fiona's retort.

Parker shook his head. "All right. Now that the tour has broken down, we're moving on." He continued to film the interior but headed toward the exit.

Wyatt's amusement faded a shade. Getting to know Fiona a little was simple. She was genuine. Parker was more difficult to crack, and a large part of it was that fucking camera. He'd cultivated a one-way personality for viewers. He didn't intend to interact, only project.

Did Parker realize he was keeping the world at arm's length, despite spending so much time exploring it? He must have at least a little bit of an idea. Wyatt hung back, watching and musing, while Parker and Fiona wrapped up the live feed.

The loudest thought in his head—and the one he didn't have an answer for—was, *Why do you care whether Parker has any level of self-awareness?* In fact, why was Wyatt lingering on any consideration beyond enjoying this moment, and the satisfaction he'd get when he landed the Grammie's contract?

Because I am.

Fiona sat next to Parker at the booth in the back of the diner Wyatt recommended for dinner. He was across from them. Even in a casual place like this— or maybe because of the casual atmosphere—he held himself with a breathtaking elegance. His suit, his posture, the shadow of a beard darkening his chin— it was intimidating and nothing like Parker.

Who had been sweet and stayed close since she swore she saw rose-guy in the hotel last night. She was pretty sure Parker didn't believe her, but his presence was comforting. She twisted in her seat to rest one leg on the bench and press it against his thigh. The contact was as nice as being able to see both men while they spoke.

They'd finished their meals, and were poking at free refills on soda while they talked.

"Hot-seat time," Wyatt said. He was no-soda-for-me-coffee-black kind of guy. Go figure. "Parker gets to be on the other side of the camera."

Parker frowned. "How so?"

"You don't drive the questions. We do."

"We?" Fiona hadn't expect that.

Wyatt looked at her. "You know more about him, so you have to help make sure I'm asking in the right direction."

Interesting. How did they go from a bland discussion about the weather in different parts of the world to this? "Right direction for what?"

"Everything."

Parker shook his head, and his smile looked strained. "That's not a direction, and you don't want to know *everything*."

"Not today." Wyatt agreed. "But I'm looking for a roadmap. A place to start."

"Do I get the same in return?" Parker asked.

Fiona thought it was a fair question. Then again, Parker wasn't an enigma; Wyatt was.

"Depends on how observant you are." Wyatt topped off his coffee from the pot the waitress had left him, then leaned in, forearms on the table. "You game?"

"Ask away." Challenge lined Parker's voice.

"We'll start easy. How long have you known you were bisexual?"

Fiona didn't expect a question like this. Then again, he wasn't going to ask something like, *What's your favorite color?* That would be too obvious. "That's starting easy?" she asked.

"Isn't it?" Wyatt kept his gaze on Parker.

Parker smirked. "It's not some sort of deep, dark secret. I don't think I've ever not known. Rather, I was attracted to both sexes growing up. My best friend... s were female, so it didn't occur to me for a long time that checking out guys with them might be considered weird."

The line of questions brought back a rush of the past for Fiona. She didn't want to linger on his hesitation around the *friends* or the past-tense *were*, so she grabbed something else. "Remember Clint?"

"Oh fuck. That was a mess." Parker scrubbed his face.

Wyatt leaned in closer. "Do tell."

Fiona should have kept it to herself, but Parker didn't seem to mind her bringing it up, so she picked up the story. "He was the only male cheerleader in school. Everyone assumed he was gay—including himself."

"I asked him out," Parker said. "I can't honestly say if I was attracted to him. He was hot, and a total douche. But he was also the only other guy in school who was openly into guys, so… I had to start somewhere, you know? It was a disaster. The night started out okay, until we got to the making out. He wasn't into it at all. I got teased for"—he scrunched up his face—"pretty much the entire rest of the year. I was the guy who turned Clint straight."

Wyatt chuckled. "You seem to have come out of it okay."

"Nope. Scarred for life." Parker's retort was playful. "Seriously, though, I hated it then. Looking back, I'm glad I took the risk. What about you? When did you know?"

Fiona expected Wyatt to deflect.

He sipped his drink, brow furrowed in thought, then set the mug down. "I wasn't as insightful and wise in my youth. Don't know if it was the difference in media and culture, or self-denial. But I did it like any *normal* guy. Got drunk in college and made out with a fraternity brother who denied after that it ever happened."

It sounded like a sad story, but Fiona caught the emphasis. "You're not normal."

"I'm hurt." Wyatt sounded anything but.

Parker rested a hand on Fiona's calf. That he did it casually and without hesitation made her smile. "She's right," he said. "You spend too much time watching and recognizing, to be one of the normals."

A frown ghosted across Wyatt's face. "You're one to talk. Except you're filtering your observations through a lens."

The words had a bite. Did the conversation take a downward turn?

"*Filter*'s not the right word." If Parker caught the shift, it wasn't reflected in his tone. "I prefer to see the world through other people's eyes sometimes."

"Or most of the time," Wyatt said.

"If you dig deep enough and try hard to uncover the depths of my soul, do you think you'll find answers about yourself in there?" Parker locked his gaze on Wyatt's.

Fiona shook away the desire to hold her breath.

"I already have those answers, and you don't want to see what's hiding in there."

"I might not mind as much as you think," Parker said.

How the hell did they wind up here? Fiona racked her brain for something to shake things up and get rid of the cloud growing around them.

Chapter Nineteen

The moment he let Parker's words get to him, Wyatt knew he'd made a mistake—reacted emotionally, rather than stepping back. And then he got defensive, instead of correcting the error. Time to change that. He looked at Fiona. "How about you? When did you know?"

"About Parker's sexuality? My answer is pretty much identical to like his."

"That you're a sex kitten." That ought to knock her off balance. And if she fumbled, Parker would too.

"No," Parker said. "You're not doing that. You can't toss out a random statement and take the conversation off track."

Fuck. "My rules. I get to steer."

"And you tasked me with making sure you pointed things in a good direction." Fiona's cheeks were pink, but there was no shyness in her voice. "You're asking a lot for someone who's not willing to give in return, but I'll answer your question. I didn't wake up one day and say, *Hey. Kinky sex sounds like fun.* It's taken years and a lot of pushing past indoctrination, to even start to be okay with it."

"See? Not so hard." Wyatt wasn't making this better. He didn't like not being in control of the conversation.

Parker shook his head. "Nope. Not nearly as hard as you're working to keep us from talking about you."

"What do you want to know? I'm an open book, though a couple of the pages might be stuck together." Wyatt hid his wince at the last bit. A casual joke. An attempt at light humor. Also, another blatant distraction.

"Why are you here?" Fiona asked.

Concern flashed through him, and his brain began dissecting the question before he even registered he was doing it. He needed to stop responding impulsively, stop over-analyzing, and stop assuming they knew anything about his background beyond what he told them. "Here? Because we wanted dinner."

"Nice. Why are you showing a couple of kids around Philadelphia?" Parker said.

Kids. He might have thought they were immature when he met them, but they weren't kids. He was fascinated by how much they picked up on. "You needed a hook for your channel, and I know the town." The canned answers made it easier to slide back into a casual posture.

"You met us in a hotel bar." Fiona straightened on the bench, turning her body toward him.

Parker nodded. "It didn't matter that we were

together. You didn't hesitate."

"You're attractive. Both of you. You said you weren't a couple—which, by the way, anyone who's paying attention can see is something you only tell yourselves."

Fiona didn't flinch. "After that fell apart, and you ran into us in the airport, you randomly handed me a business card. Which is a personal card, and not for your actual job. That didn't escape me. And then you chatted me up on the plane."

An accurate rundown of the situation, but when they laid it out like that, it didn't seem so innocent. Why hadn't he expected them to be curious about the string of coincidences? Because most people wouldn't give it this much thought. "You looked bored, and I wanted company."

"And now we're here. Half a country away from home base, and the guy who wasn't even a one-night stand is our tour guide. Why are you here?" Fiona asked again.

"I told Parker why. It's about the sex. It's good. It's fun. Why the fuck not?"

Parker shook his head. "If it was just about the sex, you'd hand over a room number, say *bring the lube*, and unpack the blindfold."

They were relentless, and Wyatt was losing track of why he was fighting this conversation. "You said it yourself—I like to observe, and you make for nice scenery."

"What was it you told me? *Lying to get laid isn't worth the effort*?" Parker said.

"Not quite my words, and I'm not lying. This is deviance. Lust. Need. Letting the anticipation build.

A little bit of fun sprinkled in with the *wham* and the *bam*." Fuck. He sounded like he was making excuses. Why couldn't he come up with something short and sweet, besides, *I'm here to secure my job, and you're the chess pieces*?

"Because it's about the sex." Fiona mimicked him.

That wouldn't do at all.

"Because from that very first night, you've worked really hard to convince us you're the bad guy," Parker added.

Wyatt definitely was, but not in the way they were twisting things. He didn't like balancing on this cusp of telling them everything. Correction—he hated that it was even a consideration. He drew in focus and locked his defensive walls back into place, then looked Parker in the eye. "I'm every bit the wolf I told you I am. I don't care if you think that's a cheesy line." His voice was steel. "It doesn't mean I don't enjoy your company." Wrong. That wasn't emotionally detached. No, it was okay. He could work with it. "The intellect is certainly a turn-on, and I don't see why *just sex* has to replace friendly conversation. Make no mistake—at the end of the week, we go our separate ways."

"Why are you trying so hard?" Fiona's soft question wrenched his thoughts out of alignment again.

"To what?"

"To reinforce this persona of *I don't care*. How emotionally immature is that?"

Ouch. A retort slid to the tip of his tongue, about their habits. The way they kept each other at arm's length. The emotional scars they didn't hide at all. But that would prove her point. "I care."

"Because we all have an intellectual connection," Parker said.

That made everything sound so cold. Then again, that was the point. "Because you're human beings."

"There's just no romance," Fiona added.

"Exactly." Wyatt wasn't sure how, but things were deescalating. What the fuck had happened? "I liked you two better when you were uncertain and dancing around each other."

"No you didn't. This is much better. You like the challenge." Fiona smiled. Fuck it all—why did he enjoy that sight so much?

"Fuck you." Wyatt didn't mean it, and the words carried no strength.

She rested her chin in her palm and fluttered her eyelashes. "There you go, changing the subject to sex again."

"Okay. I yield." Wyatt held his hands up in surrender. "I'm not sure to what, but..." He chuckled. "What was the point of all of this?"

Fiona's smile grew. "You're learning about Parker. Finding out who he is without the camera."

"Yeah. I really am," Wyatt said. Not in the way he'd inteded, but despite the confrontational tangent, and the change to tension then back to middle-ground, he liked what he saw.

He had to remember everything he'd told them. The problem was he wasn't any more convinced than they were.

"What do you want to know next?" Parker sank

back in his seat.

Nothing this intense. "What's your favorite color?" Duh. "Red," Wyatt said at the same time Parker did.

"It's not." Fiona propped her leg on the bench, to rest against Parker's leg.

An odd spike of envy jarred Wyatt, that they had this level of comfort without thinking about it. He shouldn't care. He'd been working too hard and his head was all sorts of fucked up.

"It is." Parker jabbed his straw at the remnants of ice cubes in the bottom of his glass. The sound was more *slosh* that *clank.*

"Do you have the same level of appreciation for bad horror sci-fi that she does?" Wyatt nodded at Fiona.

Parker furrowed his brow. "Not quite. And how do you know that?"

"It's what we did the other night," Fiona said. "When I was mad at you."

Parker seemed to relax further.

God, that seemed like forever ago. And apparently, there were still some things the perfect not-couple didn't share with each other.

The conversation continued to slide back toward neutral. What was Wyatt doing? Confusing lust with something more? Letting pleasure threaten business? The sooner he wrapped this up, the better. Would one more day be enough? Not unless he could maneuver Parker into violating the decency clause of either the contest or the Grammie's contract.

Sounded like a solid goal.

♥♥♥

"Hey." Fiona knocked on the bathroom door in the hotel room. "Are you going to be in there all morning? Wyatt will still like you even if you don't pretty yourself up."

The conversation last night, after the church, took an odd turn, but at the end of the evening, she felt more at ease with Wyatt than she had since they met. Like he'd finally stopped hiding.

Parker opened the door and stuck his tongue out at her.

She jabbed it with her finger.

"Give me five more minutes," he said with a laugh, then closed her out again.

She liked this so much, she didn't dare bring up the question of *is sex okay if it's just the two of us*? Probably a childish thing to fret over, but she didn't want to push Parker away after finally rediscovering their friendship.

They were meeting Wyatt again this afternoon, but they had a delivery first. It was for a wedding, so she and Parker had to look nice. If he didn't hurry up, she wouldn't have time to smooth the fly-aways out of her hair, along with the rest of what she needed to do to get ready.

She grabbed her laptop and pulled up Parker's video from yesterday. She wanted to see the chapel again—all that gorgeous light and architecture.

Her gaze drifted to the comments, and she looked away. But when she saw her name front and center, she had to read.

It was from Lumb3rjck76. A chill raced over

her. He'd written, *You're a goddess, Fiona. You deserve so much better.*

Simple words, but they gnawed at her gut until she had to swallow back the bile rising in her throat.

"Hey." Parker rested a hand on her shoulder, startling her. "You know better than to read the comments."

"Tell me comments like this are status quo." She pointed to the screen.

Parker leaned in and frowned. He took the computer from her, set it aside, and dropped on the bed behind her.

"You'll wrinkle your suit." Her protest was weak.

He draped an arm over her shoulder and tugged her so her back rested against his chest. "It's not a great suit anyway. I know this isn't comforting, but at least it's just a comment."

"You're right. Not comforting at all."

"I'll block him, so he can't comment anymore."

"Don't." Fiona hated saying that, but it was the most reasonable response.

"Why not?"

"It won't stop him from creating another account, and if he does that, I'll be wondering if it's still him, or a new creeper." She'd also rather ignore all of this and hope it went away, rather than risk pissing the guy off. Besides, blocking him wouldn't stop him from seeing the videos, just from leaving comments, and something about that was even worse.

Parker rested his head against hers, and his breath fell across her neck, soothing her. "We're in this together. I know it hasn't always seemed like this, but I'm here, and we've got this."

"Thanks." His words were reassuring. She hated to extract herself from his arms, but they were on the clock. "I'll go get ready."

Before she could leave the room, Parker took her hand and met her gaze. "It'll be all right," he said.

She gave him a weak smile. "I know." She grabbed her dress from the closet and locked herself in the bathroom. She stripped down and stepped into the shower. It was a little thing, but she'd miss unlimited hot water when this was all over.

She turned up the temperature as high as she could stand, and stood under the scalding stream, letting the heat and pressure chase away her tension. She stood there until she convinced herself this was no big deal, then finished washing up.

Fiona had her dress on and was pulling her hair into a bun, when Parker called, "You've got a text."

It was probably from Nick. "Read it to me?" she said.

"I don't know your passcode."

She smiled at her reflection, and bright green eyes, lined with enough eyeliner and mascara to make her look like a different—more exotic—person, smiled back. "Yes you do." It was the last four digits of Parker's childhood phone number. Silly. Sentimental. And the first number she'd ever memorized.

"Who's W?" he asked a second later.

"Who do you think?" *Wyatt.* Her stomach fluttered in a new way. "What does it say?"

"Looking forward to seeing you both this

afternoon. Don't wear panties."

She squeezed her thighs together and peeked out the door. "You made that last part up."

"Nope." He held up the phone.

As if she could read that from where she was. She stripped off her underwear, trying to ignore the throbbing between her legs. She emerged into the main room, and Parker's whistle stopped her.

He was looking at her like it was the first time he'd ever seen her. Her skin must have turned almost as red as her dress.

Time to be bold and have some fun, instead of cowering from an unseen stalker and letting the stranger ruin her plans. She held up her panties. Parker's eyes grew wide, and she dropped the lingerie on top of her luggage.

"Let's go to a wedding," she said, with far greater confidence than she felt.

Chapter Twenty

The wedding delivery went smoothly. Not the kind of stuff high-view videos were made of, but Parker was glad to see the couple enjoying the day with their friends and family.

But watching the celebration didn't take his mind off what Fiona wasn't wearing under her dress. It was distracting enough, seeing how the red hugged her breasts, left her pale shoulders and neck on display, and showed off the curve where her hips met her waist.

It was the amusement in her eyes that got him every time he met her gaze, though—that hint that they shared a secret no one else was in on.

After the live filming, they met Wyatt at a local winery. He said they were already dressed up, so they should do something elegant. The owner was happy to let Parker film. Since the footage would be edited before it was uploaded, Parker didn't have to go out of his way to keep Wyatt out of the shots. That made everything run more smoothly.

Except that now all three of them were in on the secret, and Parker felt like he'd spent the entire day with an erection. In reality, it was probably only half the day.

They finished the tour of the winery, and Parker stashed his camera in Wyatt's rental car. It was odd to trust Wyatt with something so valuable, but Parker wasn't worried about it.

From there, it was picking raspberries, which Parker was pretty sure was designed partly as a form of torture. At least this afternoon. He didn't know which was a bigger turn-on—the light teasing of Fiona sucking the stain of juice from his fingers, or watching Wyatt do the same to her.

Wyatt steered them toward a quiet clearing, surrounded by trees and vines and with no one else around. He grabbed a cooler and blanket from the trunk.

"You pick now to be a cheap date?" Parker teased. "Figure you've already made your best impression?"

Wyatt shook his head. "I'm a fantastic fucking date. So good, you don't know if you envy me or want to fuck me."

"A little of both," Parker admitted. Watching Wyatt move was nothing like watching Fiona, but the man did wicked things to a suit and captured a room simply by being in it.

Dinner was simple. Finger sandwiches from a local deli and sparkling juice from the winery. Afterward, Wyatt stashed the cooler. They were seated on the blanket, joking about random things, and Parker had mostly forgotten the one thing that teased him the rest of the day.

"Come here." Wyatt motioned to Fiona.

She had kicked her shoes off and sat with her legs tucked to the side. "Why?"

"I don't have to explain myself."

She raised her eyebrows and stared at him, lips pursed. "I'd like you to." Her tone was playful.

Wyatt smirked. "Fine. Because I want to see if you got my text this morning."

Right. *There* was the distraction. Parker adjusted himself as his cock pressed against the seam of his slacks.

"You see with your eyes, not with your hands." Fiona's tone was almost sing-song. "And you can see fine from there."

Wyatt chuckled. "You and I clearly have different definitions of the word *see*, and yours isn't as fun."

"It's not?" Challenge blended with Fiona's teasing.

"Fine," Wyatt said. "We'll do it your way. Show me."

She chewed her bottom lip as she glanced around, and pink crept up her neck.

Parker was captivated by the scene. Anticipation raced over him, and he clamped his jaw shut to keep from doing something like gaping.

"Well?" Wyatt prompted.

Fiona stretched her legs in front of her and raised one knee to let her skirt creep up toward her hip, exposing a triangle of smooth, bare pussy.

This was wicked. Sneaking a glimpse at porn when he shouldn't be. Peeking in on an intimate moment that wasn't necessarily meant to be.

Wyatt whistled and looked at him. "How did you ignore that? You knew."

"I did. And I didn't ignore it. I spent half the day hard and the other half trying not to be."

"I didn't mean to make you suffer." Fiona's sweet voice drew his attention again. She hadn't covered herself.

"She did," Wyatt said, "or you wouldn't have known."

Fiona slid her legs together, then rolled to her hands and knees. As she crawled toward Parker, green-eyed gaze locked on his face, her skirt hugged her hips, and he had the perfect view down the front of her dress. "Let me make it up to you?" she purred.

She really was part kitten.

"What did you have in mind?" His throat was dry. He felt like an inexperienced, horny teenager. Seduction wasn't new—he'd been on both sides— but this was different. This was *her*. Sweet, smart, always-there Fiona. And fuck, if he didn't like this side of her as much as the rest of her.

She moved up his legs and dragged his zipper down. A shudder raced over him at the release of pressure against his erection. When her cool fingers met his hot skin, he sucked a sharp breath through his teeth.

She met his gaze again, and drew her tongue up his shaft, before taking his length in her mouth.

"Fuck." He knotted his fingers in her hair and pulled her back. "Stop."

She jutted out her lower lip, and the fleshy swell was less than an inch from the head of his dick. "Did

I do something wrong?"

"No. God no. But I've been thinking about you all day, and if you do that now, I can't promise to hold back."

"Good." A wicked smile played on her lips, and she lowered her head to his lap again.

Each lick and suck sent a new wave of pleasure through Parker. He was intensely aware that Wyatt watched, silent, and that amplified Parker's desire.

He brushed a few loose strands of Fiona's hair aside, to watch her full lips glide up and down his cock. "So fucking gorgeous," he muttered.

The comment drew more enthusiasm from her, and she gripped tighter. Sucked harder. She drifted her free hand back between her legs but hesitated.

"Don't stop." He forced the words out through jagged groans. "Play with yourself. I want to watch you come with my cock in your mouth."

He glanced at Wyatt, who watched through half-closed eyes as he stroked himself.

"We're both watching," Parker told Fiona. "Getting off to the sight of you." All right, so he wasn't the dirty-talker Wyatt was, but he liked the taste of the coaxing rolling off his tongue.

She reached back and inched her skirt higher, until she could slide her finger between her legs. He felt her gasp against his skin, as much as he heard it.

He glided a hand along her chest, under her dress, to squeeze her breast. When he reached her nipple, she moaned. He pinched harder, and she returned the favor, pumping with hungry enthusiasm.

Parker's balls tightened, and tension coiled through his body as he hovered on the edge of orgasm. "Red." He tried to nudge her away.

She gave him that look again—innocence mixed with hungry desire—and watched him as she continued to lick along his shaft.

Wyatt's groans shifted to staccato grunts.

Parker's arousal hovered near one-thousand, at the knowledge that this private show had an audience. He couldn't take his eyes off Fiona though. Manners said he should push her away, but each delicious sound and touch and glance drew him closer to the edge of climax and stole his thoughts.

Sensation overrode reason, and he came hard, thrusting against her face, hitting the back of her throat, and spilling in her mouth.

She slowed her attentions, and stopped when he shuddered away from her touch, too sensitive to take any more. She glided her tongue along his skin with one last, feather-light touch, licking him clean before she pulled away.

He pulled her up, needing to taste her and himself. To feel more. And to make sure she enjoyed herself as well. She straddled his legs, skirt riding over her hips. When he gripped her hair, knocking more strands loose, she gasped. He crushed his mouth to hers, swallowing each tantalizing noise she made.

She was so wet when he slid his touch along her slit, it threatened to make him hard again. He dipped three fingers inside her without resistance, and she ground against his hand. She tasted like raspberries and cucumber sandwiches and him. Fuck. That was intoxicating.

Parker found her swollen clit with his thumb

and pressed into it while he fucked her with his fingers.

This was more than physical. It seared through every inch of him. Penetrated his thoughts. His soul. Who he was with was more arousing than what they were doing, though the way she slid her body along his, danced her tongue with his, and clung to him clenched in his chest.

Her pussy clenched around him as climax tore through her. She broke away with a cry, then bit the inside of her cheek, muffling the sound.

God, she was gorgeous. He slid out of her gently when the writhing stopped, and dragged his fingers along the grass.

Fiona met his gaze again, a shine in the emerald of her eyes that he couldn't name but wanted to see over and over again.

"You two going to go all night?" Wyatt's throaty, teasing question shattered the invisible bubble around Parker and Fiona.

Fiona giggled and dropped her forehead to Parker's chest.

"I thought we'd wrap up soon." Parker managed to find his voice. He was imagining the hint of jealousy in Wyatt's question, wasn't he?

Wyatt stood, zipped himself up, and crossed the distance between them. He offered Fiona a hand, and she accepted, wobbling for a moment when he tugged her to her feet. He rested a hand on her back to steady her, and gave her the most chaste kiss on the cheek Parker had ever seen.

When she looked stable, Wyatt offered Parker a hand too. He helped Parker stand and jerked him close.

"I told you she was yours alone." Wyatt's words were barely a whisper.

Ambivalence flickered through Parker, as he searched for a response to a comment he would have given anything to have confirmed in the past. Why didn't the words feel the same now?

"Hey," Fiona said playfully. "No fair, keeping secrets."

Wyatt faced her and gave a deep bow. "Never, my lady."

Bits of Parker's mind wanted to delve deeper into the consequences and meaning of what happened. This wasn't *just sex*. Not for him. But it wasn't anything he had words to define.

The rest of him insisted he enjoy the glow and not overthink this to the point of ruining the moment.

One thing he was certain of—he couldn't leave Fiona again. There were no answers to what Wyatt had to do with that. How he fit in. *If* he did, despite his insistence. But watching Fiona smooth out her skirt, grab her shoes rather than putting them on, and look up at him with a smile, he couldn't imagine letting her go.

♥♥♥

Wyatt needed to remember he was here to do more than show a couple people around town and watch them fuck. As he sat in his hotel room, several hours after parting ways from Fiona and Parker, the evening in the park was the only thing painting his mind.

He should be finishing his summary of local

delivery capabilities, rather than reliving that moment—that alluring instant he was both a part of and completely removed from.

The way it should be. Wyatt was a voyeur at best, and a fucking bastard at worst.

He dropped his face into his hand with a sigh and massaged his temples, as if that might coax the memory away.

His phone chimed with a new email, and he grabbed it. It was an alert that Parker was doing a live feed. That was the perfect reason for Wyatt to set his phone to *Do Not Disturb* and finish his work.

Instead, he clicked the link in the email and let the video load on the small screen. Parker had the camera trained on him, the stark neutrality of a hotel room in the background. From the shaking and angle of the shot, it looked like he had the handheld and was sitting on a bed. He'd shed the suit from earlier in favor of sweats and a battered T-shirt with the Eiffel Tower. And fuck it, if he didn't look sexy and scruffy.

"Okay. I know I already went live once today," Parker said to the viewing audience, "but I'm a billion times too wired to sleep, so, you get to put up with me. For the first time in ages, I can't tell you why. Don't you hate that? The person online who insists they have a *huge* secret they're dying to tell someone, but they can't? Tonight, I'm that jerk."

What was he talking about? Did it have something to do with Grammie's? That didn't make sense. Parker wouldn't jeopardize things by even hinting at something, if he wasn't supposed to.

"I will say this, though—this trip has been the

best thing ever. A million times better than I ever could have imagined." Parker's grin was huge and irritatingly infectious.

Wyatt realized he had his chin in his palm and was wearing a silly smile as he watched, and he wiped the emotion away. But he didn't stop the video.

"Are you talking to your internet friends again?" Fiona's voice carried from the background.

Parker looked past the camera but didn't turn it to follow his gaze. "I am. And we're live. Say *hi* to your fans?"

"I don't know. Maybe." Her tone was that light, carefree kind of playful that made Wyatt hard without any visual cues.

"Please. Pleasepleasepleasepleaseplease," said Parker.

She laughed. "All right. Only because you begged."

He turned the camera on her, and a fist clamped around Wyatt's lungs. She wore knit shorts that barely covered her ass, and a matching camisole. Her hair was pulled into a messy ponytail, with loose red strands flying everywhere. Her smile scrunched up her nose, and with the hotel lighting and the camera, made the freckles on her cheeks obvious.

What was he doing here, watching this with every other voyeur in the world, rather than sitting there with them? Right—he wasn't part of their universe. With good reason. Wyatt shouldn't have to remind himself of that.

"What's your favorite part of the trip so far?" Parker asked. "And remember—live."

Fiona laughed and shook her head. "I can't say." She waved. "Hi, Nick. Nothing bad, I promise."

"In other words, all the stuff we're doing that gets cut in post."

She ducked her face behind her hands, muffling her, "Maybe."

Wyatt didn't care that they were talking about the sex. Or that it involved him. He was watching out of idle curiosity.

And if he kept repeating the assurance, he might believe it.

"Okay. We'll compromise. Leave out the torrid details and tell us your second favorite part instead." Parker zoomed in closer and pulled back again until the image came back into focus.

"I can't pick one thing; I love all of it. The places. The people. The good, bad, familiar, and filthy."

"Keep it family friendly." Warmth mingled with Parker's warning.

Fiona shook her head. "I am. Completely and totally family friendly. I didn't even mention that thing, with the—"

"Say *goodnight*, Fiona."

She looked into the camera, grinning. "Goodnight, Fiona."

Wyatt tossed his phone aside and let it slide across the desk. The twinges of longing and jealousy didn't matter. He had what he needed to break their contract, and it was close. It would only take another nudge or two to coax them into a community-standards violation. Get one of them to say or do too much on camera, and it would all be over.

He'd move into his promotion and leave them and this entire affair behind.

Guilt joined everything else he refused to feel. There was no reason for it. Fiona was brilliant, and her app would take off without Grammie's. Especially after the coverage she'd gotten for it.

Parker was charismatic as hell, and this would be the kind of no-such-thing-as-bad-publicity, slip-up that would only further his career.

Everyone would be better for this, once Wyatt was done.

Chapter Twenty-One

Wyatt answered his phone as he walked into the local offices for work. "Wyatt. How can I help you?" A low-grade thrum ran through the base of his skull, thanks to a night of tossing and turning, accompanied by dreams of flirty redheads and charming-as-fuck vloggers.

"Hey." Chuck's too-friendly voice made Wyatt cringe. "Saw you were in town, working on proposals. What's your calendar like this morning?"

Wyatt planned to wrap up work early, check in on where Fiona and Parker were, and see how he could fuck things up for them. The thought soured in his gut, but he ignored the reaction. "I can rearrange my schedule if you're around. Fair warning—the strip clubs aren't as great here as in Atlanta. Nor do they open this early."

Chuck laughed. "I know, right? You'll still owe me in two weeks, but we're both here now and I'd like to talk face to face."

"When and where?"

"Half an hour? I've got a temporary office set up over here, at Grammie's."

"Great." It sounded intolerable, but Wyatt kept that from his retort. This was the job, and he excelled at it. He pocketed his phone, spun on his toe, and headed back to his car.

Nearly an hour later—after waiting in the lobby for almost twenty-five minutes—Wyatt took the seat across from Chuck, in a cramped office. They exchanged basic pleasantries.

"I'll keep this short. I know you're busy," Chuck said.

Wyatt's mask never wavered. "Fantastic. What can I do for you?" He'd have to dig through fractured thoughts to come up with a status on his updated proposal, but he could bullshit his way through it.

"Have you seen this ludicrous YouTube contest that's going on? This win-a-sponsorship deal all these bums are competing for?"

Wyatt's brain ground to a halt at the question, stalled on memories he shouldn't have an emotional attachment to. "Yeah. I got caught up in one of those channels and their filming. Some flashmob thing in Indiana." No reason to lie about it, but he didn't need to offer any information beyond that, either.

"What a wreck. Am I right?" Chuck snorted a laugh. "And those are the guys I wanted to talk to you about. They're supposed to be representing us, of all things. And I hear they're here, now. Fucking amateur hour at its worst."

Wyatt bit his tongue to swallow back a defense for Parker. "Hmm."

"Anyway… They're working for the company

competing with you for the contract."

"I'd heard that." Wyatt blanketed the chaos bubbling inside. The conflicting thoughts of his plan, feelings he wouldn't acknowledge, and the desire to punch Chuck for his disdain.

"Like I said, the thing is a disaster area. This app is glitching on contracts. It's a two-person circus, and we haven't even rolled out a tenth of our projected business."

Wyatt forced his chuckle. What he wanted to do was point out Fiona had dropped everything the moment there was a tiny hiccup in the system and had things back online within hours. Few businesses could boast that kind of reaction time. "So much for that family-friendly feeling you were looking for, huh?"

"Touché." Chuck grimaced. "Anyway. I wanted to talk to you about something else. I've seen preliminary work of what you've done onsite, and if you can offer that—the things you're discussing with our regional offices—and come in at your original quote, we're going to go with you."

How do I know you'll actually sign the contract this time? The question lodged in Wyatt's throat. "What about these YouTube kids? They still have two weeks, don't they?"

"This is where it gets tricky. We're going to let them run through the end of their one-month trial before we pull the plug. See out their contract. Hey, it's free advertising. You know?"

"Right..." This was about Wyatt and getting what he'd been shooting for—no mess, no fuss. He grabbed the question he should have asked. "I need a guarantee the deal is going through."

"Fair enough," Chuck said. "I'll give it to you in writing, but it has to be under NDA for the next two weeks. We'll sign the paperwork now, if it stays private."

Wyatt grinned his widest, most genuine-looking smile, to smother the doubt inside. "Great."

And, it was. This way, he didn't have to force failure on Parker and Fiona. Wyatt had accomplished his goal, he'd never see them again after this week, and he'd be long gone from their lives if they found out who he was.

Everybody won, and they'd see it too, even if it took them a little while to realize it.

♥ ♥ ♥

Parker sat on the edge of a fountain, legs stretched in front of him, letting the sun beat against his back. He'd finished filming for the day, and this was Fiona's chance to sightsee, so he'd left the equipment at the hotel.

Amid the chatter of tourists, footsteps drew closer, and then a pair of leather dress shoes moved into his line of sight.

Wyatt stood a few feet back, hands in his slacks pockets. Parker had misjudged him. Not that his initial assessment was outright wrong; Wyatt was arrogant and aggressive and not used to hearing *no*. But he seemed to have a personality under that. And he really was a sexy bastard.

"You're awfully easy to track down," Wyatt said.

Parker felt a nudge of doubt about the hints that

Fiona's biggest online fan may be following them, but he was a bit stalled on what he could do about it. "I suppose that only matters if you're looking for us."

"I was. You have room for one more in your party?"

Parker hesitated, torn between wanting Fiona to himself for the day and wanting Wyatt to stick around.

"Don't jump on an answer right away." Light sarcasm leaked into Wyatt's voice. "Take your time." And was that a trace of hurt?

Fiona skipped up to them, saving Parker from summoning a response. She squeezed Wyatt's hand. "Hey. Didn't expect to see you today."

A new batch of muddled thoughts taunted Parker, in response to her enthusiasm. It quieted when she sat next to him, her arm resting against his.

"I couldn't find it," she said.

"Find what?" Wyatt asked.

Parker shrugged. "I don't know. She won't tell me."

"It's a surprise. The guy said I should check out the gift shop on the other side of the square, but I saw you both and wanted to say *hi*." She looked up at Wyatt. "Are you sticking around?"

That helped Parker make up his mind, though he still didn't know how he felt about it. "He is."

Wyatt smiled. "Go buy your surprise. We'll wait."

"Okay." Fiona hurried away again, and Wyatt turned to watch her leave. Not that Parker blamed him. In those jeans, the view was incredible.

Wyatt looked at Parker again. "Has she always

been so…"

"Amazing? Yes." Though, that seemed like the understatement of the decade when he said it aloud.

"I was going to say *effervescent*."

"That too."

A group of kids rushed past Wyatt, nudging him aside, and a frazzled looking father chased after them, pausing for half a breath to apologize before continuing his pursuit.

"What about you?" Wyatt asked.

"I've never been effervescent."

"No. You're charismatic." Wyatt tilted his head, as if studying him. "That's the word I'd use."

Parker'd never thought of himself that way. "I'm just friendly."

A giggle caught his attention, and he followed the sound to two girls in their late teens. One balanced on the fountain wall and the other walked beside her on the ground. Every few seconds, they'd look toward Wyatt and Parker and laugh again. When the one on the ground caught Parker's eye, he gave a short wave. She flushed, turned away, and grabbed her friend's hand.

"But you're sincere about it." Wyatt's comment drew his attention again.

This coming from a guy who earned his living selling things. And as far as Parker could tell, he was damn good at it. "You're not?"

"Depends on what I'm trying to get out of the situation. I don't always *not* mean it."

Parker winced at the jumble of negatives. "That's not a convoluted statement or anything."

"May I ask you a personal question?"

"You've had my dick in your mouth. Does it get more personal?"

A couple with a baby stroller glared at Parker as they passed. He gave them an apologetic half-shrug.

"It does," Wyatt said. "And it has the potential to ruin a day, so think before you answer."

The shift in tone tightened in Parker's neck. Wyatt only knew one thing that might sour Parker's mood. Or rather, one person. "I have to know now. Ask away."

"That clip from Omaha, with the sister of your… deceased girlfriend? I saw that."

Oh. There was that, too. "Okay."

"What happened?"

Everything. Nothing. All the wrong things. God, he didn't want to relive that. But the memories were bubbling to the surface, so there was no point in pretending they didn't exist. "At least you ask the hard stuff first. Like ripping off a Band-Aid."

"You're not obligated to answer."

"It's all right." With the sun warming his skin and the laughter and enjoyment all around them, it was easier to not sink into those shadows. "Fiona, Gretchen, and I were friends growing up. Elementary school. Junior high. We made it a few years into high school, and Gretchen asked me to homecoming." This was probably more detail than Wyatt wanted, but Parker needed to pad things, to remember there were good parts, too.

"From there, Gretchen and I were a couple. Red still hung with us, and she seemed to be cool with the arrangement. After a few months, things started to fall apart with Gretchen. Mostly because we were teenagers and too young to be in love. Fiona was a friendly ear when I needed one." She'd also been infuriatingly neutral. "She had this way of making me look at things from Gretchen's perspective and talking me back from the edge of frustration. Except the longer I talked to her"—he'd been blind to it then, and he wouldn't be now—"the more I realized I was with the wrong girl."

"From a strictly biased perspective, and not to speak ill of the dead, it seems like a smart conclusion to draw. For you," Wyatt said.

Was the pause intentional? "Yeah, well… Stupid teenagers, you know? Then one day I was bitching about my problems with Gretchen, and Fiona said, *Holy fuck—just dump her already*." He could still hear her voice in his head, saying those exact words. "It caught me off guard. Fiona said it was clear we weren't happy, we weren't making things work, and we were too young to be tied down."

"Smart, on her part," Wyatt said.

She always was the bright one. "The comment made me pause and think, and then I told her *okay*. I asked Red, if I broke up with Gretchen, would she go out with me?"

"She told you *no*." Wyatt shifted his weight from one foot to the other.

"She did. How did you…?"

"Lucky guess. The story goes differently if she tells you *yes*. There's more guilt. There's less chance for you two to repair things. And there's the fact that she's not the kind of person who would do that to a friend."

"But I am?" Parker didn't know how to take a statement like that.

"You're the guy who asked her."

Fair point. Not one Parker wanted to concede, but still fair. This was the first time he'd ever talked openly about what happened. He'd expected it to hurt more, but the scars were that—pale, healed over, still there, but not painful anymore. "Fiona told me that even if I ended things with Gretchen, she'd still be there for me as a friend. That she wouldn't let that drive us apart. And maybe, down the road, we'd be more. Maybe not, but she hoped maybe. She just refused to be the rebound girl."

"And Gretchen passed away before you ended things."

That was the climax of the story. That plot twist, where it all fell apart. "Drunk-driving accident. She was the drunk. Killed a family of four." *That* still hurt. Knowing he'd been responsible for their loss, even indirectly, was a burden he'd never shed. He breathed past the grief. "So there you have my deepest, darkest secret." His chuckle was forced. "What's yours?"

Wyatt shook his head and sat on the ledge next to him, hands pressed into the concrete. He stared at his feet. "My ex—current at the time, open relationship—used me as a wingman for women he was obsessed with. I inadvertently helped him stalk and harass about half a dozen of them before I figured it out."

Parker didn't know how to respond to that, but he didn't doubt the story. It rang with a kind of truth that not everything coming out of Wyatt's mouth did. "I'm sorry," Parker said.

"Live and learn, right?" Wyatt sighed.

"What do you learn from something like that?"

"Never trust anyone too convenient to be true." When Wyatt looked at him, his neutral expression was back in place, and that hint of sincerity had vanished. Whatever he was hiding was tucked away again.

"You mean *too good.*"

"I don't."

"Hey." Fiona bounded to a stop in front of them. She looked back and forth between them. "Did I miss something?"

Yes. But Parker had, too. He'd been half a breath from chipping away at Wyatt's exterior, and he lost his chance.

Then again, did he really want to know what was underneath the mask?

Chapter Twenty-Two

Wyatt didn't know what he was doing here. He could have—should have—walked away from this, after meeting with Chuck. Maybe sent Fiona an, *it was fun, ciao*, kind of text.

Instead, when he was done with work, he found himself heading toward Independence Hall, where Parker and Fiona were supposed to be, and then getting sucked into the story of their past. And sharing snippets of his own. This was *not* how cutting ties worked.

"Did you find what you were looking for?" Wyatt asked Fiona. It didn't answer her question, but since Parker hadn't stepped up with an immediate response either, this was probably the best way to go.

"Yes." A hint of smile was on her lips, and she handed Parker a plastic bag with a gift shop logo on it. She handed a second one to Wyatt. "I didn't want anyone feeling left out."

"I can't." Wyatt shook his head.

She shook the bag at him. "It's a gift, dummy.

You don't get to turn it down. And please, don't get us into another circular conversation about how you care but don't. Take the damn bag."

"Yes, ma'am." Wyatt laughed. His smile grew broader when he looked inside. He pulled out a stuffed bear in a purple T-shirt with a Liberty Bell on it.

Fiona blushed. "They didn't have any wolves, but he's as fierce and mean as you are."

She had no idea. "Thank you." He kept his reply genuine and ignored the chaos in his head.

She looked at Parker. "Well?" she said.

He unwrapped his gift, and his mouth twisted in amusement. He pulled out a fake quill pen, with Independence Hall markings on it. "It's perfect."

"I know you don't collect souvenirs, because you don't have a home address," Fiona said, "but you can always keep it at my place. Finally start that collection. Have a reason to visit more often."

A layer of bittersweet settled over Fiona and Parker, and Wyatt swallowed back a vile cocktail of jealousy and self-loathing. "You two up for an early dinner?" he asked, more to shatter the cloud than because he was hungry.

Fiona studied him, brow furrowed. "As in, actual dinner, or euphemism dinner?"

The latter was tempting. And a thoroughly bad idea at this point. Fuck—what he wouldn't give for another night of sex with these two… Well, except his job. "I thought we'd start with actual dinner, but only if you're free. There's a place within walking distance that has amazing calzones." He stopped short of selling up the idea. No reason to come off as desperate.

A tinny song filtered into the conversation, and Fiona was already reaching for her phone when Wyatt realized it was her ringtone.

She held up a finger as she raised the device to her ear. "What's up?" Her happiness vanished in a scowl. She turned away, speaking in quiet tones.

Wyatt glanced at Parker, who shrugged. "It's Nick. That's all I know," Parker said.

A moment later, Fiona returned. Her frown etched lines in her forehead. "Go get dinner." She looked between them. "Text me the address, and I'll catch up if I can."

Parker was on his feet in an instant. "What's going on? Can I help?"

"Nick tried to *tweak something*." A growl cut through her words. "He was trying to make sure we were ready for the next leg of our trip. Now contracts are associated with the wrong accounts, and he had to take the system offline to keep it from emailing personal information to the wrong people, and...." She sighed. "It's messy. The two of you should enjoy the night. For me, if it makes you feel better. I'll see you soon."

"If you're sure..." Parker was hesitant.

"I'm positive. You'd be bored, watching me work. Go have fun."

"Good luck. Catch up soon." Wyatt kissed her on the cheek. He tried to pass it off as meaningless with a casual smile.

Parker tugged her fingertips and brushed his lips over hers. "I'll drop everything and come running in an instant if you need me."

"I know." Her smile was back, though not as strong as before. "Thank you."

Wyatt grabbed fleeting threads of joy trying to hide in the recesses of his mind and forced them to the surface. He was happy for Parker and Fiona, and they were going to need each other even more once this was over.

Because he was an asshole. Knowing it didn't change his decision, but it did leave a knot inside that was going to take several shots of tequila for him to ignore.

♥♥♥

Fiona sat in the back of the cab, only vaguely aware of the passing scenery. She was grateful the driver wasn't chatty. She hovered her fingertips over her lips, barely making contact. It was such a simple gesture—a light kiss. No expectation or demand. Parker did it as if it were the most natural thing in the world.

Which was why the silly grin refused to leave her face.

What about Wyatt?

What about him? He was in it for the sex. He never implied anything else. The only reason he popped into her head was because he'd been part of this change in her life.

But Parker... He'd always been there, even when he was somewhere else. It had never been anyone else for her.

She set aside thoughts of what it meant when she got back to their room. She connected remotely to the servers, dialed Nick, and put him on speaker.

"Okay. Talk me through this, a step at a time," she said.

First stop was to see if their backups were viable. The mirroring had gone offline and Nick hadn't noticed. No recent backups. She raked her fingers through her hair in frustration, and pulled it back into a ponytail to keep from yanking it out.

In the background, on Nick's side, she heard Parker's voice. Nick was half-watching, catching up on the shows he'd missed. He didn't say it, but she knew his schedule was packed between doing his job and keeping on top of hers.

With no way to automatically restore, she spent the next several hours manually repairing the customer database.

She sent Parker a couple of messages, letting him know she wasn't going to make it after all.

Miss you. Get a lot done, and we'll catch up later.

His reply lifted the irritation that was sinking in.

When she was confident the system was complete, she turned her attention to the app itself.

She loved Nick dearly, and he was fantastic at the business side of things. This was his idea. He made it happen. He sold it. He brought her in on it. But his coding skills weren't what they needed to be, for these types of changes.

Exhaustion was sinking in. Her eyes were dry, and the TV was lousy company compared to what she left behind.

"I know you're having a blast," Nick said, "but I'll be glad when this month is up. I can't do this without you."

Her laugh came out more bitter than she intended. But she knew things would be coming to an end soon. It was why she made Parker the offer she did earlier—to keep his souvenirs at her place. She had to go home in a few weeks, but that might be the nudge he needed, to stop by more often.

An empty pit grew inside, at the thought of going back to only seeing him on screen except for the rare in-person visit. What else had she expected, though?

Parker's next message came through about half an hour later.

I want to come back. Wyatt wouldn't let me. He said to let you work.

Ambivalence surged into the pit in her chest but didn't fill it. She typed a quick response. *He's probably right. But I'm almost done. Hurry back?*

As you wish, he wrote.

She pushed her sadness aside. If they had two more weeks, she was going to enjoy the hell out of him. She wasn't going home with any regrets, and she was taking a lot more memories of Parker with her.

And Wyatt.

Him too. But mostly Parker.

She wrapped things up with Nick. "I'm turning my phone off for the night. Don't break anything. If it's an emergency, I'll get it in the morning."

"Thanks, Red. Enjoy what little of your night is left. And you're the best."

She disconnected, set her phone to silent, and placed it face down on the table.

A short while later, she heard the latch on the

hotel door. She spun to see Parker walk into the room with Wyatt next to him. Her heart did a skippy thing she couldn't describe and didn't know how she felt about. "Hey."

Parker nodded at Wyatt. "I told him he had to at least come back with me and say *hello*, since you had to leave. And that if he needed to—for whatever bizarre, masculine or super-villain reason—he could leave right after."

Wyatt strode across the room, and moved behind Fiona. Before she could spin to face him, he rested a hand on her hip, holding her in place. He traced his fingers along the back of her neck with a touch so light, shivers raced down her spin.

"I had to come back to say *goodbye*, too." His voice was as tantalizing as his touch. The words, not so much.

"Oh?" Fiona frowned.

"I don't have any more work to keep me in town." The disappointment in his voice matched hers. "I'm heading out the day after tomorrow."

An unexpected sadness spilled inside. Was this it, then? The fun with Wyatt was over?

Chapter Twenty-Three

When Wyatt wrapped Fiona's hair around his hand and yanked, she gasped at the sting that raced along her scalp.

He nipped her neck. "I want to leave you with something to remember me by, though."

The shift in his voice and promise in his words made her pulse hammer in her ears. A whisper of concern joined it. Wyatt was fun, but Parker is real, and she couldn't sacrifice that. Wouldn't surrender her best friend—and more—for a little hot sex.

She met Parker's gaze, to find him watching the exchange with a lazy smile.

"I like the sound of another incredible memory." He stepped in and kissed her bottom lip, before crushing his mouth to hers.

She moaned into the intensity. Parker glided a hand under her shirt to tease a nipple, while Wyatt sucked on her neck, his erection digging into her back.

Fiona didn't know which way to press, so she hooked a hand around each of their necks, holding them in place and sinking into all of the sensations.

"What do you want to do that you've never tried?" Wyatt's lips vibrated against her skin with the question.

She stalled on a response. It was a long list, but some of it terrified her. She didn't know if she just liked the idea of half the things that turned her on, or if she'd actually enjoy them in practice.

Parker brushed a strand of hair behind her ear as he searched her face. "You're overthinking things, aren't you?" There was no accusation in his question. He pulled her shirt off in a single fluid motion.

Wyatt unclasped her bra, and she let the garment tumble to the floor. Need ignited across her skin everywhere Parker dragged his gaze. The look in his eye made her feel like a stunning piece of art.

Wyatt undid her jeans next, and glided his thumbs under the waistband. "You can start simple. There's no judgement."

"Wouldn't judgement come from starting too kinky?" she asked.

"I suppose it depends on your insecurities." Wyatt's touch was playful, slipping along her hips, but no lower.

Parker kissed along her collarbone. "There's no judgement either way. How's that?"

She should pick something. Being pinned between them was incredible, but if she got to push boundaries a little further… "How about being tied up?" As soon as the words passed her lips, hesitation was back. "That's really tame, isn't it?"

Wyatt's hands fell away from her waist.

Parker pushed her jeans and panties to the ground, leaving her naked between two fully-dressed men. At least one of whom was fucking her with his eyes. "No one's measuring this on a scale," Parker said.

"If it's what you want, it's the right answer." Wyatt trailed his hands down her arms, drawing them together behind her back. "Is it what you want?"

"Yes."

Wyatt slipped something soft and silky around wrists—his tie?—and tightened the restraint.

Fiona's next request stalled in her throat. It was one of those that scared her, but she was safe with these two. In multiple ways. "And used." Her voice cracked.

A whisper wickedness flashed across Parker's face.

Wyatt sucked in a sharp breath. "In that case, kneel on the floor, Red. What you did to Parker the other day? I can't stop thinking about it. I want to see your mouth wrapped around my cock. Watch you take my entire length while I fuck your face."

She didn't know which part of that she enjoyed the most—the description, the command, or the idea he couldn't get them out of his head. She knelt in front of Wyatt. When she squeezed her legs together, dampness coated her thighs. She looked up at Wyatt. "Do you want me to swallow, too?"

"We'll figure that out when we get there." He slid his zipper down, and worked himself free.

Her core pulsed with the same need that sparked along her skin. Wyatt knotted his fingers in her hair, holding her captive, and thrust in her mouth.

He hit the back of her throat, and reflex made her eyes water.

"Relax," he coaxed.

She focused on letting him slide in her mouth. And then the gentleness was gone. He slammed against her.

She traced her tongue along his shaft when she

could. How was this so arousing? She didn't want to think about it. She just wanted to enjoy it.

When Parker's bare chest pressed into her back, she started, but once again she was pinned. His cock dug into her ass. He must have stripped off his clothes.

He cupped her breasts and squeezed her nipples. Tenderness slid toward rough. She moaned against Wyatt's cock while Parker pinched and twisted.

Wyatt thrust his hips fast, and his grunts said he was close.

She was surprised when he pulled out. He stroked himself slowly, holding her gaze.

Bending at the waist, he gripped her face and kissed her hard. "God, it's so tempting to lay you out and fuck every hole."

Fiona couldn't find her voice, so she settled for a nod. She licked her lips. "Whatever you want," she managed to croak.

Parker's hands on her hips urged her to rise a little, but not stand. He slipped two fingers inside her, and she clenched around the penetration. She pressed back into his touch, and Wyatt growled.

"No," he said.

Parker slipped out of her again. She whimpered when he slipped along her ass, spreading her juices as he moved.

He nudged her rear entrance with his cock. He eased in slowly, an inch at a time, waiting for her to adjust between each slide.

Wyatt watched them with hunger in his eyes, keeping a steady rhythm on with his grip on his dick.

Fiona didn't remember ever being so aroused. One brush against her clit, and she'd probably come.

"I love that this turns you on as much as it does me," Wyatt murmured. "Both of you."

And then Parker was all the way in. He pulled her back, so her weight half rested on his knees, as he rocked inside her at a gentle pace.

Pleasure built inside her, creeping toward ecstasy. She wouldn't reach climax this way, though.

Parker slammed inside her faster, and friction built. His grunts said he was close. She wasn't sure if she could take much more. He slid out of her, and hot wetness hit her back when he came.

Wyatt pulled her forward, to drive his cock into her mouth again. The non-stop pace, being pushed and pulled between them, made her squeeze her thighs together again. It didn't sate the throb between her legs, though.

This time when Wyatt's groans became punctuated, he didn't pull out. Salty spurts hit the back of her mouth and slid down her throat.

She licked him clean as he withdrew, smirking at his shudder when she traced her tongue around the swollen head of his dick.

Parker tugged her back, twisting her head to kiss her. Driving his tongue deep, and tasting Wyatt on her lips. Pressing into her still-slick back. "Every fucking inch of you is incredible," Parker murmured against her mouth.

He untangled himself and stood.

Fiona frowned when something occurred to her. She was bound and desperate to get off, and they were done. Not quite what she had in mind.

Wyatt leaned in and bit her earlobe. "You wanted to be used." He slipped his hand between her legs, and brushed her outer labia, but didn't penetrate her.

The game wasn't over yet, then. She whimpered and tried to press into Wyatt's touch.

He pulled back, and *tsked*.

"Can I add to my answer?" she asked. "I'll beg."

"What are you begging for, Red?"

"Let me come. Make me scream. I want the neighbors to be jealous."

"Hmm…" As Wyatt considered, he unbuttoned his shirt. He stripped it off, then removed the rest of his clothing. Watching him undress was a new flavor of anticipation.

Parker joined him. As she'd assumed, he was already naked. Wyatt whispered something in his ear, and Parker smirked.

"I'll help you stand." Parker helped her to her feet. Her legs were stiff, and her balance tentative. He was gentle, though.

She looked around. "Where did Wyatt go?"

The sound of the shower curtain being yanked open answered her question.

"You're a mess. You need to get cleaned up," Parker said. He led her into the bathroom.

Wyatt had covered the floor in front of the tub with towels, and set a couple more on the far corner of the counter.

"Tub. Both of you," Wyatt ordered.

Fiona turned so he could see her still-bound hands. "What about your tie?"

"It's a fucking tie. I can replace it."

Parker helped her step into the tub, and Wyatt stayed on the other side. Parker turned the water on, and let it run hot before switching it to the shower head.

The men soaped Fiona up, hands gently slipping and sliding everywhere until she sank into the warmth and lost track of who touched where.

None of it distracted her from the need pulsing through her.

Wyatt's kiss was tender this time. "My turn to choose. I *am* the one leaving."

Before she could ask what he picked, he trailed his mouth down her chest, sinking to his knees as he went.

He hooked one of her legs to rest her foot on the edge of the tub. When he glided his tongue along her slit, a low groan tore from her chest, and she pressed into his mouth.

This time, he didn't push her away from the touch she craved.

He spent several minutes licking and exploring every bit of her pussy except those that wanted attention the most.

"Please," she whimpered. Her head was light, and she was pretty sure Parker pressed against her back was the biggest reason she could still stand.

Parker slipped his hands to her breasts again, kneading lightly. Her nipples were still tender from earlier, and each caress zinged through her.

Wyatt plunged two fingers inside her, and pumped with the sway of her hips.

She wanted to knot her fingers in his hair. She

twitched her hands uselessly against her restraints instead.

Wyatt reached her clit and sucked. Fiona screamed as climax sped up and crashed through her. She rocked hard, grinding into his face, until his touch was too much. She tried to pull away, but he gripped her hip, and kept his mouth buried between her legs.

He nudged her past *too much* and into another orgasm. Stars danced behind her eyes and her thoughts evaporated in a haze of pleasure.

When Wyatt finally pulled away, her legs threatened to give out. Parker loosened and removed the tie, and tossed it in the sink. He rinsed her the rest of the way clean, his touch light. Wyatt patted her dry.

Fiona wasn't sure how she stumbled into the bedroom, but being half-carried was part of it.

The sex had stolen her chaotic thoughts and loosened the tension running through her. It left her body free to melt into the mattress.

Parker lay next to her, and it was natural to rest her head on his shoulder. Wyatt slid in behind her, his naked body pressing into her back. What was arousing to the point of frustration just a few minutes earlier was comforting now. It all felt right.

She settled deeper into the blankets and the security of the men on either side. She didn't want to talk about this, but she had to know. It shouldn't be hard to think of Wyatt leaving, but it was. "Do you have a lot of work tomorrow, before you head out?"

"Oddly enough, no. I wrapped things up today, and I'm slacking tomorrow and cutting work."

Her next question froze on her lips. She didn't want to push Parker away with this. She couldn't lose him.

Parker brushed a thumb over her bottom lip. "If you don't have to get back to your hotel, we'd like the extra company."

She loved that Parker knew what she was thinking without her saying a word.

Wyatt's hesitation wasn't so great.

"Is something wrong?" She couldn't ignore the pit settling in her gut.

His easy laugh settled her thoughts again. "Exactly the opposite. I was about to say *one hotel room is the same as any other*, but that's too dismissive. This one has you in it, so there's nowhere else I want to be more."

The sentiment stole her breath, and sent a tremor running through her. That was adoration and desire, right? Not doubt and fear?

Chapter Twenty-Four

When Fiona woke the next morning, it was almost eleven. She didn't know if she'd ever slept that late. They left the hotel long enough for Wyatt to go back to his own, and to grab some food.

She, Parker, and Wyatt spent the rest of the day alternating between watching bad movies and having incredible sex. Fiona did her best not to think about the fact this would be over in just a few hours.

Night crept up on them, sliding past sunset, and no one had mentioned that Wyatt needed to leave soon.

She was trying to find the strength to bring it up, when Parker's phone rang.

"It's Nick," he said.

Fiona rolled her eyes. She wasn't in the mood for another emergency. "Tell him, if it's broken, it's his fault."

Parker answered. "Hey. Fiona says— Oh, okay." He frowned. There was a few seconds' pause, and he looked at Wyatt. "No shit."

She followed Parker's gaze in time to see a shadow cross Wyatt's face. Odd.

"Yeah, no. We didn't have a clue." Concern leaked into Parker's voice.

Wyatt's smile was frozen in place.

Fiona didn't like the pins creeping under her skin.

"Thanks for the heads-up. We've got it. It's all good. Talk to you soon." Parker disconnected.

"Is everything all right?" Fiona wasn't sure she wanted to know the answer.

Parker pointed a narrow-eyed glare at Wyatt. "What is it you do, again?"

"I'm in sales." Wyatt's response sounded mechanical.

That was extra curious. "Fill us in on the details there." Nervousness clawed at Fiona, telling her not to ask. She needed to know.

"I'm head of East Coast Distribution, for the company you're competing against for the Grammie's contract. Once your deal falls through, the sale is mine." His reply started off with a waver, but his words were ice by the end.

Disbelief surged inside, and Fiona clenched her hand, digging her nails into her palm, to give her something external to focus on. She didn't trust herself to speak. What was she supposed to say?

Parker didn't seem to have the same concerns. "And you didn't say anything, because…?"

"NDA." Wyatt looked past Parker, rather than at him.

"Fuck me." The words slipped past Fiona's lips. She glared at Wyatt. "No. Wait. Fuck *you*. Really?"

It was all sinking in. He worked for the competition. He knew all along who she and Parker were. He'd never said anything. That didn't scream *good intentions*.

"Nick says he met Wyatt the morning after we did. Wyatt offered him a deal. Some kind of collaborative effort. Nick told him *no*."

"And you didn't think to mention that two weeks ago?" Fiona was stating the obvious at this point, but she didn't know what else to do. Why had he done this?

Wyatt shrugged. "It never came up."

"It never came up?" Fiona didn't care that her voice rose. It was easier than admitting how much this hurt. She'd assumed Wyatt was keeping things from them; it was *just sex*. But something like this? "What were you hoping to accomplish?"

"Getting laid?" Wyatt said.

"No. Fuck you, and bullshit." Fiona refused to believe it was that simple. "If that were the case, there was no reason to lie about who you are. Why. Didn't. You. Say anything?"

He clenched his jaw. "I was looking for a way to trip you up. To cost you the contract." His eyes went hard. "Lucky for me, you did that on your own."

"You need to go. *Now*." The threat in Parker's voice all but shook the room.

"Yeah. I do." Wyatt turned on his toe and left.

Fiona bit the side of her hand, to keep a scream of frustration from slipping out. Her throat burned, and tears pricked her eyes. She refused to cry over this fucking asshole.

"Can you believe—" Parker turned to her and stopped. He crouched, which brought him to eye-level. "Red. Talk to me?"

What was she supposed to say? She didn't even know what to tell herself. She felt stupid and betrayed and blind and crushed.

He grasped her wrist and tugged it down. She stared at the bite marks in the fleshy part of her skin, then turned her gaze to Parker. "I know this is the worst possible time to say this." The words formed, and they tasted right. "I love you, Parker, but—so help me—I need to process what happened. Let me go."

His pained look matched the churning inside her, but he dropped his grip.

Not trusting herself to say anything else, she climbed from the bed, slipped on her shoes, grabbed her phone and purse, and left.

Fiona's footsteps beat out an uneven rhythm, as she walked down the hall.

She should have stayed. Talked this through with Parker. He'd listen, and he'd mean it.

But she couldn't look at him. Not with the intense combination of guilt and stupidity that boiled in her veins, both because she loved Parker and because she'd been falling for Wyatt, too.

Giving words to the feeling made it hurt more. How did she miss the signs they were being played? What was wrong with her, that she fell into things as easily as she did, never questioning?

God, how idiotic was she?

She couldn't lose Parker again; she had to make things right with him. But she felt disloyal. Like she'd been cheating on him.

Fiona needed to find a way to get Wyatt out of her system, because she wouldn't subject Parker to the same thing she accused him of, all those years ago.

She refused to use Parker to fill any sort of void inside. He deserved better.

Chapter Twenty-Five

"Red."

The voice nudged the edges of Fiona's fractured thoughts, but she didn't register it as significant. She headed toward the elevator. Or maybe the stairs would be better. Less chance of having to face other people. Then again, not many people were up at this hour.

"Fiona." Footsteps pounded behind her, and a moment later, someone stopped next to her.

She looked up to see the man from the flashmob—rose-guy. She pasted on her most neutral expression, despite a fresh flurry of nausea. "Hey."

"Hi." He grinned. "I never introduced myself before. I'm Tim."

"Nice to meet you." She shook his hand. Still clammy. Still disconcerting.

"I can't believe I finally caught you alone."

Speaking of which— How? Had he been watching through a peephole all night or something? "Amazing." She kept her tone cool, though nervousness churned inside. She didn't know if he was the same guy who commented on their videos, but the fact he was in their hotel, on the same floor as them, hundreds of miles from where she last encountered him, set off warning bells. "It was great running into you again. I'm so sorry, but I remembered I left something in my room." Like Parker.

"Don't go yet." Tim shifted his stance when she turned, blocking the path back to her room. "I just want to talk to you for a minute."

"What's up?" She didn't have the emotional capacity right now to turn this into an argument. If she maneuvered right—talked and walked and kept him distracted—she'd be back safe and sound before panic fully set in.

She tried to step around him, and he adjusted his position again.

Her back was to an open door. Why didn't she see that before? *Scream and run.* Good call. Fiona opened her mouth, and Tim drove an elbow into her stomach.

Pain spread like a shockwave from her gut, stealing her breath and forcing tears from her eyes. Instead of a shout, a pitiful squeak tore from her throat. Before she regained her senses, he crammed a rag in her mouth.

She choked at the sudden intrusion, bile rising in her throat. Panic built inside. She forced herself to breathe through her nose, to keep from gagging.

Tim grabbed her wrist and twisted, forcing her the few more steps needed to enter the room. He pressed her face to the wall and wrenched her arm behind her back. A new wash of agony tore from her shoulder, which was held at an awkward angle.

"You said we could talk." His breath was hot on her neck. "Screaming isn't talking."

She nodded, trying to force back the panic and pain. She could kick him or step on his foot or something. She just had to get away long enough to tear out the gag and make noise. It was a fucking hotel. Someone would hear.

"I only need you to hear me out." He pressed his weight against her, squeezing more air out of her lungs, and rested a foot between hers, keeping her off-balance.

Something plastic and thin, with sharp edges, dug into her wrists, accompanied by the *zip* of the restraint being pulled tight. "I didn't want to do things this way. I need you to see what I see."

Tim yanked her farther into the room, and she stumbled, hoping to knock herself loose. Instead of letting go, he gripped her arm tighter and half-dragged her until she found her footing.

Her knees burned through her jeans, her shoulder screamed in pain, and she struggled to draw breath. When he yanked out a chair and helped her into it, she collapsed with relief.

"The first time I saw you on camera, distraught and tormented, I knew I could help. And when we met at the cafe, there was a spark. You felt it too."

Holy shit. This guy wasn't just nuts; he was borderline movie-villain delusional. Fiona stomped her feet against the ground as hard as she could, hoping to make enough noise to piss off the neighbors. To get someone's attention.

"*Stop.*" Tim's bark rang in her ears. He slapped her, and her head jerked back from the impact. "Jesus. I wish you would stop."

He wanted *her* to stop? A new wave of tears welled up in her eyes, and she blinked them back with anger.

He grabbed her forearm, digging his fingers in so hard she expected it would leave bruises. "We'll do it this way instead." He hauled her onto the bed and laid her on her side. Her legs dangled over the edge, but before she could kick, he zipped a second tie around her ankles, and cinched it until it dug into her tendons.

He moved behind her and dragged her further onto the mattress. A second later, he was in front of her again, lying next to her, on his side, looking her in the eye.

When he rested a hand on her cheek and traced his thumb under her eye, she wanted to jerk away, but she didn't want to antagonize him further.

"It's been a long week for you." The sympathy in his voice made Fiona want to retch. "That asshole, *Wolf,* following you around. Your supposed *best friend* dragging you along on his adventure. Neither of them thinking about you."

The reminder of Wyatt might hurt if she wasn't sinking like a stone in a pool of terror.

"You should sleep," Tim said.

No. She didn't know what he meant, but it couldn't be good. She squirmed and tried to scream through the gag, but he used his weight to pin her down and searched her eyes. "I'm not like Wyatt," he said.

That made this so much worse. Parker had never used Wyatt's name on camera. No one watching their videos should know it.

"I won't touch you until you're ready."

Fuck. She wanted out of this. She wanted Parker. She wanted to go home.

"Get some sleep, Red."

She felt a sharp jab in her arm, and clouds swam into her head. She clawed to stay above them. To not surrender. But consciousness slipped away.

♥♥♥

Parker wanted to stop Fiona before she walked out the door, but her words stalled his thoughts. If she needed space, he'd give it to her.

I love you, Parker. The declaration echoed in his head. Hearing her say it made his heart soar and his mind numb. He needed to tell her he felt the same.

But it wasn't that simple. He wanted it to be. Those four words should be what they needed to solidify things between them.

They each had their own baggage to deal with still, though. And Wyatt. Red crossed Parker's vision. He wanted to track the smug fucker down and grind his face into the pavement.

It wouldn't solve anything, but it would make Parker feel better.

Wouldn't it?

It certainly wouldn't get Fiona the Grammie's contract back. Which was where his thoughts kept drifting. He'd never forgive himself if he cost her this chance. Or if he let her leave without telling her how he felt. He needed her to come back, so he could say it. *I love you too, Fiona.*

The minutes ticked away, turning into hours, as the clock passed midnight, and then one. Concern bled in. He understood she was upset, but where the hell was she at this time of night?

He sent her a quick text. *Making sure you're all right. Send me an OK at least?*

Fifteen minutes later, she hadn't replied. He scribbled a note and left it on the table, then wandered downstairs. Maybe she'd settled into one of the chairs down there and was reading, or fell asleep. It was a long shot, but as concern grew inside, he had to do something.

No one was in the lobby except the guy working behind the counter.

"Hey." Parker painted on a friendly smile as he approached. "Have you been working all night?"

They clerk gave him a flat stare. "Since ten. Why?"

"Did you see a redhead come through here, in the last couple of hours? Maybe she called a cab?"

The guy shook his head. "Haven't seen anyone tonight except you. Sorry, man."

Fuck. Parker's smile wavered. "Thanks anyway."

He returned to their room, hoping she'd be waiting when he opened the door.

When the room was empty, he wasn't surprised. Where the hell was she? It was almost two. Did he need to call every Denny's, Waffle House, and IHOP in the city until he found her?

That was probably a bit obsessive.

The word plummeted in the hollow pit growing

in his gut, gnawing a hole into a thought he couldn't quite grasp or ignore.

Obsessive. Like a guy who'd follow someone he saw on YouTube across several states? Nah. Parker was grasping at straws now—looking for an excuse, when Fiona left on her own and would be back when she was ready.

The self-assurance didn't work. He looked up the local number for the police and dialed.

"Dispatch. May I help you?" The voice of the woman who answered was a blend of bored and sympathetic. Odd combination.

"Hi. Yeah. My friend is missing." Way to be specific.

"I'm sorry to hear that. When did you last see… What's your friend's name?"

"Fiona," Parker said. "It was about three hours ago."

Her sigh was so faint, he might have imagined it. "I see." The woman's voice softened. "Did the two of you fight?"

"No. She was upset, but not at me. But we're not from around here. It's the middle of the night. She wouldn't just vanish."

"I'm sorry, sir. She'll be back when she's ready, but right now, there's nothing I can do."

He should have known that. "Thanks anyway." He disconnected and dropped his phone on the bed. He scrubbed his face, hoping to drag more ideas to the surface or push the gnawing ill-ease away. Either would work.

He could ask his viewers for help, finding her.

That seemed stupider than contacting the police

after only three hours. He didn't need to sic a bunch of people on the city, or have to wade through shit answers that didn't lead anywhere. And if one overenthusiastic fan was a problem, he wasn't sending more to find Fiona.

He paced a short path, until it threatened to make him dizzy. It didn't matter how hard logic argued that things were fine; he couldn't shake the feeling they were the opposite.

His gaze landed on something poking out of the pocket of Fiona's luggage. A business card. He plucked it out, and scowled when he saw Wyatt's name and number scrawled across it.

The bad taste Wyatt's name left in his mouth didn't stop Parker from grabbing his phone and calling.

"Do you know what fucking time it is?" Wyatt's irritated growl almost made Parker smile.

"Did I wake you?" Parker couldn't keep the sarcasm from his voice.

"Parker?"

He wasn't in the mood to ask forgiveness or get into lengthy explanations. "Fiona's missing."

"And?"

Parker swore he heard a tremor in the question. Fuck holding back or not sounding like a loon or any of that. He didn't give a shit what Wyatt thought. "She left right after you did," he said. "Told me she needed to think. Maybe she's just out, but it's almost three in the morning."

"I noticed."

Parker ignored him. "The guy from Indiana, the one who approached her after the flashmob, has been sending her texts. She thought she saw him in the lobby a few days ago, when we checked in." He didn't know why he was sharing that information.

"Call the police." Wyatt barked the words.

"I did. They won't do anything."

"Fuck. I'll be there in ten minutes. Meet me in the lobby."

The line went dead. It wasn't the assurance Parker was looking for, but at least someone was as concerned as he was.

Seven and a half minutes later, headlights shone through the glass of the hotel doors before turning into a parking spot and blinking off. Parker strode toward the entrance, for lack of anything better to do.

Wyatt stepped inside and locked his gaze on Parker. He crossed the distance between them in a few long strides, grabbed Parker's T-shirt near the shoulder, and slammed his back into the nearest wall. "She's being stalked, and you let it slide?" Wyatt growled.

"I didn't..." What? Think it would be a problem? Take it seriously?

"Hey. I'm calling the cops." The nervous clerk's voice cut through the tension.

Wyatt's snarl morphed to a twisted grin. "Good." He let go of Parker and walked to the front desk. "Did you see a redhead leave here in the last couple of hours? Attractive? Terrifyingly furious?"

Parker followed him.

"I already told that guy *no*." The clerk shook his head.

Wyatt turned to Parker. "If she didn't leave, she's still in the building. You said you saw the creeper here."

"Yes." Parker should have thought of that. Something else occurred to him. He grabbed his phone and pulled up the video from the flashmob. He scrolled to the end, tapping his toe on the tile as he waited for the clip to buffer. When rose-guy was in frame, Parker showed the screen to the hotel clerk. "Is he staying here?"

"Like I know? That's some really shitty resolution. And if he was here, I wouldn't be allowed to tell you."

"Fine." Wyatt shrugged. "We'll knock on every door in the place until we know for certain."

"I *will* call the police."

"You threatened to do that before," Parker said. "I'd start dialing. By the time they get here, we may have our friend back."

Wyatt was already walking toward the first-floor rooms.

"Wait," the clerk called as his phone rang. "Let me deal with this first, and then I'll see what I can do. I swear to God—worst fucking night ever. You psychos, plus some asshole I keep getting noise complaints about. Front desk. How can I help you?" The clerk's tone shifted from irritated to sweet in a breath.

Noise complaints? The look Wyatt gave him made Parker think they were on the same wavelength.

"At least you assholes, aren't thumping so loud every neighboring room has bitched about you tonight." The clerk stepped from around the desk. "Stay here. I'll be back."

Chapter Twenty-Six

Wyatt didn't know what compelled him to follow the clerk, but he was glad Parker fell into step without argument.

"You can't come with me." The clerk entered the elevator and pushed the button for Parker's floor.

Bullshit, they couldn't. "We're still talking." Wyatt let the threat leak into his conversational tone.

The clerk shook his head. "Whatever."

The elevator slid to a stop, he stepped out, and Wyatt and Parker followed. The clerk stopped in front of a door, only a few rooms away, and hammered on it with the side of his fist.

"*Do not Disturb* means do not disturb." A male voice came from inside.

"Sir, I need to speak with you, please."

The door opened a crack. "Go away."

Wyatt recognized the sliver of the face that was visible. Rage spilled inside, and he didn't care if he was jumping to the wrong conclusions.

The clerk crossed his arms. "I've been getting noise complaints—"

Wyatt shoved past him and kicked the door, knocking rose-guy back with an *oof.*

Fiona sat on the edge of the bed, wrists and ankles bound and a gag in her mouth.

Parker rushed into the room, and as much as it ached to not be the one to comfort her, Wyatt knew she was in good hands. Wyatt whirled on rose-guy, and slammed him into the wall. His new favorite move, and he was liking the outlet for his fury. "Call 911," he said to the clerk, who looked between everyone, shock on his face.

"*Now*," Wyatt yelled.

The clerk sprinted for the phone in the room.

Rose-guy yanked out of Wyatt's grasp, and Wyatt grabbed his wrist, twisted his arm behind his back, and pulled until the man gasped.

Wyatt let all of his frustration with the evening, with Parker, with every single moment in the last few hours, spill into his grip and his words. "If you do that again, I'm not above breaking bones."

"This is assault," Rose-guy said through clenched teeth.

"It's self-defense. And I guarantee I know better lawyers." Wyatt glanced into the room, to check on Fiona.

The rag was gone from her mouth, and she worked her jaw up and down, but she was still bound.

Parker sifted through luggage.

"Hey. Don't touch that," Rose-guy protested.

Wyatt applied more pressure to his shoulder, eliciting a yelp.

Parker produced a utility blade and two sets of plastic restraints. He handed the latter to Wyatt, then turned to Fiona.

The moment she was free, she fell into Parker's arms with a sob and buried her face in his shoulder.

The exchange devoured Wyatt, chewing through heart and stomach and—he was pretty sure—the soles of his feet.

It was exactly what it should be—not that this situation should exist to begin with. The handsome prince rescued the fair maiden. Or in this case, the rugged woodsman saved Red Riding Hood.

Giving them ridiculous names was much easier than acknowledging the envy and longing that rocked inside.

The police showed up, and the clerk begged them to take things downstairs, to not disturb the guests. It was almost four in the morning, and a low-grade ache thrummed in the base of Wyatt's skull.

After about five minutes, Rose-guy—Tim apparently—was led to a patrol car. An officer pulled Wyatt aside, to get his version of things. A second one wanted to talk to Parker and Fiona, who refused to let go of each other's hands.

Wyatt didn't blame them. He even had a hard time being upset about the glares Parker shot his way each time their gazes met.

Wyatt gave his version of the events to the officer as best he could, only half-focused on the conversation.

Parker and Fiona looked good together. True, the circumstances sucked, but it was more obvious than ever that they were a couple. Wyatt had made the right decision, every step of the way. It didn't matter that a voice nagged from the back of his head. The only thing wrong about any of this was the attempted fucking kidnapping.

He wished he'd done something about those comments on the videos. Said something. It was his one regret about the last couple of weeks.

"I think that's it for now." The officer—Jones? Johnson?—handed Wyatt a card. "Give me a call if you think of anything else."

"Thanks." Wyatt turned toward the front doors.

"Wyatt."

He glanced over his shoulder to see Parker kiss Fiona on the forehead, then jog to catch up with him.

"Thank you for your help," Parker said when he reached him.

Wyatt nodded. Nothing seemed appropriate on the wit-scale. "You're welcome."

Parker's smile thinned. "And if I ever see you again, chances are good I'll deck you."

"I think that's fair." Wyatt gave Fiona one last look, then headed for the parking lot. The sun was creeping over the horizon. He was going to go back to his room and sleep the rest of the day.

He dropped into his car and closed the door. With the world shut outside, a fracture ran through him, and then shattered.

Everything he'd been ignoring—convincing himself he didn't care about, pretending was insignificant—squeezed the air from his lungs until he gasped.

The impulse to run inside was so potent it almost stole his reason. He didn't want to walk away.

He wanted to crawl back and ask for forgiveness. Be there for Fiona, the way Parker was. Stay up the rest of the day, talking to them, even though he hadn't slept half the night.

And he wanted to tell Chuck to shove the Grammie's contract up his fucking ass.

Instead, Wyatt started the car. He wouldn't do any of that, because a feeling like this was fleeting. It wasn't real, regardless of the chanting in his head to the contrary.

He put the vehicle in gear and headed toward his hotel. Once he got back to his old life, he could bury this intense, deep ache, until it didn't exist anymore.

None of the logic stopped him from feeling shitty, but he was stronger than that. This wouldn't break him.

♥♥♥

It was almost noon when Parker and Fiona got back to their room.

Her every limb and joint felt like lead. Walking took effort. Talking was work. Breathing meant summoning inner strength. She wanted to collapse in bed and pass out for a month, but she didn't know if she'd ever sleep again.

Parker's fingers were intertwined with hers. From being questioned by the police, to heading to the hospital to make sure she was okay, to another round of talking at the police station, he'd only pulled away when he was required to.

She was so grateful for that.

He guided her to sit on the edge of the bed and

crouched in front of her. "You look tired." Sympathy and concern lined his voice.

"So do you." She tried to keep her tone light but didn't have the energy.

He pulled off her shoes and set them by her bag, then stripped off her socks. "You need to rest."

She shook her head. With exhaustion gnawing at her senses, she couldn't shake the terror of last night. Thank God they found her when they did. A detached part of her was happy to see Wyatt there, but the rest of the night made her want to curl up in a ball until the world vanished and took the memory with it.

"Just rest. You don't have to close your eyes or sleep if you don't want to." Parker lay on the bed behind her, on his side. He propped himself up on one elbow and patted the blanket. "Come on."

Fiona nodded and made herself as comfortable as she could, with her back to Parker. He draped an arm over her hip, and a thin layer of comfort settled over the raging bedlam inside.

She pressed closer and pulled his arm tighter. If she could vanish here, it would be perfect.

He rested his head against hers. "Just close your eyes for a little while, okay?"

"Okay." Her answer came out as a dry croak.

Having him so close, without question or argument or hesitation, scared away more of the shadows lurking in her thoughts. If he was here, she'd be fine. Wouldn't she?

She was too tired to answer her own question.

Fiona was jarred awake when the bed shifted and a chill hit her back. She forced her eyes open to the sunlight fading from the room. The clock on the nightstand said it was almost seven.

Parker strode toward the room door.

When he undid the latch, she scrambled to sit, her heart hammering in her throat. She forced herself to breathe. Calm down. Consciousness rushed in, helping her grasp clearer thoughts.

"Can I help you?" Parker asked.

"You're the guy, right?" It was a man's voice, but not one Fiona recognized. "With the kidnapped girlfriend?"

She clenched her jaw. *Kidnapped.* The word filled her with shame.

"Who the fuck told you that?" Parker asked.

"I know a guy."

"Your *guy* needs to fuck off." Parker let the door slam shut, then threw the locks back in place. He whirled toward the bed, and his expression softened. "I'm sorry he woke you."

Fiona rubbed the sleep from raw, dry eyes. "No harm done." Not since last night. The reminder brought back fear, but it wasn't as strong now that she could think more clearly.

The problem was, if she tried to focus on any single thought, her mind protested. She didn't want to linger on Tim. His name was nauseating.

Then there was Wyatt, and the mess that drove her out of the room last night. She couldn't deal with that right now.

And she definitely couldn't think about And Parker, who watched her, concern painted on his face. Because being with him meant one of them had to give up their life.

There was no way she'd ask Parker to surrender his vlogging. Not with this contest. Not given how much he loved the work. But she couldn't stay on the road. Nick needed her. The app needed her. And she was terrified of encountering someone else like Tim.

She shook away the thoughts.

Parker was watching her. Crap. He said something, and she missed it. "I'm sorry, what?" she asked.

"Do you want to get dinner? You haven't eaten since yesterday."

Her stomach grumbled in response. "Yes. Definitely. But I don't want to go out." *I don't want you to leave, either*. She was allowed to be childish for a little while, after her ordeal, wasn't she?

"Pizza?" He reached for his phone on the desk and swiped the screen. "Oh. Shit."

Fiona didn't like that. "What?"

He gave her a wilted smile. "It's from Nick."

"Oh?"

"He says, *Why the fuck aren't you answering your phone? You promised to keep Fiona safe, you fucking asshole.*"

The sentiment almost made her feel better. "I guess we should have called him. Wait. We didn't call him, so what's he talking about?"

Parker was already dialing. He put the phone on speaker, and Nick's, "Tell me I don't have to kill you," filled the room.

"I'm fine," Fiona said. *In a way, I suppose.*

Nick's sigh was loud. "Thank God. They said you were kidnapped."

"Who did?" Parker asked.

"Trending headlines. Social media. National news. Where the hell have you two been?"

Fiona didn't like juggling the conversation without more information. She hated to worry her brother, but he was past that point. "It was a long night. We were sleeping it off."

"You couldn't have called?" Concern bled into Nick's anger.

"That's my fault." Parker took him off speaker and moved the phone to his ear. "I panicked when she disappeared, and I wasn't thinking straight... Some psycho fan followed us ... I know. Trust me, I haven't stopped blaming myself."

And guilt joined the jumble in Fiona's thoughts.

"Yeah. Hang on." Parker handed her the phone.

"Hey," she greeted Nick.

"I want to hear it from you. How are you?" His voice in her ear should be another reason to feel calm. Nick represented home and family and everything she missed.

It notched her tension instead. "I'm okay. I mean, mentally I'm a little screwed up, but I'm okay. This creeper held me in his room for a few hours, but that was it." It was more than enough.

"I'm glad you're safe," Nick said.

"Me too. I'm sorry to cut this short, but I'm starving. I promise not to get in any more trouble." Hell, at this point she'd promise not to leave the room again until it was time to go home. *Home.* The word made her heart ache. Looking at Parker made the feeling worse. "I'll talk to you soon." She said goodbye to Nick, and hung up.

Parker found a local pizza place and called to

place their order. She didn't mind that he did it without asking her what she wanted. He knew what she liked.

She watched him chatting up the person on the other end of the line. They wouldn't hear the strain in his voice, but Fiona saw it written all over his face.

This entire thing was a mess. She felt stupid for getting nabbed. Hated the idea of leaving Parker's side. Couldn't justify walking away from life back in Salt Lake. And missed Wyatt.

That seemed like the fucked up icing on a multi-layer cake of confusion. She already had one amazing man she loved and was considering walking away from. What the fuck was wrong with her that she was thinking about the asshole who lied his way into their lives and bed for personal gain?

She massaged her temples, but it didn't clear away the pain of *what am I supposed to do next*?

Chapter Twenty-Seven

Parker and Fiona sat on the bed, backs to the headboard and box of half-eaten pizza in front of them. She'd positioned herself so she was always touching him. Arms brushing. Legs pressed together.

Parker was good with that. He would be even if he wasn't riding a hard line of never wanting to let her out of his sight again.

Wyatt had been right. If Parker'd taken this stalker more seriously—done something at any point, when Fiona voiced concern—last night could have been avoided.

"TV?" Fiona grabbed the remote.

Good idea. Background noise, to drown out the nagging in his head. "Sure."

He was grateful Wyatt dropped everything to help find Fiona. Not that they had to go far, but the support was nice. Parker was also glad the fucker was gone. As far as he was concerned, Wyatt and Tim had too many things in common.

That's not true, and you know it.

Wasn't it? The guy followed them from State to State—or at least arranged things so they'd continue to end up in the same places—to take advantage of the situation.

Except you wanted Wyatt there. Both of you did.

That wasn't comforting.

"It's straight out of a modern horror movie…" The chipper female voice caught Parker's attention, and he snapped his gaze to the TV.

It was cable news, and the picture to the anchor's right was a still of Parker and Fiona, from one of his videos. Nick wasn't kidding.

"Wonderful." Broken sarcasm dripped from Fiona's voice, and she dropped the remote.

He grabbed the device and pushed the *Up* arrow to change the channel.

"…like an episode of Black Mirror…" Another image of them.

No wonder Nick had been worried. Why the fuck did they make national news?

Parker changed to another station.

"…questioning the wisdom of Rinslet Media, in holding a competition…"

This was why. Fiona made for a good poster girl, and the news got to tear into a company who thrived on any media attention they received.

Parker turned off the TV and reached for his laptop. "Whatever you want to watch," he said.

"It's okay. I'm not in the mood, after all." Fiona closed the pizza box, shoved it aside, and turned to face him. "Are you going on a Grammie's run tomorrow?

"Fuck them. I'm not their free advertising lackey." Not that he would phrase things that way to them, but things like *breach of contract* weren't high on his list of concerns with Grammie's. His contract was valid for thirty days or until they opted to work with a different vendor, and he had a feeling that was the one thing Wyatt was telling the truth about.

"What about footage for the competition?" Fiona asked. The shadow of fear that lingered behind her gaze since he found her, grew darker.

He wasn't going out without her, and there was no way he'd invite her to tag along. Not yet. They'd have to figure out when, but it wouldn't be tomorrow. "There's a clause in the competition that allows me to opt out of filming for a few days, in case of extreme emergencies. I think this qualifies. I'll call tomorrow and invoke it, and we can do whatever you want. Including nothing."

"I need a little time. A day or two, to pull myself together." She smiled. It was weak, but it was still one of the best things he'd ever seen.

"I get it. You don't have to explain or justify yourself."

Fiona lay down, setting her head on his thigh and her hand next to it. He trailed his fingers through her hair, unable to ignore the churning inside. This should be perfect. Everything he wanted, all right here.

But it was fractured, and he didn't know how to fix it. Or if that was possible.

The conversation faded in and out, until Fiona was yawning more than talking, and Parker convinced her she needed sleep. It seemed natural when she fell into bed with him, curled up against him the way she was earlier.

He'd never shared a bed for more than a night before. Traveling meant any hook-up was temporary, and everyone involved knew it. He'd always been grateful that those rare instances of someone spending the night never happened more than once with the same person.

But now he hated the thought of ever falling asleep alone again.

♥♥♥

Parker dialed the contact number he had for Chloe Nielson, expecting to be sent to voicemail. He'd leave her a short message, and then he and Fiona could spend the rest of the day watching movies.

"This is Chloe."

It took him a moment to adjust to hearing a human voice. "Uh… yeah. Hi. This is Parker Carney."

"Hey." Her voice brightened. "How are you doing? How's Fiona?"

It was odd to hear someone who didn't know Fiona ask about her in such a friendly tone. It was nice Chloe cared, or at least sounded like she did. "Surviving. I'm sorry for any bad press this is bringing Rinslet."

"Pft. You know our unofficial motto—there's no such thing as bad publicity." Was that a hint of bitterness in her voice? "Something like this only draws more eyes to our contest. Great for us, not so much for you."

"We'll be all right." Parker didn't know if that was true, but he had to believe it. "Thank you for the concern. I don't want to take up too much of your day, though. I'm calling to see if I can invoke the hiatus clause in my contract."

"Absolutely." There was no hesitation in Chloe's voice. "I know the news exaggerates and gets things wrong, but I don't doubt you need a few days. If you'd like, I can speak with Legal and fast track you past this round of voting. Give you a pass for the month."

"No. I want to do this fairly. I appreciate it, though. I just need a week or so, and I'll be back in the swing of things."

"If you need more, call me back. And while I have you… I don't suppose you'll be in town again anytime soon?"

Rinslet was located in Salt Lake City. Their offices were a few blocks from where Fiona and Nick worked.

"I'm not sure yet what my schedule will be like," Parker said. "Why?"

"I, uh… I was going to call you anyway, and I hate to ask this of you…"

He didn't like the sound of that. "What?"

"Speaking of Legal, they'd like you to sign and have notarized paperwork that indemnifies us from anything to do with what happened."

Parker choked on a bitter laugh.

"I know." Chloe sounded apologetic. "I don't want to bring it up, but the job is the job. I can overnight you the paperwork, or if you'll be here anyway, you can come by the offices."

"I'll think about it." Disbelief rocked in his head as he disconnected. He understood where they were coming from and didn't blame Chloe for the request, but it still reeked of ballsy to the point of unbelievably unsympathetic. He dragged his fingers through his hair with a shaky sigh.

"Is everything all right?" Fiona's soft question pulled him back to the room.

He flopped onto his back next to her and placed his hand on her leg. "People boggle my mind sometimes. But they're granting the hiatus, so that's good."

"Then what did she want?" Fiona studied him, emerald eyes digging into his soul.

Parker didn't want to say, but he also didn't like the idea of keeping secrets from her. He laid out Chloe's request.

"You have to sign." Fiona didn't look as bothered as he felt. "I'm not planning on pursuing anything against them, anyway. This isn't their fault."

No. It's mine. "I know."

Her attention drifted away, and she fiddled with a loose thread next to his head.

That wasn't good. "Red? What's up?"

"I've been thinking… about a lot of things, really, but a few specifically." Her hesitation put him on edge, and he sat up. "If they'd prefer you sign the paperwork in person…"

He didn't like where this was going. He wanted to protest before Fiona could finish the thought. His trying to convince her to leave home behind was what started this whole thing though. He grasped her fingers, drawing her gaze. "Tell me," he said.

"You could fly back with me. Keep me company when I go home."

The request sliced through him like a knife. He wanted to talk her out of leaving. Beg her to stay. He hated the thought of not being with her. Instead, he said, "I can do that."

"Yeah?" She gave him one of those tentative smiles that widened the cavern in his heart.

"Of course." He forced cheer into his voice. "And maybe I can stay." Whoa. Where did that come from? He didn't know, but it wasn't a bad idea.

"You're always welcome. You know that. I'd love to have you stick around for a few days." Her expression brightened.

This was what he needed to do. "I mean for good. As in, moving back home." Saying the words took more strength than he expected, but it would hurt more to not make the offer. "If I have to pick between this life and you—or between anything and you—there's no question. It's you. Every time. I love you, Fiona. I don't know how long I've felt this way. Maybe always."

He settled a hand on her cheek and leaned in to kiss her. The light brush of his lips on hers hummed through him. It was amazing. Intense. Like no other kiss, but the way it always should have been.

The taste of salt, wet and bitter, hit his lips, and he pulled back. Tears traced tracks down her cheeks.

"Shit. I'm sorry." He didn't know what else to say.

She gave a dry laugh. "Please, for the love of all that's holy, don't apologize. Take it back."

"Okay. I take it back. I'm not sorry." He didn't get it, but he'd do whatever he had to, if it meant she stopped crying.

She returned the kiss—feather light, with whispers of the unknown—and pulled back to look at him. "Damn straight, you're not."

"Then what's wrong?" He drew a thumb across her cheek, smearing a tear. "This isn't happy crying."

"You can't stay with me." Her voice cracked. "You can't move home. I mean, if you really wanted to, I'd take it in a heartbeat. You could crash at my place until you found your own. Or maybe my apartment would become ours. I love that idea. But that won't work for you."

What kind of mixed signals was he giving off, to make her think that? He thought he was being clear. "Of course I do. Two nights ago, with you missing, it was horrible. I can't even begin to imagine what it was like for you. But the rest of this trip, having you with me… You made it what it was. I can't let you go after seeing what we have."

"But the trip is part of that experience. And you live for the new places. If you stayed in Salt Lake—set up a real, *permanent* physical address—it would drive you insane."

That was probably true. "We can still travel."

"Vacations aren't the same as a new city every week." Fiona hooked her fingers with his, sending warmth and doubt scurrying over his skin. "Besides, you're in the middle of an incredible opportunity. This is your career, and you're good at it. Like, *really* good. Only twelve of you were picked to compete, so I'm not the only person who thinks so. You can't throw that away. You'll never forgive yourself or me if you do."

Fuck. He hated that she was right, but she was. It felt so selfish of him. "I can change my brand up. I'll set up shop there. Film myself doing food reviews of local places. Save the travel culture for trips."

"You'd be in hell and, we both know it." She crawled closer until she could bury her face in his chest. Her breath was hot through his shirt, searing a hole in his lungs and stealing his air. "I don't want you to leave me. I'd rather keep you by my side forever. But you can't stay. We both know that."

"Fuck." He was out of arguments. Anything else he tossed out would be a lie. "What are we going to do?"

"Facetime every night. You stop in whenever it's not out of your way, and maybe things change in a year or two. I'm not going anywhere."

He kissed her on the top of the head. "That's it, then. I'll fly back with you and make sure you're safe and settled. After that, you'd better expect to see me on a regular basis. In person. Every single time I have spare days in my schedule."

"I'd be heartbroken if it were any other way."

He already was, and believed it was the same for her. He hated this so hard. It wasn't right or fair, but he didn't see a way around it. Fuck it all to hell.

Chapter Twenty-Eight

Wyatt didn't have a preference for where he spent his workdays. On the road it was in someone else's building, and at home it was in the office. Or on the golf course. At whatever restaurant people were in the mood for.

Today, each time he glanced out his window, he was treated to memories of the winery in Philadelphia. Raspberry picking. A church under renovation. And he'd rather be in any of those places than here, as long as the company was good.

Speaking of… He dragged his focus back to his boss, whose office he was in, and whom he sat across from. So far, Wyatt had only gotten a few things from the half-hour long monologue. *Good job with the Grammie's contract*, and, *Why the hell did you need all the travel to make this work?*

Wyatt explained why. Again. It didn't matter what he said; Brett had heard the same rumors as everyone else—this contract was going to land Wyatt the promotion he wanted, which would make him

Brett's boss.

Brett was squirming, searching for any way he could shift credit to someone besides Wyatt.

Wyatt was getting tired of this never ending… whatever it was. "I'm curious," he said. "You've been a director of sales for… what? Three years now?"

"Four." Brett frowned.

"Before that, you had colleagues you were friendly with and others not so much?"

"As most people do."

Wyatt kept his posture friendly and his smile the same. "After you were promoted, some of those people reported to you, I assume. You ever make life difficult for those not-so-muchs, after the balance of power shifted?"

Brett narrowed his eyes and clenched his jaw. "I don't think retaliation is appropriate for people who are doing their jobs, and I don't like the threat."

"I didn't threaten you. And I agree. Anyone doing their job should be recognized for it. Are we done?" Wyatt stood without waiting for an answer.

"Yes." Brett's response hit his back, and Wyatt let the door swing shut between them.

Then it was back to more paperwork and phone calls for Wyatt. Normally he loved chatting up prospects. It was fun to read them—figure out what they needed to hear, to say *yes* and twist the conversation in the direction he needed it to go.

Today he wasn't feeling it. He shook his head to rattle loose what was sticking. What he needed was a new city, a new hookup, and a fresh memory to overwrite the old ones. He was done trying to convince himself either Parker or Fiona was just a piece of ass. That bullshit wasn't flying.

But maybe he could make this stubborn hold they had on him fade into the background, if he willed it away hard enough.

His phone rang, and Chuck's name flashed on the screen.

Wyatt snarled and answered. "Chuck. Great to hear from you." His grin radiated in every word. "You calling to finalize on that contract?"

"As a matter of fact, you'll have a copy in your email in about ten minutes. Legal promised me."

Wyatt was almost as shocked as he was pleased. "So soon. Glad to see we're moving forward."

"Yeah. We're done playing games with this two-bit operation from Salt Lake. We canceled their contract today. This Parker kid was guilty of so many levels of breach, starting with missing several days of posting footage."

Wyatt wasn't surprised. Mostly because he hadn't been able to shake the habit of checking Parker's channel every morning, and it had been bereft of updates.

But even without direct knowledge, given what Fiona went through, radio silence for a little while made sense. "Fiona Walters was kidnapped. It seems reasonable that they'd take a little time to get their shit together."

"Ms. Walters doesn't have her name on either of the contracts." Chuck's tone was snide. "Though she seems to be at the root of disrupting both of them. Mr. Carney needs to honor his obligations."

Fury nudged Wyatt's senses. He was glad all

the cards were on the table, regarding Grammie's and Parker's work. There was no reason to keep up the facade, to yank everything away from Fiona and Nick in a couple weeks. But he didn't care for Chuck's indifference.

"Besides," Chuck said, "dumb cunt was stupid and got herself snatched. That's not our fault."

Rage seared white hot through Wyatt's veins. He was both grateful and disappointed Chuck wasn't in the room, because Wyatt's fist needed a target. "I misheard that." His voice was a low growl. "I must have."

"Excuse me?"

"It sounded like you blamed an innocent woman for having the nerve to live her life. But I know you didn't just do that. What you really said was that you have nothing but sympathy for her being in a situation she's in no way responsible for, and you understand her friend has chosen to support her, rather than selling your overpriced fucking cookies."

The line was silent, except for the sound of breathing. Wyatt might be worried he'd fucked up the contract, but the anger needed to fade first.

"No. That's not what I meant. I have another meeting. Enjoy the rest of your day." Chuck bit off the words.

Wyatt was fuming as he disconnected. He itched to drive his fist into something. It would wait.

Once he found his rhythm, it was easier to keep working than risk looking up and getting lost in his own head again. He stayed at his desk through lunch, shrugging away offers from a couple of colleagues to pick something up for him.

His desk phone rang, jarring him. *Lee Benedict* flashed on the display. The company CEO, or rather, his assistant.

"Wyatt Lindberg," he answered.

"Hey." Roni's voice was chipper. "Lee is wondering if you've got time on your calendar to meet with him. He's sorry for the short notice, but he's got a gap between meetings and wants to squeeze you in."

Very few circumstances would let Wyatt turn down a request like that. "I can make time. When?"

"Five minutes."

In other words, *now*. "I'll be there." He shouldn't hope this was about the Senior Vice President position, but he did. He'd earned it. Anticipation and excitement spilled inside, and he refused to let anything else mute it.

Fifteen minutes later—after ten minutes of waiting outside for Lee to finish—Wyatt sat across from the CEO in the other man's office.

They exchanged a few pleasantries about work and the weather, and then Lee dove into the conversation. "I talked to Chuck Edwards a short while ago."

"How is he?" Wyatt didn't like that as an opener, considering how their conversation went this morning. That incident didn't have to be related to this, though.

"He's well, but he expressed concerns about how you handled the sales process."

Wyatt summoned a thin smile. "I'm sorry to hear that." The contract couldn't be sunk. Not now.

Not after everything Grammie's invested. They couldn't afford it. Wyatt couldn't afford it.

"I was too. He tells me the entire thing would have gone more smoothly, with none of this hesitation on his part, if someone besides you was handling things." Lee's expression gave nothing away. There were circles under his eyes, and his expression was drawn, but he usually looked like that.

Wyatt wasn't going to roll over and play dead on this. Fortunately, he knew who he could speak his mind with in this company. "That's bullshit. No one could have handled this the way I did, and Chuck waited until now to complain because we have a difference in opinion."

Lee cracked a smile. "I figured. I know what you can do, and this didn't sound like you. I am curious, though, why you had any opinion that wasn't his. That's not like you either."

"This was important." Wyatt had to force himself to not speak through clenched teeth.

Lee waved his hand with a *pfft*. "It doesn't matter. He asked to work with someone else during implementation, so I'll shift him to Brett. Great job with this contract, by the way. I don't think I've said that yet."

"Thanks. Is there anything else I can do for you?"

"As a matter of fact..." Lee grabbed a folder from its spot to his right and slid it across the desk. "Despite what Chuck says, you nailed this thing with Grammie's, as you have a tendency to do. As you know, we've been looking to fill the Senior Vice

President of Sales position since Mags moved on." He nodded at the folder. "That's an offer letter. If you're interested in the position, it's yours."

"I'd be honored." This was perfect. Exactly what he'd worked for.

"Fantastic. Get that signed and leave it with Roni. We'll announce it to the office this afternoon, and a press release will go out tomorrow."

Wyatt signed the offer, shook hands with Lee, and returned to his office. He was proud of this. He'd pushed hard for it. And he refused to acknowledge the empty pit inside, trying to take away his joy.

♥♥♥

An unfamiliar knot grew in Parker's stomach as Fiona took the airport exit. The last two days with her were amazing. And not enough. He left her place to sign the paperwork for Rinslet, and they spent the rest of the time enjoying each other's company.

He shouldn't have let her talk him into this. She had a point—he wasn't going to be happy if he surrendered the travel. But was it worth leaving her behind?

She pulled up to a loading spot in front or Terminal Two and put her car in park. She popped the trunk, and he grabbed his bags to set them on the sidewalk.

"Call me as soon as you get to your hotel," she said. Lines marred her forehead.

"Absolutely." Fuck, he hated this. *Goodbye* had never been hard before. He cupped her cheeks and pressed his lips to hers, searing the sensation into his mind.

She groaned and gripped his T-shirt in her fists. Desperation flowed between them, carried on sparks. When she pressed closer, sliding his body against his, he wrapped an arm around her waist. He gripped her ass, holding her as tightly as he could, and memorizing every inch of her body and the way it molded against his.

When they broke apart, he gasped. It wasn't only from the kiss. The idea of leaving had squeezed the air from his lungs, and they refused to re-inflate.

"You should go." She squeezed his fingers.

He nodded and forced himself to pick up his bags. This would get easier. It had to. Or he'd be back in a few weeks, contest and dreams be damned.

He looked over his shoulder every few seconds, until he stepped inside. She was still waiting by the curb, watching him, when the doors closed between them.

Parker trudged his way through the security line. The problem with flying out in the afternoon was that *everyone* flew out in the afternoon. Even with the option to skip the long line, it was half an hour before he stepped through the metal detector.

He sat in front of his gate. His phone whistled—Fiona. He grabbed it, smile threatening.

The first text said *Pussy for you*.

When he saw the photo of one of her stuffed cats, he laughed. *Sexy,* he typed.

Her response came seconds later. *Ask nicely tonight, or maybe not so nicely, and I'll send you a real picture.*

A sliver of sadness joined his amusement. That was Wyatt's influence. It was still Fiona—she wasn't putting on a show—but this was a side of her Parker might not have unlocked on his own.

He replied, *I'm holding you to that :**

The gnawing inside, at the thought of leaving her behind, grew. He sent one more message. *Signing off for now. Talk in a few hours. I love you.* He switched his phone to airplane mode and resisted the urge to check again for her reply. He had to give it time. It would get better. Or he'd convince himself it had.

Chapter Twenty-Nine

Signing off for now. Talk in a few hours. I love you.

Fiona hovered her thumb over Parker's message, not touching the screen. *I love you too.* She sent the reply, then pocketed her phone.

She leaned against the doorframe to her bedroom. It was so empty, and the space behind her was so big, compared to the hotel rooms they'd stayed in.

Time to adjust to life in the real world. She doubted she had the attention span to focus on reading. Instead, she settled at her desk and opened her laptop.

YouTube loaded when she clicked her browser. Which made sense—it was the last site she'd visited. Hell, it was one of the few she'd been on regularly on the road.

And it was on Parker's channel, of course. Nothing new to see. She'd come back when he had new content. When it didn't gnaw at her to see his face not here.

There was a link to the main contest page, and she clicked it. The Top Ten contestants were featured. Parker was up there. Barely, according to his score, but it still meant extra visibility. She tasted the bitterness in her smile.

One of the other top contenders was a sex-toy vlogger. She looked interesting. Fiona clicked over to her channel. How did she get away with reviewing vibrators without violating community guidelines?

The vlogger was pretty—curvy, generous cleavage. Fiona wasn't surprised the woman utilized her breasts as assets. Parker went shirtless for the views.

Ms. Pleasure was about to go live. Good timing.

"Hey, boys and girls." Ms. Pleasure sat in front of her webcam, similarly to the way Parker did when he was in a fixed location. Her blouse was cut low, and her lips were lined to enhance how full and pouty they were. "Today I have this dual-purpose stimulator." She held up an object that looked like a stainless-steel U, with a ball on each end. "And you're going to like what I have to say about it. This hits both the clitoris and the Gräfenberg spot, and whoa-baby… Whew." She puffed out a breath that blew her hair out of her eyes.

That explained how she skirted guidelines— medically appropriate terminology. Could she keep it up the entire show?

Ms. Pleasure leaned in, blue eyes wide and gaze locked on the camera. "But before I get into it… I can rant to you for just a sec, right? Just you and me?" She spoke with a conspiratorial tone. Another thing

Parker did as well. "This whole kidnapping thing? You know what I'm talking about—that *other* channel I'm not going to name. It's complete and utter crap."

Fiona's world tilted, and she gripped the edge of the desk to make sure she stayed upright. Wounds she thought were superficial, ripped wide open, aching inside with a memory of that night.

"Think about it." Ms. Pleasure continued, as if she hadn't just cut the bottom out of Fiona's thoughts. "This guy is pure bull. I mean, he feeds that stuff to his viewers. He hits the competition, and he bombs. I mean, delivering cookies? What kind of dull-as-freak, goodie-two-shoes crap is that? So he figures *pretty girl should help*." She shifted her weight, and her arms pressed her breasts together. "He totally stole that from me. But y'all love me more, right?"

Fiona wanted to reach through the monitor and slap her for trying to pull off *y'all* with a West coast accent. It would be better than drowning in this.

Ms. Pleasure pursed her lips, then continued. "That still doesn't do the trick for him. I mean, look at the guy—he's barely in the Top Ten. He decides he needs a better gimmick. Get the pretty girl kidnapped. Think about it. They found her less than five hours later. On the same freaking floor she was staying on. I'm seriously surprised they didn't try and sneak in some rope action, just for the repeat clicks. I mean, that crap would have gone viral. I call bull—"

Fiona slammed the lid shut on her computer, nausea and fury simmering inside.

Reading was a good idea after all. Something to bring her blood pressure down. People thought she was faking it? That it was a hoax? Who the fuck was that kind of twisted?

She bit the inside of her cheek, to give her an external pain to focus on. Books. She'd pick one. Not "The Siren." She'd read it, and the last thing she needed was to be reminded of Wyatt.

Something not sexy and not scary. She also didn't need to be jumping at shadows. Kick-ass space pirate. That sounded good.

She was a few pages into the book and losing herself in someone else's world, when a loud *crash* jarred her.

It came from next door. The neighbors had noisy kids. She'd spent two weeks with thin, shared walls. Loud neighbors were no big deal.

She took a few breaths to calm her hammering heart and dove back into the story.

The next sound came from inside the apartment. She was sure of it. Pulse hammering in her ears, she grabbed a tennis racket out of her closet and crept from the room. She flipped on every light as she did a thorough survey of the place. The locks were still in place on the front door. The windows were sealed up tight.

She'd overreacted. It was nothing.

The assurance didn't stop memories of Tim from slamming into her. Catching her in the hallway. Maneuvering her into his room. The binding. The drugging. The threats.

She sank to the floor, massaging her temples, trying to force the past away.

Something struck the window.

Fiona yelped.

It was a bird.

She couldn't do this.

She grabbed her still-packed bag and dialed Nick as she walked out the front door.

"Hey." His warm greeting helped chase some of the shadows to the back of her mind.

She headed for the parking garage. "Hey. I have a favor."

"Sure. Whatever you need." He'd been extra sympathetic since she told him she was coming home. And profusely grateful she'd be back on the clock full time.

"I'm a little freaked out. Lingering bad mojo. Can I crash with you for a few days?"

"Totally. Guest room is yours for as long as you need."

Fifteen minutes later, she was settled in his place instead of hers. It wasn't home. It wasn't comfortable. But it felt safe. She'd take that.

When Parker called, she forced a smile. His looked just as strained, before a frown slid in. "That's not your room in the background," he said. "Are you at Nick's? What's wrong?"

"I'm fine." She forced herself to sound like she meant it. "Adjusting to life back, that's all. I promise."

"If you're sure…"

She nodded, grateful he could see her. The conversation slid along the basics. His flight was bumpy but good. She was going back to work tomorrow. He was looking forward to filming without Grammie's restrictions.

He didn't bring up her text from earlier, and she was grateful. The mood was gone.

"I think I'm getting tired." She didn't want to lie to him, but it hurt too much to see him this way.

"Me too. I'll call you tomorrow. I love you."

"Love you too." She disconnected and let her phone drop to the mattress. Damn it. This sucked in the worst possible way.

♥♥♥

Wyatt spent his day fielding the waves of *congratulations* from his colleagues and clients. Some were sincere. Others were kissing his ass. He didn't care. He was going to revel in the moment.

The day was winding down when he got a text. From Fiona. *Saw the press release. Congratulations. You earned it.*

Her words gnawed at him. It was worse because he suspected she was being sincere, rather than passive-aggressive.

Someone knocked on his office door. Gary from accounting? "Going for drinks. Want to join us?"

The worst thing he could do tonight was remove his reservations. "You can buy me a beer on Friday. I've got plans tonight."

"Got it. Catch you later."

Wyatt texted Ginny, as Gary walked away. *You up for some fun before work?* This was the kind of distraction he needed.

You want me to walk into that club and spend the night taking off my clothes with your scent all over me? You're such an alpha dog.

He chuckled at the note. *Damn straight. Besides, I owe you for the asshole a few weeks ago, and I miss the way you taste when my face is buried between your legs.* This was what no-strings was. He could do this. The only expectations with Ginny were that he give as good as he got, and he tip well when he was in the club.

You're such a charmer. Your place in thirty?

I'll be there, he typed.

When he strolled up to his condo, she was waiting outside, in the hallway. Her T-shirt hugged her tits, and her skirt barely covered her ass. When he was close enough, she grabbed his wrist and slid his hands between her legs, to let him know she wasn't wearing panties.

Red hair framed a deceptively innocent face. Just like Fiona's. Apparently, Wyatt had a type.

He banished thoughts of Fiona, pulled away from Ginny to unlock the front door, and nudged her inside with his full body. He closed up behind them and spun to press her against the wall and pin her arms above her head, her wrists captured in his hands.

He kissed her hard, pouring every ounce of need he had into crushing his mouth to hers. She gasped and squirmed under him, getting closer. Each time she moaned, she rubbed her hip against his cock. He tried to dive headfirst into the physical, but whispers of the past kept pulling him back.

"*Fuck.*" He growled against Ginny's skin, nipping then biting the pale flesh of her neck.

She broke free of his grip to drop her hand

below his waist and tease his cock. He was only half-hard. She stroked. It felt good. Right. Why couldn't he get into it?

"This is about you tonight. Not me." He grabbed her wrist again and hitched her skirt over her hips. He danced his fingers along the inside of her thighs, drawing closer to her heat but never touching her pussy.

Her moans were musical, dancing along his senses. They weren't Fiona's— *Fuck*. He needed to stop that. To be here, rather than in the park. Or back in the hotel.

Wyatt stepped back, but the rush of cool air didn't clear his thoughts. "We should take this to the bedroom."

Ginny grabbed his hands and jerked him, to force his gaze to hers. "Where are you right now?" she asked.

"Here. Only here."

"You're a better liar than that, handsome." She clucked her tongue against the roof of her mouth.

She was right. The fact that he could pull off the most eloquent, foul bullshit was part of the problem. "I don't know." It was the only answer he had.

She smoothed her skirt down, and her hips swayed as she crossed the room to drop onto his couch. "Yeah, you do. Want to talk about it?"

"You didn't come here to talk."

"No. But it seems you didn't invite me over to fuck." She patted the cushion next to her. "Lie down and tell the doctor all about it."

This time his smile felt more sincere. Ginny was working on her psychology doctorate and used stripping to pay for college.

"I can't afford your fees tonight," he said.

She crossed her legs at the knee, managing to keep from showing any hint of what did and didn't lie underneath. "This one's on me. You'll owe me double next time."

He took the seat across from her, so he could watch her reactions. He'd give her a couple of high-level snippets, to satisfy her curiosity and get things off his chest, and send her on her way with an apology.

Except, when he opened his mouth, the entire story spilled out—from what happened with Chuck after the last time they saw Ginny, to the congratulatory note from Fiona earlier.

Ginny studied him for a moment when he finished, her lips pursed and eyes narrowed. She sighed and leaned back. "Doesn't sound like you need my help."

Because he had a handle on things. "I need to get my head on straight, and then I'll fuck the hell out of you."

"Not what I mean. And no. We're done with that."

He raised his brows. "You're cutting me off?"

"Like an infected limb. Pardon the analogy." She smirked. "But you don't need me to tell you what you're thinking. You already know what and who you want."

He did. "But that's not an option."

"It's never stopped you before." She glanced at the clock behind him. She'd make a perfect shrink one day. "I'm sorry, but I need to get to work. You gonna be okay?"

He nodded. "Thanks for listening to the word vomit."

"Anytime. I'm going to use your bathroom. Feel free to keep brooding when I'm gone."

He laughed and shook his head. There wasn't a solution on the table, but he couldn't keep pretending what happened was meaningless. Or that it was going to go away. He had two choices—fix things with Fiona, or push through this unreasonable attachment.

Neither was happening anytime soon.

Chapter Thirty

Fiona settled into Nick's guest room more easily than she should have, but she didn't realize it until several days later. She hadn't left the house since she arrived. Working from home was easy; there were no distractions here. The nightly phone calls from Parker hurt, but they also made her smile.

It was Monday, Week Four of the competition. This was the only way she kept track of time now—by the number of days until he had his next layover. Until he knew if he was going on to the next round. Which he would be, she didn't doubt that.

The sun was settling lower in the sky, and she logged off the remote work machines for the day. Nick had left the office a while ago, according to his messenger note, asking if she wanted him to pick up dinner.

His knock on her door drew her attention. Two plastic bags hung from his arm, and the scents of mango and curry wafted toward her, making her mouth water. "Dinner," he said.

"Thank you." She pushed back from her desk and stepped toward him, but he shook his head and moved back a few feet.

"Nope. You hear me out first."

"Before I can eat? All right, boss."

Nick grinned. "That's better. So we have a meeting with Rinslet Media tomorrow."

"*We*? You and the mouse in your pocket?"

"You and I. They want to discuss our app, and I need you there with me."

She shook her head, before her brain finished processing why. She wasn't ready to leave the house. It was pleasant here. "You're the Sales and Scope guy. I'm just a developer. You don't need me there."

"We're meeting with their CTO. I do need you there." A hard edge lined his voice, catching her off-guard. "You can't lock yourself away forever, Red. I'm worried about you."

"I'm fine. I just need a little time. But do this meeting tomorrow. Tell me how it goes, and if they need specs, I'll write them up for you."

Nick sighed and scrubbed his face. "Fine." He extended his arm, to hand her the two bags. "First one is food. Second one is mail."

"You're the best brother ever." She gave him a quick hug, then took the delivery from him. She settled back at the desk, and he left. Despite her stomach's growls for food, the mail had her curious. The second bag held two packages.

She pulled out two padded envelopes, one much thicker than the second but lighter. The first one had her name and Nick's address, scrawled in Parker's familiar handwriting. A fist clenched around her heart, but she ignored the pain.

She tore the flap open and emptied out the contents. A magnet from Baltimore, a spoon from Providence, and a handwritten note on hotel stationary.

You promised I could keep my souvenirs safe with you, for when I visit. There was a hand-drawn heart at the bottom of the letter. She traced the line, doubt and confusion bubbling inside. Was this really it? She'd relegated herself to seeing the man she loved once a week if she was lucky, so she could stay in a city she knew by heart and let him see the world?

No. So they could both be responsible and do what they dreamed of. She didn't question for an instant that she enjoyed her job.

But she missed life with Parker.

She couldn't think about that without answers. She turned her attention to the other envelope instead. Her name and the office address were printed on the front, in neat, block letters. There was no return mailing information.

Odd. She tore into the bubble-wrap padding. The familiar scent hit her first—Wyatt's cologne— and she dropped the package. A purple, fuzzy foot poked out. She lifted the corner of the envelope, and let the bear slide out the rest of the way, along with a note. It was a postcard from Atlanta, with more block lettering on the back.

Red,

I think you need this more than I do.

Wyatt

A sob tore from her throat, and she threw the bear across the room. It hit the wall with an unsatisfactory *poof* and slid to the ground. She rubbed her eyes, but it didn't stop the tears from spilling out.

Fucking asshole. It was a gift. He wasn't allowed to send it back.

Vision blurring, she looked at the things from Parker, laid out on the desk. They made her cry harder.

She didn't know what to do. She pulled her knees to her chest and rested her forehead on them. Tears spilled freely down her cheeks, and her nose was a snotty mess. She didn't care about that.

She cared about the guy on the other side of the country, who sent her silly trinkets and got on Facetime with her every night. She cared about the company she'd built from the ground up with her brother. She definitely didn't care about the jerk who had the nerve to return the gift she bought him.

Yeah, because that was what made Wyatt a jerk.

She rocked and cried until she was spent and her eyes were dry and her stomach ached. It left an odd kind of clarity in its place.

The one thing she'd liked about Wyatt above all else, was that he seemed like a no-regrets kind of guy. He made his decisions, and he lived with them.

If she couldn't have her cake and eat it too, she wasn't going to wallow over getting half the good stuff. She forced herself to wander into the guest bathroom. The face that stared back at her in the mirror was a wreck. Blotchy cheeks. Runny nose. Red-rimmed eyes.

But she could fix that. Wallowing wasn't doing her any good. She ran the water until it was cold, and cleaned her face, letting the icy shock drive more sense into her.

She scrubbed her skin dry and wandered into the apartment to find Nick. He was on the couch, feet propped on the coffee table, watching a Fortnite Battle Royale tournament. She rolled her eyes but couldn't help her smile. "You're such a dork."

He looked up with a grin. "I learned it from watching you. I heard you just now. How are you?"

"A mess. But better than I was." She summoned her resolve. Fortunately, this next bit was easy. "I'll go with you tomorrow, if I'm still invited."

Nick gave a single clap. "Absolutely. This is going to be awesome."

It would be. Not the adjusting, but she'd find a way to make everything work. One step at a time, backpedaling when she needed, but not getting stuck in the mire again.

♥♥♥

Fiona and Nick sat in the Rinslet lobby. An entire wall was covered with TVs. The outer row played clips from Rinslet's games, and the inside screens were snippets of YouTube videos from the contest. The clips of Ms. Passion made Fiona grit her teeth, but those with Parker were the perfect way to forget Ms. Sex-toy-vlogger-with-the-big-tits.

"Nicholas?" The man who approached them wore a battered TRON T-shirt and jeans with ripped knees and frayed seams. They sent a... developer to meet with them? Nick said something about the CTO, didn't he?

"Just Nick. And this my sister, business partner,

and genius coder, Fiona." Nick shook the man's hand.

TRON turned to her with a smile that probably disarmed the right women. "You're the brains, then. Pleasure to meet you." His grip was warm and firm. "Scott McAllister."

She knew that name. *Everyone* knew that name. He was one of the co-founders of the company. Supposedly built their graphics engine from scratch, back in the day. She tried to hide her shock. "Yeah. Hi. Right. Pleasure. Definitely." Now who was the dork?

Scott chuckled and nodded toward a set of doors. "Thanks for making time for me. I've got a conference room set up for us, so we can talk."

Fiona and Nick followed him into a room with an oval table in the middle and several chairs around it. Standard conference room. A counter lined the back wall, and a coffee pot, cups, and donuts sat next to it. "Help yourselves." Scott gestured.

"Are you expecting someone else?" Fiona asked. They didn't roll out this kind of red carpet for two people, did they? She picked a chair and sat.

Scott gave her a funny look. "Nope. Just you."

Nick didn't seem fazed by the situation. He made himself a cup of coffee and took the seat next to Fiona. "What can we do for you?" he asked.

"That's simple. Or rather, I hope it is." Scott grabbed a remote off the table and strolled to the front of the room as he turned on screen on the wall. "I'll lay out the basics, and if you don't laugh me out of the room, we'll talk details."

A few pieces clicked in Fiona's head. Nick had

said something about an investment opportunity. Wow, she was dim. Rinslet wanted to invest in them? But the app was for scheduling local deliveries. That was who their contracts were with. It didn't have anything to do with video games or multimedia.

"We like what you did with the contracts part of your application," Scott said. "And the way this contest is going, we're going to need something similar to protect our asses. Especially if we run the thing again next year. Bottom line is we're willing to put up the capital you need, to grow you to the point where it's useful to us."

"No you're not." The words slipped out of Fiona's mouth before she could consider them, and heat flooded her cheeks.

Scott raised his brows. "I'm going to say that doesn't count as laughing me out of the room. Yes, we are."

"I'm intrigued," Nick said. "Let's talk details."

And that was why he was the face of the company. Fiona listened to Scott and Nick toss around terms and figures for the next hour, and chimed in whenever things got technical.

When the meeting was up, nothing had been signed, but there were handshakes and an agreement to pursue things further. Nick was beaming as Scott walked them to the front door, and Fiona felt better than she had in days. She was glad she decided to attend.

"Fiona," a voice called from behind.

Fiona spun as Chloe Nielson jogged to catch up to her.

"Hey. I heard you were in the building. I'm glad

I caught you." She extended her hand. "Chloe."

"Nice to meet you." Fiona shook her hand.

Chloe glanced at Scott, then back at Fiona. "Meeting went well?"

"It didn't go badly," Scott said.

"Can I talk to you for a minute?" Chloe asked Fiona.

"Sure." They stepped away from prying ears, and Fiona's curiosity grew.

Chloe was watching her with an expression Fiona couldn't read. "How are you doing? Like, really. You've been through a lot." Chloe sounded genuine. It was a nice change from Ms. Passion's doubt.

"I'm surviving." The concern didn't compel Fiona to spill her guts to a stranger.

"Can I ask you something only barely business related?"

Fiona didn't know what that meant, or if she wanted to answer. "Sure."

"Why did you cut out of the show? I know you weren't originally part of it, and Parker holds views on his own, but the two of you had off-the-charts chemistry on camera."

And off. "The whole stalker incident… It freaked me out." That was as much detail as she was willing to share.

"I get it. Are you doing better now that you're back?"

Fiona started to say *yes*, but the lie stuck in her throat. She was doing better than yesterday. That wasn't a high bar, though. She didn't feel safer. She missed Parker so much it hurt… "I'm good."

Chloe seemed to relax. "I'm glad. And I hope the contract negotiation, due diligence—all of it—goes well." She handed Fiona a business card. "You can call me if you can't get hold of the guys up top, or if you have any questions. And..." She frowned.

"What?"

"Nothing." Chloe shook her head. "It was good meeting you."

"Thanks. You too." Fiona wandered back toward Nick, the odd advice echoing in her head. It was another version of *think outside the box.*

She only had the one big issue, though—how was she supposed to do her job and be with Parker and let him do his job, all at the same time? Outside-the-box thinking didn't seem like a solution, unless it came with the ability to bend space and time or alter reality.

That didn't stop Fiona from getting stuck in a loop of *how* as she got into the car.

"We're here." Nick's announcement made her realize they'd finished the drive back to his place.

"We're not going to the office?" She was surprised.

"I figured you did your socializing for the day. Honestly, we don't *need* the office. I like the structure of it, but you work fine wherever you are."

"Is this your way of getting out of paying rent on my spot in the shared space?" Fiona teased.

Nick chuckled. "No. And if this Rinslet deal goes through—fingers crossed—I won't have to consider things like that anyway. It's up to you, though. You're not some nine-to-fiver I have to watch, to make sure you're working. You have as much vested in this as I do, and you bust your ass regardless of your location."

She hopped from the car. "Thanks for the ride. Talk to you when you come back online?"

"Yup." Nick pulled away from the curb.

Something tickled Fiona's thoughts, but she couldn't grasp it. What was it?

Chapter Thirty-One

Fiona wasn't surprised when Parker made it to the next round of the competition. Despite his detractors, and her critics, he was putting out a solid show, and his fans loved it.

She watched the new coverage around Tim, and was relieved when they denied him bail, and then two weeks later, arraigned him. He was behind bars for at least a little while, and she prayed it would be a long while.

After a week at Nick's, she told herself she needed to go home. After two weeks, she realized she didn't want to. Not because she was terrified—the fear was still there, but not as potent as before—but what Nick said about her working remote refused to leave her.

She didn't want to move back to her place, because she wanted to be with Parker. To see more of the world. To learn more about the man she'd called best friend. To explore their new relationship.

Each time she thought about it, terror tried to

convince her to stay here. There were more people like Tim in the world.

But she refused to let him terrify her into hiding her life away. She'd done enough of that to herself.

♥♥♥

Parker worked as best he could in the confined storage room. He was grateful the bar owner gave him a place to set up, but the folding table tucked between boxes of beer wasn't exactly prime real estate.

A knock made him look up.

A thin guy, sporting dreadlocks and a goatee, stood in the open door. "You Parker? I'm Jeremy."

"Yeah. Good to meet you." Parker shook his hand.

Jeremy was another of the contestants, and he and Parker had a joint Week Four challenge. Jeremy did death metal covers of popular songs. He was performing in a New Orleans bar, and Parker had to broadcast to both channels. The challenge was, they each had to keep the other's audience entertained. The longer the average live feed view, the better their scores.

"You have any idea how this tech works?" Jeremy nodded at Parker's camera and tripod.

"Not beyond the standard. I'll run through a Rinslet cloud, so technically we're broadcasting on a several-second delay. They do their magic—wands or some shit, I don't know—and all our viewers see it."

Jeremy shrugged. "That works for me. You need anything from me before I go on stage?"

"Don't fuck things up for us.".

"Me? Man, everything else will pale in comparison to what your subscribers see tonight."

"Big words. Bring it, guitar boy." Parker laughed.

Jeremy clasped Parker's hand one more time and clapped him on the shoulder. "I'll break a leg for both of us," he said. "And for what it's worth, I don't think the two of you faked anything."

"Thanks." Parker's smile was thin. He was so sick of the rumors that Fiona's kidnapping wasn't real.

He grabbed his camera and tripod, and headed to the club floor, to set up. The bar had sectioned him off a square, a few feet back from the stage. Parker expected to get jostled, but he'd deal with it. It was part of the magic of live streaming.

He let his thoughts wander as the crowds poured in. He didn't know how much longer he could deal with the whole *Fiona isn't here* thing. He wasn't sure how he'd gone so long in the past.

But he'd been rearranging his travel schedule. Going home for good was a no-no. He wanted to argue with her logic, but it was true. However, Parker had put plans in motion that would let him be with her two to three days a week. He'd surprise her with the news next time he was in town. Which might be sooner than expected if he didn't make it through today's elimination round.

Parker excelled at his work, and he'd seen Jeremy's videos. The guy was hardcore talented.

Before go-live, Parker turned the camera on himself to talk in the act. He didn't switch over to the dual-feed yet, though. He wanted to address his audience.

"Hey, guys. In a few minutes, you're going to see the most kickass show on the planet, but first I have to say something." The words flowed easily once he started talking. He was glad he decided not to script them. This way his sincerity would show through.

"Everyone's heard a billion rumors by now, about what happened in Philadelphia with Fiona. You can believe what you want, but I'm not sharing personal details to prove a point. I'm also not going to give you some sort of lengthy *this is why it's true* kind of diatribe. Take me at my word or don't. A monologue won't change what happened.

"The thing is, I'm grateful to all of you who watch and support. You guys make this so worth it. And to those of you who watch and don't support me— Thanks for the hate clicks." He winked at the camera, then switched to the dual feed.

He spat out another introduction and focused the camera back on the stage when Jeremy stepped up to the microphone.

For the next hour and a half, Parker, the audience, and over a million YouTube viewers were treated to an incredible live performance. Parker didn't have to address the fans; the music spoke for itself.

When someone pressed against him from behind, he adjusted his weight. It had been happening all night. Then a warm breath caressed his cheek, next to the ear that didn't hold the Bluetooth mic.

"I know you're live. Don't turn around."

Fiona. He grinned. She pressed her chest against him, slipped her hands into his front pockets, and rested her cheek against his back. Everyone else in the club fell into the background, and heat surged through him, to tug at his cock.

He was glad he had the camera trained someplace besides them, but—fuck—he wanted to shut it off.

"Don't you dare blow this because of me," she said, as if she could read his mind.

Damn it. He covered one of her hands with his, tangling their fingers together. It would do for now.

Jeremy wrapped up his set and worked the crowd a little more.

Fiona said, "Find me in back when you're done."

Parker managed to sign off for the camera without stuttering or skipping too many words. He had no idea if he hid his excitement, though. He powered everything off, stashed his gear in the messenger bag hanging from his shoulder, and went in search of Fiona.

She was leaning against a far wall, looking as incredible as he'd ever seen her in jeans and a T-shirt. "Hey," she said, when he was within hearing distance.

Yeah, words weren't going to work for him. He cupped her cheeks in both his palms and crushed his mouth to hers. Her whimpers mingled with his groans and the chatter of club goers. Her body molded to his, soft curves yielding in all the right ways. Fuck. Why were they someplace public?

They broke apart, and he rested his forehead

against hers, still holding her face.

"I missed you too," she said with a giggle.

"Are you real? As in, actually here? I'm not hallucinating?"

"I'm real."

He grabbed her hand and tugged her toward his temporary staging room. He was kissing her again, as he kicked the door shut and pressed her against the wall. In the background, the next band introduced themselves. He let his camera equipment slide to the ground and toed it aside.

She draped her arms over his shoulders and interlocked her fingers at the base of his neck.

Maybe they should slow down. Talk. Catch up.

Fuck that. They caught up every night, and she felt and tasted and smelled better than his memories.

He undid her jeans and slipped his hand over her panties. Heat and dampness teased his fingertips.

She adjusted her weight, grinding into his touch. He wanted to watch her get off. See the way her face screwed up with pleasure and abandon when she came.

He nipped along her jaw, up to her ear. "This door doesn't lock," he warned. "Someone could walk in on us any minute."

"You're such a tease." Her reply faded into a moan when he pressed against her clit.

She bit her bottom lip and her eyelids fluttered. Hand over his, she shoved her underwear out of the way. She was slick and eager, and he returned his attention to her swollen button. Circled and stroked. Watched her expression shift from playful to lost.

His dick was hard enough to drill a hole through

the wall, and begged for release. Fiona's lips parted slightly, and when she came, her gasps blended with guitar riffs and screaming crowds.

Parker kept up the stroking until she jerked away from his touch. He pulled his hand back, and she relaxed more of her weight against the wall.

He nibbled her bottom lip, drawing her gaze. Bright-green eyes studied him with lust and adoration. "Can you stand?" he asked.

"I think so. Do we need to go?"

"Not yet. I need you. To feel you." He gripped her hips and spun her to face the door. Desperation clawed inside him. How did she cause this effect on him? This all-consuming drive? He wasn't in the mood to analyze it.

He dragged her jeans halfway down her thighs, then cupped her full ass. "Bend over." He nudged her forward, and she placed her hands on the door.

He fumbled with his zipper, the strain against it making it hard for him to think. When he worked his cock free, he expected relief. *Not yet.* He fisted his shaft, dragged the head between her legs, along her slippery slit, and thrust inside her without further fanfare.

The way she arched her back and pressed back into him almost made him blow his wad.

Gripping her hip, he worked to a slow, steady pace. Every time she tried to increase the rhythm, he forced her to slow. He tangled his fingers in her hair and jerked her head back. "At least let me enjoy you for a minute or two." He dug his teeth into her shoulder.

She moved a hand under her shirt. Though he

couldn't see, knowing she squeezed her breast, the mental images of what lay underneath sent a new cord of desire tugging through him.

She pounded against him harder, and this time he didn't try to slow her down. The flush on her skin and the way she was lost in the moment were intoxicating. His balls tightened, and he held back. Need built inside, nudging and screaming for release.

Fiona climaxed again, clenching around him, her groans reaching his ears on the beat of a snare. She drove against his cock with a force that pushed him over the edge.

He tightened his grip in her hair when he came. He spilled inside her, thrusting until he was spent, and only slowing to a stop when his legs wobbled and threatened to give out.

He wrapped an arm around her and buried his face in her hair. The faint scent of soap filled his head. They both used the door for support.

Someone knocked. "You okay in there?"

Fiona giggled—fuck, he adored that—and ducked her head.

"Fine." Parker found his voice. "Just packing up. Be right out."

Fiona untangled herself to spin and face him, still leaning against the door.

"What are you doing here?" he asked.

"Finish what you're doing. We'll go back to the hotel, and I'll explain."

He kissed her. "The explaining better happen on the trip, because I don't see a lot of talking when I get you back to my room, at least for a little while."

"I'm good with that. Great, even." Mischief

danced in her eyes, and the flush on her cheeks almost made him hard again.

He forced himself to calm down. The faster they finished here, the sooner he'd have her all to himself.

♥♥♥

Fiona followed Parker to the bench at the back of the half-full bus. The lack of privacy wasn't ideal, but the way he never let go of her hand for more than a few seconds was pretty decent.

He sat and pulled her into his lap. His palm was warm against her stomach, and she leaned her head on his shoulder.

"Spill." There was a hint of force to his voice. "How long do I have you for?"

"Forever. Duh." The words carried more weight than they had the right to.

He brushed her hair aside, to trail his fingers down her neck. "Be serious for—like—two seconds and give me a straight answer."

"Spoil sport." She rolled her eyes. "Do I still have an open invitation to travel with you for the rest of the competition?"

"Always."

"Then—short answer—forever. Longer answer—that deal I told you about with Rinslet? It looks good. Nick's pretty sure he'll sign. There are other offers coming in too. People who want to invest and are looking for custom development."

"So you decided to throw in the towel and leave Nick to fend for himself?" Parker sounded confused.

Never. That was a concession she couldn't

make. Fortunately, the alternative was more attractive. "We—he and I—are hiring more staff. Including developers. I'm going to move into a consulting position. Remote work. Part time, except for those rare instances where more is needed."

"I like the sound of that."

The bus stopped for more passengers, and an older man rambled toward them, shot them a glare, and dropped onto the far end of the bench.

"So, surprise," Fiona said.

Parker drew his nose along her skin and followed that with a row of tiny kisses. "Best. Surprise. Ever."

She wanted to be alone with him. Fortunately, the bus trip didn't take long.

Fiona had left her things with the front desk, and Parker insisted on carrying her bags upstairs. The moment they were in his room, talking faded in favor of groping… Kissing… Stripping off their clothes…

The lovemaking—she liked the sound of that—wasn't so frantic and desperate this time. Parker was tender and took his time, playing with every inch of her body, making her skin hum and her thoughts evaporate.

Round Three was in the shower, scrubbing each other clean. Playing and slipping and sliding. With Parker kneeling at her feet, licking and sucking her clit, and fingering her until she couldn't stand.

She had no idea how much time had passed when they collapsed in bed, half-clothed and tangled up in each other. She just knew it felt right.

He spooned her, arm draped over her hip and lips brushing her neck. A happy thrum danced along her nerve endings.

"You miss him, don't you?" Parker's question caught her off guard.

She didn't have to ask who he meant. "Not the best pillow talk."

"It's one of those things the new boyfriend never wants to hear. I shouldn't ask. But… I did."

She didn't want to get into this. Things were finally right. She snuggled closer. "I mean it when I say I love you completely. I'm not making that up or exaggerating."

"I know." There was no hesitation in Parker's reply. "But you also just avoided my question."

She didn't want to tell him the truth, but couldn't stand the thought of lying. "Yes."

"Fuck."

She'd hoped to avoid the topic of Wyatt until it wasn't necessary. When she could honestly say, *I felt something, but I'm better now*. She rolled over, needing to look Parker in the eye. "I'm sorry. I wish I didn't feel this way." She searched his face, looking for clues about his reaction.

He stared back lovingly, with traces of hurt and concern, but he didn't say anything.

She pushed forward. "I can't flip a switch and shut it off, but I'm working on it. I don't even know if the man I was falling for was a real person, or if it was part of the scam. But I don't love you any less."

"I get it." He brushed a strand of hair from her face. "I wish I didn't, but I do. It doesn't change my feelings either."

She pressed into him. This—Parker, the job, the travel, the opportunities—was perfect. The longer she lived it, the easier it would be to forget that bump in their past. That unfortunate incident that was only good because it brought them here. Together. "I love you," she murmured against his chest.

"Me too, Red."

Chapter Thirty-Two

Parker's phone chimed with a new email, as he and Fiona stepped out of the cab. He swiped to see who the message was from, and his thoughts froze.

"What's up?" Fiona stopped next to him.

"Rinslet. Month Two contest results." It killed him to do so, but he put the device back to sleep and dropped it in his pocket. "It'll wait."

Since Fiona and Parker had a stop planned in Atlanta anyway, Nick had asked Fiona for a favor. A prospective client wanted to sit down face to face and discuss options for the app. They were supposed to be meeting the contact here.

She pulled his phone from his pocket and handed it to him. "We've got ten minutes. We're early. Watch it now. Neither one of us will be able to focus during lunch if you don't."

"Thank you." He clicked the link to pull up their announcement video, and she pressed her arm to his, so they could both watch.

It was Chloe. She promised to keep her intro

short, because she knew everyone was only here for the list anyway.

Even that made Parker itch with impatience.

The names of the channels progressing to the next round flashed on the screen, one by one. She insisted they were shown in no particular order, but he had a feeling it was related to their total score, highest to lowest, based on what he'd seen of views.

He kept a mental tally as she scrolled through the list. Fiona squeezed his hand, and he returned the gesture.

Only five left, and he wasn't up there yet. Disappointment and disbelief filled him.

When his channel flashed up last on the list, he let out a choked laugh of relief.

"*Yay.*" Fiona wasn't as restrained. She threw her arms around his neck and squeezed. "Never doubted it for a second."

"Not even one? You did better than me."

She kissed him on the cheek. "Get me through lunch, and we'll celebrate after."

"Deal."

When Nick had called with his request and told her the name of the shipping company, Fiona had hesitated. Nick said she didn't have to fill him in on what happened with Wyatt, but the guy wasn't involved with this deal. She'd be speaking with someone in technology.

Parker wanted to hate the way she stalled or paled or fumbled at anything that reminded her of Wyatt, but he'd meant it when he told her he understood. He and she agreed a meeting like this was a good way to move past the shipping company being a reminder—working with someone else in the company—it wasn't as though the company sanctioned Wyatt's actions.

Parker and Fiona strolled toward the restaurant, glee flitting through Parker. He'd done it. Round Three. He had no idea if he could hold out for the full year—he'd have to step up his game, to keep his views up—but his chances seemed a lot more promising than when the contest started.

They waited their turn once they got inside, and then she stepped up to the host podium. "I'm meeting with a London Draxon."

"Mr. Draxon couldn't make it." Wyatt's familiar voice cut through the chatter and sank in Parker's gut like a stone.

He and Fiona spun. The Big Bad Wolf himself stood off to the side of the crowds, looking as incredible and dangerous as ever.

Wyatt extended his hand. "London asked if I'd step in for him, just this once. I hope you don't mind. There's something we need to discuss."

The End (But Not Really)

Fiona, Parker, and Wyatt's story continues in Red Consumed (Subscribe, Live, Love, Book 2. Keep reading for a free sneak peek of Chapter One.

Red Consumed

Chapter One

Wyatt wasn't surprised to see Parker standing next to Fiona, in the restaurant lobby. That didn't mean he was interested in hearing the sappy details of how they finally climbed over the baggage that composed their past, to end up in a place where they were comfortable holding hands in public.

Fiona glared at Wyatt, a storm of irritation raging in her green eyes, and her jaw set. "No," she spat the word out. "If you want to talk to me, you call me like a normal person."

Fuck, she looked incredible. Even when she pointed that kind of venom at him, his body reacted without his permission, flames of need licking across his skin.

"If I'd done that, would you have taken my call?" Wyatt expected hostility. He wasn't sure how raw and open she'd be about it, but given he lied about being her competition for a career-making contract—his career specifically—seduced her, literally fucked her while her best friend watched…

Her reaction was probably tame all things considered. She shook her head. "And you definitely don't set up a bullshit meeting, complete with a bullshit offer, to drag me into a public place and ambush me. Fuck you.”

Inside the restaurant dining room, more heads turned toward them as her voice rose. He didn't mind the confrontation, but spilling the details for the world to hear wasn't quite on his list of ways this should go down.

“The meeting is sincere, the offer is real, and I didn't set this up.” He kept his tone even and professional.

Parker gave a barking laugh. “Right. Because your company just randomly decided they needed this app, that happened to be created by the woman you were fucking.”

He looked good too. Wyatt hated to admit that. He was pretty sure if Fiona was his Achilles Heel, Parker was the arrow that would kill him. Parker's demeanor had changed on camera in the past week. The dark shadows under his eyes faded, and his smile reached his eyes again.

He didn't talk about Fiona in his videos anymore, but Wyatt would bet money the shift coincided with her being back in his life.

“I don't suspect the decision was random, but it wasn't mine.” Wyatt turned a pointed gaze on Parker. “Why are *you* here?”

“You expected me to come alone?” Fiona asked.

“Too easy.” The innuendo slipped out before Wyatt could stop it, and it summoned images of just how enticing she looked when she was coming.

She clenched her jaw. “Don't.” At least she'd lowered her voice enough the diners weren't watching them anymore.

"Fine." He needed to yield somewhere or this conversation wouldn't get them anywhere. "I didn't expect you to come alone, but I hoped you'd leave the guard dog home. The two of you together are impossible." He hid a wince as the confession slipped out. Impossible in the most tantalizing way, but only if they weren't pissed off at him.

Parker's smile was thin. "Tough shit."

Wyatt kept his focus on Fiona. "Can we get a table and talk?"

"No." She clipped off the response. "In fact, *we* as in you and us, aren't doing anything. *We* as in Parker and I, are leaving." She spun on her toe and pushed outside, Parker next to her, arm around her waist.

Wyatt followed, a few feet back. "The offer is sincere. There really is a business proposal on the table." If she wasn't interested in talking about what happened between them, that was fine. He wasn't going to let her throw away a real opportunity because of him. Especially since he tried to destroy the last one.

"So… she sucks you off, and she can have the contract?" Parker asked.

"Fuck you." God, this was getting old.

Parker smirked. "Not with a stolen dick."

"Is this a business meeting, or a playground fight?" Wyatt struggled to hide his frustration.

Fiona met his gaze again. "You tell me."

"That's what I'm trying to do."

"I'm listening." She crossed her arms, pressing her breasts together and giving him a perfect view of the way her shirt hugged her torso. His attention drifted down before he could stop it. She let out a tiny growl, that did nothing to curb his sneaking arousal, and jammed her hands in her pockets instead.

He forced himself to look her in the eye. "The company is evaluating apps like yours. They found you without any input from me. The department making the purchasing decision doesn't have anything to do with me except that we keep offices in the same building. If you go through this proposal process, I won't be involved."

"Then why are you here?" Parker asked.

"I saw Fiona's name on a budget request, and called in a favor with the evaluating director. That's the one-hundred percent, honest-to-God truth."

Fiona studied him, eyes narrowed and lips pursed. The deep furrow in Parker's brow and the way he clenched and unclenched his fist implied he was considering making good on the standing threat to deck Wyatt next time they met.

Fiona crossed the distance between them in a few quick strides, grabbed the lapels of Wyatt's jacket, and crushed her mouth to his.

His shock at the gesture didn't stop his dick from hardening in an instant. Fuck he missed this. Her smooth lips. Her faint scent. The tiny gasps she made when she was lost in the moment.

He reached out to pull her closer, and she stepped out of his grip. She slapped his hand away, the sound echoing through the parking lot, and the sting ringing through his wrist. He was glad she didn't do that to his face. Wyatt pasted on a mask. "Feel better?" He removed all emotion from his voice.

"Getting there."

"Can we talk now?"

"Business, yes. Everything else is off the table." Fiona matched his tone.

Wyatt was happy to make that concession for now. She could have walked away the moment she saw him. Asked to reschedule with the Draxon. Told Wyatt forget it, she wasn't doing business with any company associated with him.

Instead, despite the grief, she was still here. And the way her kiss lingered on his lips, she wasn't completely Parker's.

Wyatt strode back to the restaurant entrance with them, and held open the door. He wasn't sure what he hoped to accomplish, and it bothered him going into this without a full-blown plan. He saw the bond between Parker and Fiona, and it was strong. One of those lust-, time-, and reason-defying connections.

And if anyone could sever it, he could.

Parker had to press his legs into his chair to keep his knee from bouncing. The adrenaline racing through him was ebbing slowly, leaving it gnawing in his stomach and prickling sensation under his skin.

He had half an ear on the conversation between Fiona and Wyatt. Enough to know it was actually business. The rest of his attention slid around the chaos living in his head. The elation of making it to the next round of the competition. The smug assurance every time Fiona squeezed his hand, which was muted by the scrape behind his ribs at the memory of watching her kiss Wyatt.

And the jealousy. He expected that when it came to Fiona. Just because they were together didn't mean they'd worked past all their issues. There was a twinge at knowing Wyatt was only here for her, and disappointed to see Parker, that was fucking with his head.

"We need to know you can handle that kind of stress and load," Wyatt said.

"As long as I've got the appropriate warning, we're prepared for any size data package." Fiona's reply was smooth and professional.

Parker wanted to think it was an overactive imagination hearing innuendo in a large part of what they said, but he had a feeling they knew what they were saying. Underneath the entire exchange though, was the reality that this could be big for Fiona and Nick. Game changer kind of stuff for their app. Parker wasn't going to ruin that for her.

They finished lunch and the meeting, and the three strolled outside. Wyatt shook Fiona's hand. "One of my colleagues will be in touch."

"Will you?" she asked. Her voice was devoid of emotion.

Parker didn't hate hearing the question the way he expected to.

Wyatt smirked. "I planned on it."

Parker wasn't opposed to that either, which he didn't understand at all.

"You need to call. I won't be so kind next time about being ambushed." There was no teasing in Fiona's voice. No room for negotiation.

As Parker and Fiona walked away, ambivalence

raced through him. "You can't do this with him if you're going to do business with this company." As they strolled, they wove through small groups of people, wandering the outdoor mall.

"I'm not doing anything." The edge from warning off Wyatt was still in her voice. "And I know how to conduct myself with a client."

The last thing he wanted to do was turn this into an argument. "That's not what I meant." Sun warmed his face, but it didn't sear away the questions with no answers.

"It is, but I get it. The question about him being in touch was a warning, not an offer."

So Parker *was* reading too much into things. "I'm still trying to figure out how this works." He kept the apology in his tone. It was easy enough in theory to accept that she was with him because she chose to be, even if she still had feelings for Wyatt. Seeing it actually play out would take some adjusting. "I'm sorry."

"Me too. To both." She slipped her hand into his and pressed closer, leaning her shoulder on his head as they strolled down the street. "Let me make it up to you?"

The sugar and seduction in her voice turned his irritation to desire. "This is on him, not you. But if you had something in mind..."

"I'm sure we could come up with something you'd enjoy." She rested enough weight against him to steer him toward a shadowed alcove between shops. When they were out of the flow of traffic, she leaned back against the brick, watching him with her bottom lip caught between her teeth.

The playful smirk erased the negatives of the afternoon. He dipped his head to brush his lips over hers. "I enjoy a lot of things."

"Pick a couple. Or more." She hooked a finger in his waistband and tugged him closer.

Every inch of his body lit up like a live wire, as he pressed his body against hers. The chatter of foot traffic drifted from just a few feet away. A tiny whisper echoed in the back of his head, asking why sex with Fiona was more tame, unless Wyatt was around.

She slid her hand lower, tracing the outline of his erection through his jeans, drawing him from semi-hard to painfully so.

He gripped her wrist, pulling her away from his cock, grabbed her other hand, and pinned her arms above her head. The giggle-squeal that tore from her throat was gasoline on the flames licking through his veins. He crushed his mouth to hers, devouring her groans and loving the way she ground her hip against his dick.

She was incredible regardless, and he wasn't going to over-analyze things because she was playful and aggressive.

He nipped a line of bites up the side of her neck, to her ear. "You make me think you want to be pinned to the wall right now and fucked."

"It's tempting, isn't it?" Her soft question fell across his cheek.

Christ it was. She was going to be the death of him. Or at least, a couple of days in jail for indecent exposure. And it would be worth it.

He glided his free hand under her shirt, using

his body to block them from the view of casual passers-by. He cupped one breast, and squeezed as he dragged a thumb over her bra and the nipple underneath.

Her gasp rocketed through him. "More." Her plea was breathy.

He caught her earlobe between his teeth. "More what?"

"Finger fuck me. Here. Please?"

The teasing. Her recklessness. Was it because they'd just walked away from Wyatt?

That was jealousy trying to rear its head again. Parker and Fiona hadn't been a couple long enough for him to have a feeling for the ebb and flow of either of their moods when it came to sex.

And God damn it if her words didn't unravel his control.

The story continues in Chapter Two.

Acknowledgements

Thank you to my two writing partners in mischief, who also happen to be my critique partner, and my editor, Sofia and Sotia. (And double thank you to Sotia for not cringing too badly at the construct of that sentence).

A huge thanks to Vanessa, for being an amazing beta reader. For loving my books, but still helping me find their flaws.

And thank you to Shannon, Elizabeth, Angie, and Addie, for lending me the vivid descriptions of their hometowns and favorite places to visit, so I could send Parker, Fiona, and Wyatt on a fantastic our around the United States.